"She deserves bette[...] some game. She's a woman, not a pile of coins."

"She's *my* woman." Scaevola leaned forward slightly. "Unless you win the game, that is. What do you say, Varro, why don't we make this interesting? I thought you might actually appreciate the chance to win her. I suppose I can see the appeal myself in a rustic kind of way, even if she does look like a savage. I wonder if she acts like one in bed, too?" He grinned suddenly. "But then I suppose I'll find out after we're married. After I've dealt with her behavior tonight, of course. I haven't thought of a punishment yet, but..."

"How much?" Marius slammed his fist onto the tabula board.

"I knew it!" Scaevola cackled. "I knew that you wanted to bed her."

"Not to bed her. To win her. That's what you said." He fixed the other man with a challenging stare. "That means if I win, she's mine completely."

JENNI FLETCHER

The Warrior's Bride Prize

HARLEQUIN® HISTORICAL

Recycling programs for this product may not exist in your area.

ISBN-13: 978-1-335-52292-4

The Warrior's Bride Prize

This edition published by arrangement with Harlequin Books S.A.

For questions and comments about the quality of this book, please contact us at CustomerService@Harlequin.com.

Printed in U.S.A.

Jenni Fletcher was born in the north of Scotland and now lives in Yorkshire with her husband and two children. She wanted to be a writer as a child but became distracted by reading instead, finally getting past her first paragraph thirty years later. She's had more jobs than she can remember but has finally found one she loves. She can be contacted on Twitter, @jenniauthor, or via her Facebook author page.

Also by Jenni Fletcher

Harlequin Historical

Married to Her Enemy
The Convenient Felstone Marriage
Besieged and Betrothed
Captain Amberton's Inherited Bride
The Warrior's Bride Prize

Visit the Author Profile page at Harlequin.com.

For Helen & David

Also a big thank-you to RomanArmyTalk.com
as well as the staff at the Roman Army Museum
and Chesters Roman Fort on Hadrian's Wall for
answering my many questions so patiently.

Historical Note

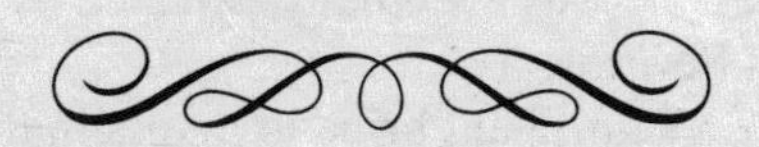

One of the best but hardest things about writing a story set in the Roman era is that although we're constantly learning more about this fascinating period, there's still a lot that we don't know. While this allows for greater imaginative freedom, it can also be frustrating when dealing with real-life events, such as the Caledonian rebellion of AD 197.

What we *do* know is that Hadrian's Wall was built after the Roman Emperor's visit to Britain in AD 122. Comprising forts, mile-castles, ditches and turrets, it stretched for eighty Roman miles—seventy-three modern miles—from Wallsend on the north-east coast of England to Bowness-on-Solway on the west, and took fifteen thousand soldiers six years to complete.

It had several purposes, functioning as a frontier, a military bulwark and a customs barrier, although the Romans also made several forays into the area they called Caledonia—now Scotland—even building another shorter fortification, the Antonine Wall, between the Firth of Forth and the Firth of Clyde, though this was abandoned after only twenty years in AD 163.

In spite of these efforts, the northern tribes were never completely subdued or brought under the Pax Romana and there were numerous uprisings throughout the second century AD. Matters came to a head in AD 182, when the then Governor of Britain, Clodius Albinus, proclaimed himself Emperor of the Roman Empire and took a large part of the British garrison to Gaul, where he was eventually defeated by his rival Septimius Severus.

Despite a significant bribe to maintain the peace, the Maetae tribe north of Hadrian's Wall took advantage of the Romans' absence by launching a series of raids and destroying large parts of the fortifications.

In AD 197 the new Emperor Severus sent commissioners north to rebuild the wall and re-establish control—although archaeological evidence shows continued fighting around this period. The exact sequence of events is unclear, but the Sixth Victorious Legion was based in York—the Roman city of Eboracum—at this time, and the Emperor himself finally came to Britain to suppress the uprising in AD 208.

Hadrian's Wall wasn't abandoned by the Roman Empire until the early fifth century. Consequently, although we know that there *was* a Caledonian rebellion, and it affected the real forts of Coria—Corbridge—and Cilurnum—Chesters—which feature in this story, all the specific incidents and characters are fictionalised.

I've tried to keep place names accurate—Lindum is Lincoln—but to avoid confusion I've referred to the collective northern tribes simply as Caledonians, although there was an actual Caledonii tribe in central Scotland, in addition to the Maetae, Picts and Selgovae, to name just a few.

As the heroine's hair colour is an important aspect of the story, it's also worth noting that several Roman sources, including Tacitus's *Agricola*, describe the northern tribes as having red hair.

Chapter One

North Britannia, AD *197*

'Halt!'

Livia woke with a gasp, startled back to her senses by the shout. With a lurch, the carriage rolled to a standstill, jolting her forward on the bench at the same moment as she heard a dull clanking of armour and a heavy thud outside, like dozens of feet all stamping the ground at once.

Quickly, she pulled herself upright, tightening her arms around the four-year-old girl asleep in her lap. To her amazement, their unscheduled halt hadn't disturbed her, though Livia had the ominous feeling that something was about to.

'What's happening? Are we under attack?'

Porcia, her maidservant sitting opposite, sounded on the verge of hysteria. Despite the presence of an armed escort, the girl had been a bundle of nerves ever since leaving Lindum a month ago. Perhaps with good reason, Livia thought grimly. Her own anxieties had been gathering in strength the closer they travelled to Coria, though for very different reasons.

And now this! Whatever *this* was… She felt a shiver of fear, as if an icy claw had pierced its way through her chest and was clutching her heart, making her feel cold all over.

'I don't think so.' She leaned over, trying to see out of the carriage window, but whatever was happening was taking place at the head of their small procession. 'I don't hear any fighting.'

'What if it's Caledonians?'

'They're on the other side of the wall. This side is under the Pax Romana, remember?'

'Barely.' Porcia's bottom lip trembled. 'They say only savages live this far north.'

'Who say so?'

'Civilised people. Romans…like us.'

'Like us.' Livia repeated the words sceptically. 'Well then, it must be true.'

Not that now was the time to be debating the merits of Roman society with her maidservant, she admonished herself, though somehow the words themselves gave her courage, forcing the claw to relax its grip slightly. If *civilised* Roman society said that she ought to be afraid then she'd be more than happy to prove *civilisation* wrong.

In any case, there were still no sounds of combat, no clamour of weapons or shouting. If they were really under attack from Caledonians or outlaws, surely they'd know it by now?

'Stay here. I'll go and see what's happening.' She slid herself out from beneath the sleeping child. 'Take care of Julia for me.'

'Shouldn't we wake her...just in case?'

'No.'

Livia shook her head emphatically, bending over to press a kiss into the spiral curls of the little girl's hair. It was every bit as wild and untamed as hers had been at that age, as well as the same shade of blazing copper red, a legacy from her own mother that she wished Julia might have avoided.

If only her daughter could have had dark hair like Julius, she thought regretfully. If only Julia could have looked anything *at all* like him, then mother and daughter might never have been in their current perilous situation. Julia might have been a rich heiress and she an independent widow, safe from her brother—*half-brother*, she corrected herself—Tarquinius and his scheming. Strange how great a difference something as trivial as hair colour could have on a person's life...

She straightened up again, dismissing the thought as unhelpful. Now wasn't the time for regrets. *Now* she had bigger problems to worry about and she had to be brave for her daughter as well as her terrified maid.

'There's nothing to worry about, I'm sure of it.'

She squeezed Porcia's hand reassuringly and then climbed down from the carriage, glad to be out of the confined space for a while, no matter what the circumstances. It was more comfortable than horseback, better for Julia, too, but her muscles were still cramped and stiff from so much prolonged inactivity. Cautiously, she looked around, searching for some sign of an enemy attack, but there was none. On the contrary, it was hard to imagine a more peaceful, springlike scene than the one before her. The sun was high in a cloudless sky and shining for the first time in days, warming the air and giving the woodland road along which they were travelling a fresh, almost sparkling appearance. The trees on either side were starting to bud, too, if not yet bloom, and the birds within chirruping loudly, as if to celebrate the fact that the long, hard winter was finally coming to an end.

It was a whole different world to the makeshift camp they'd left, shivering and cold that morning, as if some enchantment had fallen over the carriage during her brief nap, turning the hours into weeks. But then time seemed to have been working differently during the seemingly endless days of their journey north. Hardly surprising when they were travelling as far from Rome as they could possibly go, following the great road beyond Eboracum to the very limits of the Empire and the great wall built less than a century before by the Emperor Hadrian—a massive eighty-mile structure stretching from one side of the country to the other.

Despite the relentless pace of their journey, however, there'd been days when she'd had the uneasy feeling they might be travelling for ever, trapped in some never-ending loop. Then again, there'd been days when she'd hoped that they might never arrive in Coria, one of the northernmost settlements of the frontier. Being sent to marry a stranger of her half-brother's choosing wasn't an experience she'd relished the first time. It certainly hadn't been one that she'd wanted to repeat, yet now it was happening all over again, barely two months after Julius's funeral, as if her past were repeating itself in the present and she was powerless to do anything to stop it.

How many more times would Tarquinius use her as a bargaining tool? she wondered. How many more times must she be humiliated? Bad enough that he had so much power over her life, but now he was controlling Julia's, too. Her only hope was that her new husband might prove a different kind of man to Julius. If not, then it was surely only a matter of time before her second marriage turned just as sour as her first... If he *did* prove to be different, however, then there was still hope. If he turned out to be good and honourable, then perhaps she could talk to him, perhaps even tell him the whole truth about herself *before* Tarquinius got a chance to interfere.

Of course, that was supposing they survived their current danger and made it to Coria in the first place. Not that it sounded very dangerous, she reassured herself, heading around the front of the carriage in search of Tullus, the leader of the small band of men entrusted with delivering her safely to her new husband. She could already hear his voice at the front of her escort, talking calmly enough—in Latin, too, which was another good sign—though oddly without his usual bravado.

She caught sight of his back at last and then stopped, rooted to the spot in amazement at the view before her. The road was blocked by tens upon tens of Roman soldiers, a whole century of them by the look of it, all standing in perfect formation and dressed in full military regalia, shields and spears at the ready, as if they were marching into battle. They looked even more impressive and imposing than the ones she'd seen on parade in Lindum, their burnished shoulder plates and polished helms gleaming like molten gold in the spring sunshine. And there at the front, wearing a transversely plumed helmet that immediately signalled him out as a

Centurion, stood their leader, the man—*surely it had to be him*—that she'd come to marry.

'Oh!'

She didn't intend to utter the exclamation aloud, but it came out anyway, too loud in the silence that greeted her arrival, and the Centurion's gaze shifted towards her, sweeping briefly over the long folds of her *stola* before their eyes met and held. For a few moments he didn't move. Then he inclined his head, courteously enough, though his gaze never left hers. His eyes were dark, she noticed, like pools of black tar, deep and mysterious and compelling, though the expression in them looked strangely arrested.

'Livia Valeria?' He broke the silence at last.

'Yes.'

This time her voice sounded too quiet as she forced her feet to move forward again. She couldn't think of a single other thing to say either. How *was* she supposed to greet the man she was going to spend the rest of her life with? A simple *Ave* seemed insufficient.

'I trust that you've had a good journey, lady?'

'Yes,' she repeated, wincing inwardly at the repetition. 'At least, as good as we might have hoped for in springtime.'

He glanced up at the sky. 'The weather's been milder than usual.'

'Ye— True.'

She corrected herself just in time, tucking her red curls back behind her ears self-consciously. In her haste to discover what was happening outside, she'd left her *palla* behind in the carriage, leaving her hair uncovered. Now she felt uncomfortably exposed, wishing she'd brought a shawl to cover her *stola* as well. The silken fabric felt too thin and flimsy in front of so many men, but then she'd dressed to impress her new husband, just as Tarquinius had instructed her to…

As awkward as their first encounter felt, however, at least this got it over with quickly. It wasn't exactly the way or the place that she'd expected to meet him, on a woodland road in the middle of nowhere, but perhaps it was as good as any. She'd sent a rider ahead with news of their imminent arrival the day before, though she hadn't expected any response. Having never met him in person—Tarquinius not having considered a meeting necessary prior to their marriage—she'd had no idea what he thought of their union, but surely *this* had to be a good sign, his coming to greet her with an honour guard of soldiers.

'Are we close to the wall?' She asked the first question that sprang into her mind.

'About ten miles away.'

'So close? Then we should be there before nightfall.'

'Even sooner. It's barely half a day's march from here, lady. We'll get you there for dinner.'

'Thank you.'

She smiled nervously and he reached up to remove his helmet, revealing a head of light brown hair, close-cropped like most soldiers', above a ruggedly handsome face, with prominent cheekbones, a slightly crooked nose that looked as if it must have been broken at some point and a resolute-looking jaw. Judging by the ingrained frown lines between his brows, he didn't smile very often, but taken as a whole his face was stern, not cruel, as if whatever burden he carried—and she had the sudden conviction that he carried something—was his alone.

He wasn't as young as she'd feared he might be either. Tarquinius had said that he was newly enrolled in the army, but the man before her looked both older and more experienced, closer to her own age of twenty-four than that of a raw recruit. The realisation was both a relief and a fresh source of anxiety. After marriage to a man almost three times her age, the last thing she'd wanted was to go to the other extreme and marry a boy—something this soldier most definitely wasn't—though there was something powerfully disconcerting about him, too.

There was his sheer size, to begin with. Even without his helmet he was as tall as the next tallest of his men, with broad shoulders and, she couldn't help but notice, an almost equally wide torso. Then there was his overtly military appearance. His long blue cloak, trimmed with a yellow band and fastened at the front with a bronze *fibula*, was swept back over his shoulders, revealing a contoured breastplate and metal greaves over a pair of form-fitting *braccae* that only emphasised his muscular thighs. He'd placed his oval shield to one side, but he was still holding a spear, allowing her a glimpse of hefty forearms decorated with bronze *armillae*, decorations for valour, as well as an intricate silver scabbard on the left side of his belt, paired by a dangerous-looking dagger and three-foot-long *vitis* on the right.

She curled her fingers into her palms, beset by a confusing blend of emotions. Ironically, now that she'd discovered they weren't in any danger, she felt as though she were under a different kind of attack. Her legs felt as weak and tremulous as if she'd just run a race and she felt too hot all over, as if it were the middle of summer and not a mild spring day. Julius had never made her feel this way, not even at the start of their marriage, as if her abdomen were full of tiny, fluttering butterflies, each of them beating their wings in unison. She'd never been so keenly physically aware of another person. Could this Centurion tell? Was it obvious?

It *felt* obvious, as if her body's shameful reaction were writ clear on her face for everyone to see, but at least he was her betrothed, the man she'd come to marry. That was her one consolation. If he'd been anyone else, she might surely have died of shame on the spot.

'I'm honoured to meet you, Lucius Scaevola.' She addressed him by name at last. 'We're grateful for your escort.'

Chapter Two

The Centurion didn't answer at first, his only reaction being a slight tightening of his jaw muscles, and Livia felt a hot pink flush spread up over her cheeks and into her hairline until surely the skin beneath clashed with her curls. Had she displeased him by speaking? Staring into those deep, dark eyes, she had no idea what he was thinking, but surely she hadn't said anything so shocking?

'Pardon, lady—' his stern features became even sterner than before '—but my name is Marius Varro, Second Centurion of the Fourth Cohort of the Sixth Legion. I'm here to escort you and your men the rest of the way to Coria.'

'Varro?'

Her voice seemed to have abandoned her again, emerging as a stricken whisper while she stared at him in dismay. His name was Varro? For some inexplicable reason, it hadn't occurred to her that he might *not* be her future husband. She'd simply assumed that he'd be the man who'd come to greet her—and then once she'd seen *him* she hadn't thought to question his identity at all. Perhaps because she hadn't wanted to.

She closed her eyes and sucked in a deep breath. As it turned out, it wasn't *actually* possible to die from shame and mortification, or disappointment for that matter, though continuing to talk to him at that moment seemed just as terrible.

'You mean…' somehow she forced her eyelids open '…you're *not* Lucius Scaevola?'

'No, lady.' His tone was brisk now, as if he were trying to dispel her embarrassment. 'He's waiting for you in Coria.'

'Oh… I see.'

She stiffened at the sound of Tullus smirking beside her, obviously enjoying the scene. No doubt he'd enjoy telling Tarquinius about it, too, at some later date. They could both laugh at her together… She felt her insides plummet, the ball of tension she'd carried all the way from Lindum curling up like a fist in her belly. But what was one more humiliation, after all? Where men were concerned, she'd already experienced so many. She ought to be immune to the feeling by now, though having this Centurion be a witness to it made her feel even worse somehow.

'Is something amusing?'

She froze at the glacial tone of his voice, half-opening her mouth to protest before she realised he was speaking to Tullus.

'No, sir.' Her escort jumped to attention, visibly startled.

'Then perhaps you can explain to me why you're laughing?'

'I…' Tullus spluttered ineffectively. 'I'm sorry, sir.'

'Are you?' The Centurion's eyes narrowed dangerously. 'If I had time, I'd make sure of that fact. You're lucky I don't. Now get your men ready. We're leaving.'

'Yes, sir.'

Livia felt the corners of her mouth tug upwards as her escort scuttled away like a frightened rabbit. He wouldn't be telling *that* to Tarquinius! She'd never seen him respond to orders so quickly.

'Your men are insolent.' The Centurion turned back to face her and her smile faded at once.

'They're not my men. They're my brother's.'

'All the more reason for them to treat you with respect.'

She gave a murmur of assent, unable to frame an answer to that. Tullus simply took his cue from Tarquinius. He knew exactly how much respect her half-brother would expect him to show, as well as how much he could get away with.

'We'll march for another hour and then rest.' The Centurion—what had he called himself again? Varro?—surveyed the woodland on either side of them suspiciously. 'If that's convenient to you, of course?'

She blinked, surprised to be consulted. 'Yes, if you think that it's best.'

'I do. Now allow me to escort you back to your carriage.'

She didn't move, regarding him warily instead. His eyes were actually green, she noticed, but of such a dark shade they seemed to blend into the wintery foliage around them. She had no idea what he thought of her, but she had the distinct feeling that if she went back to the carriage then she'd only spend the rest of the journey fearing the worst, reliving the scene of her humiliation over and over in her head. Whereas if she stayed…well, hopefully then she might find some way of salvaging her dignity, not to mention of overcoming this strange physical effect he seemed to be having on her. What did Aesop's tale say, something about familiarity breeding contempt? She only hoped that was true.

Besides, even if he wasn't her new husband—a thought that, to her renewed shame, did nothing to relieve the fluttering sensation in her stomach—perhaps he could tell her something about the man she *was* going to marry. Apart from his name, all she knew about Lucius Scaevola was that he came from a senatorial family in Rome and was heavily in debt to her brother. Since those debts had most likely been accrued drinking and gambling in one of Tarquinius's establishments, neither fact was particularly reassuring, and she didn't want to spend the next few hours cooped up in a carriage, her nerves stretched even tighter than before. Julia would be safe with Porcia and surely her skittish maid must have realised they weren't under attack by now.

'I'd prefer to walk for a while.'

One eyebrow lifted at the same time as the furrow in his brow deepened. 'We march at a fast pace, lady.'

'Then I'll march, too.' She felt determined not to be thwarted. 'I have two legs as your soldiers do and no armour to weigh me down.'

His gaze dropped at the mention of her legs, lingering briefly before he pulled his helmet back on with a jerk.

'Pulex!' His shout was so loud and yet so seemingly effortless that she took a surprised step backwards.

'Yes, sir?' a voice from somewhere within the mass of legionaries answered.

'Lead from the front. I'll march at the rear.'

'Yes, sir!'

Livia heaved a breath of relief, taking up a position beside him as the column of soldiers all turned around at once, moving in unison as if they were one and not many individuals. Then she looked down at her feet, belatedly wondering if she were making another mistake, after all. Her thin sandals were completely impractical for marching over hard cobbles and as for her pristine white *stola*… She threw a surreptitious glance towards her companion and then tugged the hem up around her calves, hoisting it out of the dirt.

'Have you changed your mind, lady?'

She whipped her head up in chagrin. She hadn't thought that he was looking at her—he wasn't even looking at her now, staring straight ahead as if he were keen to inspect the tops of his soldiers' helmets—and yet apparently he still knew what she was doing. She had the distinct feeling he didn't miss anything.

'Not at all.'

'As you wish.'

She narrowed her eyes at his insouciant tone, then had to start the march at a near run as the column started forward abruptly.

'I thought that centurions usually rode?' She looked around for a horse, increasing the length of her stride to match his.

'Some do, some don't, but I never ask my men to do anything I wouldn't do.'

'Like march in full armour on a warm day?' She wondered how heavy each man's equipment was. 'It doesn't look very comfortable.'

'If there's one thing the Roman army's good at, lady,

it's marching.' There was a hint of amusement in his voice. 'As for the armour, it's something a soldier gets used to. If we were attacked, we'd be glad of it.'

If they were attacked? She felt a flutter of panic, Porcia's earlier words echoing in her ears. Was such a thing really possible, then?

'I thought the frontier was peaceful again?' She tried to keep the nervous tremor out of her voice.

'It is, for the most part, but it's still wise to be cautious.' He glanced downwards, as if detecting the fear behind her words. 'You're safe with us, lady.'

'Yes…thank you.'

She threw a swift glance over her shoulder at the carriage. Now that she'd insisted on walking, she wished that she hadn't. She wanted to be near her daughter instead, holding her safe in her arms. The thought of Julia being in danger made her feel physically sick. More than that, it made her furious, too. Tarquinius had assured her that it was perfectly safe this side of the wall and she'd been fool enough to believe him. As if she didn't know that almost every word out of his mouth was a lie! But how *could* he? She'd never deceived herself into believing that her half-brother cared a fig for her happiness, but she'd assumed he might at least want to keep her and his niece alive. Now it seemed even that much was beyond him! All he cared about was money and social advancement—allying himself to people who might prove useful to him. In his eyes, she and Julia were nothing more than commodities to be traded. Roman or not, they were little more than slaves.

She clamped a hand to her throat, as if there were actually a shackle there that she couldn't unfasten, determined to ask her questions of this disconcerting

Centurion and get back to the carriage and her daughter as quickly as possible.

'Is the pace too fast, lady?' He was looking down at her again, she noticed suddenly. If she wasn't mistaken, he even looked faintly concerned.

'No.'

She dropped her hand to her side. The pace *was* too fast, forcing her to take two steps for every one of his, but at least it distracted her from her anger at Tarquinius. Besides, she still had questions to ask…

'I was just wondering who sent you to meet us. Was it Lucius Scaevola?'

He twisted his face to the front again, the muscles in his neck and jaw bunching visibly before he answered.

'No, lady. Fabius Augustus Nerva, the Legionary Legate at Coria, sent me.'

'Oh.' Even though she'd sent her message directly to her new husband… 'Then is Lucius Scaevola away on some kind of mission, perhaps?'

'None that I know of.'

'Is he unwell?'

The few heartbeats it took for him to answer told her the truth before he did.

'No, lady.'

'Oh.'

She felt the last vestige of hope crumble away. If Lucius Scaevola wasn't away or unwell, then it seemed he had *no* desire to come and meet her himself. The thought was depressing even if not unexpected… Well, she'd wanted to know what he thought of their union and now she did. Apparently he was just as enthusiastic about it as she was.

But at least she was *there*, she thought with a renewed burst of anger. She was the one who'd come all this way, doing her duty to her family, which in her case meant following Tarquinius's orders. Scaevola might at least have come to greet her. Just when she'd thought she couldn't be any more humiliated! Only now that she'd made herself a hole, she seemed unable to stop digging…

'What is he like?'

'Lady?' The tone of the Centurion's voice conveyed a distinct reluctance to answer.

'Scaevola. We never had a chance to meet in Lindum. I'd like to know what kind of a man he is.'

The jaw muscles tightened again. 'I can't say.'

'Can't or won't?'

She surprised herself with the question. She was being too insistent, too demanding, but her nerves were stretched almost to breaking point and she couldn't seem to help herself. She didn't care what this Centurion thought of her now. His very reluctance to answer was alarming. Surely he could tell her something. *Anything!* Even Scaevola's hair colour would be a start.

'It's not my place to answer, lady. He's a senior officer, a tribune.'

'A *tribune*?'

She stopped so abruptly that he was a few paces ahead before he noticed. She'd assumed that her new husband must be a man of rank for Tarquinius to want an alliance, but Tribunes outranked every Centurion in the army. Only the Legate ranked above them.

'But I thought he'd only just joined the army?'

'He has.' If she wasn't mistaken, his lip curled slightly. 'But he has good family connections. Men like that don't enter in the ranks. Or fight much either.'

'No, I suppose not.'

She put a hand to her head, thoughts whirling. Not just a tribune, but a senatorial one, too? Such a man was more than a few steps above her on the social scale, more like a whole ladder away. The debt to her half-brother must be huge indeed for him to accept her as a bride, but what exactly did Tarquinius want from him? What was her half-brother planning?

She twisted her face to one side, vividly aware of the Centurion's stern gaze. They'd climbed out of the woodland while they'd been talking on to a plateau overlooking the rugged moorland to the north. The landscape in this part of the country was noticeably wilder than the flatter marshlands around Lindum, with jagged crags and rocky outcrops dotting a spartan terrain that seemed particularly suited to the man beside her.

On any other day she might have admired it. Today she felt as if a black cloud had passed over the sun, obscuring any warmth or beauty and making her feel powerless and vulnerable, like one of the reedy-looking trees clutching the sides of those same rocky outcrops, holding on for dear life in a wind-battered world that offered no respite. She'd as good as voiced her fears about her future husband out loud and this Centurion's answers had only confirmed the worst. As grateful as she was for his honesty, she didn't think her spirits could sink any lower.

'Perhaps I ought to go back to the carriage after all.' She felt a sudden, overpowering urge to get away from him.

'Very well.' He hesitated briefly before continuing. 'He's young, lady. He has a lot to learn, that's all.'

She bit her lip, fighting the impulse to laugh. Not a demure, ladylike laugh, but a hysterical, high-pitched scream of a laugh, one that would vent all her rage and frustration and probably convince him that she was mad, too. He was trying to placate her, she could tell, using the same tone she'd been using all this time to reassure Porcia, but there was nothing reassuring about it.

A lot to learn... What could that mean except that she was going to marry a boy after all? How would a boy react when he saw her? In marital terms, she was ten years past her prime. More important, how would he react to Julia? She only hoped that Tarquinius had told him about her in advance, though surely he had... If nothing else, *surely* he would have mentioned her daughter?

She gave a curt nod, not trusting herself to speak as she turned and made her way hastily back to the carriage. She didn't want to look at him any longer—him or any other man. All she wanted was to be left alone, to be a widow and mother, to find a place to belong and to raise her daughter in peace. Was that so much to ask?

Yes.

She knew the answer because Tarquinius had made it clear to her before she'd left Lindum. No matter what kind of man was waiting for her in Coria, she had to go ahead with the marriage. She had no freedom, no money and no choice. She had to do what her half-brother ordered or he'd cast her and Julia off from his protection for ever. She was heading for the northernmost frontier of the Roman Empire, to the very border with her mother's homeland—one of the many facts she was specifically forbidden to mention—to the place she'd spent her whole life wanting to see and now dreaded the sight of. There was no turning back and nowhere else to go. Worse than that, there wasn't the slightest hope of escape.

Chapter Three

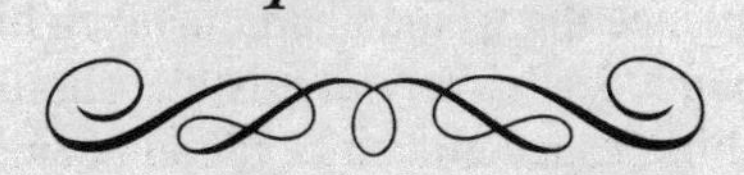

What kind of man was Lucius Scaevola?

Marius waited until the woman had climbed back inside her carriage before storming to the front of the column, stamping his hobnailed boots so violently that it looked as if he were trying to hammer the cobbled road to pieces.

What kind of a man was he?

What the hell kind of question was that? What *could* he say of a nineteen-year-old wastrel who hadn't even had the decency to come and greet his new bride himself? He knew what he *ought* to have said, what he was expected to say of a senior officer, but honour had prevented him from lying and now he had the uncomfortable suspicion that he'd only made her feel ten times more anxious than she clearly already was.

'Anything to report?' He fell into step beside Pulex, glaring ferociously.

'No, sir.' His Optio did a double take at the sight of him. 'Something the matter, sir?'

'No.' He forced his jaw to relax. After all, his bad temper had nothing to do with his second-in-command.

'Have you seen any signs of unrest? Anything out of the ordinary?'

'Nothing, sir.' Pulex shook his head. 'Do you really think there's something to worry about?'

'I don't know.'

Marius rubbed a hand across his forehead, trying to ease the band of tension that seemed to have settled there ever since the woman had mistaken him for her new husband. Such a trivial mistake shouldn't have bothered him, especially since it had been addressed and dealt with. There was certainly no need to still be thinking about it when there were bigger, far bigger, matters at hand.

A Caledonian rebellion, for a start.

Not that anyone believed him. Quite the opposite—most of the Roman officers in Coria thought he was being alarmist, but then they treated the local Briton tribes with contempt and dismissed any rumours that came from them. Now that Septimius Severus had been declared Emperor and the bulk of the British garrison had returned from fighting in Gaul, most simply assumed that the threat from the northern tribes had gone and the wall was invincible again.

Marius wasn't so sure. He'd been sent back to Britannia earlier than most, three years before when a distracted Rome had started to take the threat to its northern borders seriously again. He knew what the tribes were capable of, knew that the wall had been breached on more than one occasion, with mile-castles burned down and even a few forts destroyed. The idea of a lasting peace was still fragile. During the past decade the tribes had not only learned that Rome wasn't infallible, but they'd discovered exactly where its weaknesses lay—

and there were still sections of the wall that needed repair and reinforcements.

'All we can do is stay alert.'

'Yes, sir.' Pulex gestured towards the carriage. 'What was all that about?'

The band around Marius's head tightened again. 'She wanted to talk about Scaevola. She's worried about meeting him.'

'She ought to be. You have to pity the woman.'

Marius made a non-committal sound, fixing his gaze on the horizon with a scowl. Pity wasn't exactly the emotion he'd been feeling, though he supposed it was one among many. On the whole, however, his mind, not to mention his body, had been governed by a far different emotion, one that was still making him feel too hot beneath his mail shirt and armour.

To say that he'd been caught by surprise was an understatement. He hadn't wanted to be there in the first place, regarding the whole mission as a waste of both time and resources, but he'd expected a girl, not a woman, and especially not one who was quite so stunningly beautiful, albeit not in a conventional or fashionable way. Her face was too round, her forehead too wide, her nose and cheeks dotted with clusters of tiny brown freckles, but there was something mesmerising about her none the less, an inner radiance accompanied by an air of sadness that gave her face a deeper beauty than that of any other woman he'd ever come across. She'd seemed strong and yet vulnerable at the same time, the proud tilt of her head putting him in mind of an empress, a woman he might feel honoured to serve. His first thought upon seeing her was that Scaevola was the luckiest dog this side of the Tiber.

As for her hair… He'd seen red hair before, of course, though nothing quite so resplendent. If he didn't know better he would have thought she was Caledonian. Trailing over a bosom that had raised his temperature by a few more painful degrees, it had looked like some kind of lustrous dawn-kissed waterfall, rippling with amber lights. He'd been acutely aware of her womanly figure, too, all the curves and contours barely disguised by a tight-fitting, silken *stola*, though he'd tried his hardest *not* to look, losing himself in the depths of her luminous blue-green eyes instead while he'd tried to pull himself back together. Surely no more than a minute could have passed while he'd simply stood and stared, though it had been long enough for her to come to a mistaken assumption about his identity.

What on earth had caused her to jump to such a ludicrous conclusion? Annoyance warred with self-recrimination. She might have *asked* who he was before simply assuming! But then it had been an easy mistake, especially for someone who didn't know anything about her betrothed, as she clearly didn't. And *of course* she'd assumed that the man who'd come to greet her, not to mention one who'd stared at her quite so openly, was the man she was going to marry! It had been a natural misunderstanding, though one that might have been avoided if only he'd introduced himself sooner. If only he hadn't been rendered temporarily speechless at the sight of her. Now he wasn't sure who he was angrier with, himself or Scaevola, but it was no wonder she'd looked so flushed and self-conscious. He could hardly have behaved any more inappropriately!

Perhaps that explained why he'd felt unable to refuse when she'd asked to march alongside him. Granting such a request was against protocol, not to mention his own better judgement, but he'd agreed anyway, distracted by the mention of her legs and the realisation that he wanted, very much, to see them. When she'd tugged her *stola* up around her calves he'd felt an almost overpowering urge to glance downwards. Besides, he'd been impressed by the fact that she hadn't simply run away after her mistake. Embarrassed though she'd been, she'd stayed anyway, asking her questions about Scaevola with an air of quiet determination. Clearly she was no shy and retiring Roman maiden, even if he'd been unable to give her the answers she'd wanted. Even his attempt at consolation had failed. Damn it all, he knew how to address a whole cohort of soldiers, to send men into battle when necessary, but he'd been unable to offer comfort to one woman!

He quickened the marching pace, muttering a series of increasingly vehement denunciations against Lucius Scaevola under his breath. *He* was the one who ought to have come to greet her—she was *his* bride, after all! Albeit an unwanted one, if the look on that good-for-nothing's face as they'd passed on the steps of the Legate's villa that morning had been anything to go by. Nerva himself had looked none too pleased either when Marius entered his office a few moments later, his usually phlegmatic expression tense and agitated, as if he'd just been arguing.

'You summoned me, sir?' Briefly, he'd wondered if he ought to have waited outside, but Nerva had beckoned him forward with a wave.

'Ah, Marius, a man of sense at last! Come in, I need your help. That boy is taking years off my life.'

'Whatever you need, sir.'

'What I need is a drink.' Nerva had poured two cupfuls of wine and then given him a shrewd look. 'You'll have gathered by now that Scaevola wasn't posted here by accident. His father is an acquaintance in the Senate and he asked for a favour.'

'Yes, sir.' Marius had nodded discreetly. He'd already guessed as much. It wasn't uncommon for rich sons to be made Tribunes in the army, doing a few years of military service before joining the Senate, though Nerva's tone made it sound as if, in this case, it had been more of a punishment.

'His father wanted Scaevola out of Rome and out of trouble for a while.' Nerva had dropped into the chair behind his desk with a sigh. 'Only trouble found him before he ever reached us, it seems. You might recall that he was late arriving? Well, it appears that he broke his journey in Lindum for a week or so, tallying up a considerable gambling debt in the local taverns. Fortunately for him, the entire debt was bought up by the tavern owner. Unfortunately for him, he still couldn't pay.'

'Surely Scaevola's family can afford it, sir?'

'I get the impression that his father thinks he's already paid more than enough. I'll send a message to Rome, but it won't get there in time.'

'In time for what, sir?'

Nerva's expression had darkened. 'It would appear that the tavern owner is a cleverer man than our Lucius. He's an important man in Lindum, too, one of its wealthiest citizens with political ambitions to boot. If I had to guess, I'd say he's after a brother-in-law in the Senate.'

'A brother-in-law?'

'Quite.' Nerva had tossed back the last of his wine with a flourish. 'The tavern owner offered his sister as a bride in exchange for discharge of the debt and Scaevola agreed, though needless to say he's not happy about it. In any case, the woman's on her way here now. A messenger arrived last night. She ought to be arriving today.'

'But Scaevola arrived a month ago. Why didn't he mention it before?'

'Doubtless he thought that out of sight was out of mind, but if you're asking me to explain what goes on in his head then I can't. He's a disgrace to the army and to Rome. It's absurd that a man like that can be a tribune while you—' Nerva had stopped mid-sentence. 'Forgive me, Marius, that was tactless of me.'

'It's only the truth, sir.' He'd pulled his shoulders back purposively. 'My father's dishonour is mine, too. It's only right that I pay for it.'

'You've already done more than enough. If it were up to me, you'd be a senior centurion by now. There's not a finer soldier in the whole Roman army.'

'Thank you, sir.'

'Which is why I'm trusting you to go and meet the woman. We need to do the right thing, but Scaevola is too reckless. Unless he finds another way to clear the debt then she's his only way out of trouble, but I can't trust him not to do something stupid. Meet her on the road, bring her here and then we'll see if we can't find a way to resolve this situation…'

So that was what he was doing there, Marius thought bitterly, marching his men through Carvetti territory—friendly territory, at least—in order to clear up another man's mess. It had seemed an easy enough mission at first, but now his peace of mind was shattered and not simply because she was arguably the most desirable woman he'd ever laid eyes on. The worst of it was that she was clearly anxious, too, and with good reason. He wouldn't wish a spiteful, mean-spirited youth like Scaevola on any woman, let alone her… The very thought brought him to a standstill.

'We'll stop here for a while.' He raised a hand, bringing the column to a halt. 'Tell the men to get something to eat.'

'Already, sir?' Pulex looked faintly surprised. 'Shall I send out some scouts?'

'No.' He frowned at his own order. Usually that would be the first thing he'd do, but today his priorities seemed to have shifted. 'Post sentries, but keep the men here as protection.'

'Yes, sir.'

He waited for Pulex to walk away before turning his attention back to the carriage. Scaevola's bride was already climbing down, accompanied by a girl of around fifteen with waist-length black hair, a winsome face and the expression of a startled deer—a slave or a maid most likely. Seconds later, another smaller figure followed them, a child with flaming red hair around a face that looked strikingly familiar, an almost identical miniature of the one he'd seen earlier. He felt a jolt of surprise, his feet moving before he'd even ordered them to.

Nerva hadn't mentioned anything about a child.

'Centurion?' The woman regarded him steadily as he approached. She seemed to have recovered from her earlier distress, though there was a distinct wariness in her manner now.

'Lady.' He was irritated by how stern his voice sounded, but he needed an explanation at least.

'This is my maidservant, Porcia…' she gestured to the black-haired girl before placing her hands firmly on the child's shoulders '…and this is my daughter, Julia.'

'Daughter?'

'Yes.' Her gaze flickered slightly. 'Is that a problem, Centurion?'

He didn't answer for a few moments. *Was* it a problem? Not for him, but Scaevola was another matter. Was this something else the fool hadn't bothered to tell Nerva or didn't he know himself? Marius had the discomforting suspicion that it was more likely the latter. He wouldn't be pleased, that much was certain… He was still considering what to say when he noticed the girl's frightened expression.

'It's not a problem at all, lady.' He crouched down, bringing his face level with the child's. 'I just wasn't aware that we had such an important guest travelling with us. Pardon my neglect. Are you enjoying the journey?'

'No.' The girl pressed her cheek against her mother's skirt. 'It's too long.'

'It is.' He nodded in agreement. 'When I first came to Britannia I thought the road north would never end, but it's a great honour to come here. Not many Romans ever get to see the great wall. Even our new Emperor hasn't yet. You're very lucky.'

The girl smiled shyly and then leaned forward, studying his face with a serious expression. 'Are you my new father?'

'Me?' The words almost made him tumble backwards in surprise. Apparently both mother and daughter had a knack for asking difficult questions. 'No, my name's Marius.'

'I'm Julia.'

'That's pretty. You know our new Empress has the same name. Should I call you Empress, too?'

She giggled and he inclined his head with a feeling of satisfaction. At least he'd made someone feel better. 'But now you need to stretch your legs and eat. We have tack biscuits and dried bacon.'

'Perhaps I can offer something else?'

The woman sounded different all of a sudden and he looked up, surprised to find that she was smiling as well. It made her look even more alluring and his sense of satisfaction increased tenfold.

'We have olives and bread, baked fresh in Vindomora yesterday.'

'That sounds delicious.' He stood up to face her again. 'I haven't had olives for a month.'

'Then we'd be happy to share, wouldn't we, Julia?'

The girl nodded and skipped happily away, following the maidservant around the back of the carriage.

'You have a good manner with children.' The woman was still smiling at him. 'Do you have many of your own?'

'None.' He stifled a bark of laughter at the very suggestion. 'But I like children. They see the world in a different way to adults.'

'Maybe in a better way.' Her face clouded for a moment and then cleared again as Porcia and Julia came back with a basket, spreading a blanket over the ground beside them. 'Will you join us?'

Marius threw a quick glance over his shoulder towards his legionaries. There would be comments later if he sat down to eat with a woman. Not in his hearing, perhaps, but it didn't take long for gossip to spread round a camp. He wasn't known for being sociable at the best of times, especially with women. But surely there was no harm in a short respite…

'I won't ask any more awkward questions, I promise.'

The obvious embarrassment in her voice decided him. Clearly she thought it was her earlier behaviour making him hesitate and he felt the strange need to reassure her.

'Then I'd be glad to, lady.'

'Livia.' She sat down on the blanket, curling her legs up beside her and tucking her *stola* beneath. 'Mother of the Empress Julia.'

'Livia,' he repeated. He liked the name, not to mention the way her tongue flicked to the front of her mouth as she pronounced it. 'Then you may call me Marius.'

Her lips curved again and he crouched down on his haunches beside her. That seemed a reasonable compromise. He wasn't sitting down, not exactly, and if anyone asked—not that anyone beside Pulex would dare—he could say that they'd simply been discussing the journey.

'She seems like a good child.' He gestured towards the girl, leaping and dancing around the moorland now like an animal newly released from a cage.

'She is.'

'How old?'

'Four years last autumn.'

'You're a widow?'

'As opposed to?' Her smile vanished and he winced at his own tactlessness.

'Forgive me, I didn't mean to imply anything else.'

She gave him a long look and then shrugged. 'It's all right. At my age I suppose I could just as easily have been divorced.'

He lifted an eyebrow at the words. A lady didn't usually mention her age, let alone the possibility of divorce. The laws around marriage had been tightened considerably over recent years, so that a man could no longer readily divorce his wife unless he could prove adultery, but for some reason he didn't want to think about that.

'Have you been widowed long?'

'Two months.'

'Only two?'

He couldn't keep the surprise out of his voice. If Scaevola had arrived in Coria a month ago and the betrothal had been arranged *before* he'd left Lindum then it meant that her brother must have betrothed her within weeks of her husband's death.

'Only two.' She repeated the words quietly, though with a distinct edge of bitterness.

He frowned at the implication. Bad enough that she was being sent to marry Scaevola, but to betroth her while she was still in mourning… He felt a flicker of anger towards the unseen brother. What kind of man would do such a thing?

'You looked surprised when you saw Julia.' She sounded anxious this time. 'Weren't you expecting her?'

He hesitated briefly and then shook his head. So much for not asking awkward questions…

'No, but I only received my orders this morning. Perhaps it was simply an oversight.'

'It wasn't.' She clasped her hands together in her lap with an air of conviction. 'My brother must not have mentioned her.'

'I understand it was your brother who arranged the betrothal.' He wondered what on earth was compelling him to pursue the subject.

'Yes.' She gave a bleak-sounding laugh. 'He knows an opportunity when he sees one. But I suppose there's no turning back now...'

He felt an obscure sense of discomfort. The wistful note in her voice made the words sound like a question, as if she were actually asking him to let her turn back, to let her escape.

Escape? The word entered his head unexpectedly, increasing his sense of unease, though he resented its meaning. He wasn't her captor and Coria wasn't a prison. He was only following his orders, escorting her to a new life with a new husband, that was all. There was no coercion or force on his part. If anything, he was protecting her. There was certainly no need for him to feel guilty, even if something about her made him feel strangely defensive.

'Is that what you want, to turn back?' He asked the question before he could think better of it and saw her eyes widen with a look of surprise.

'Yes...no... I don't know.' She looked and sounded genuinely torn. 'That is, I want to see the wall. I've always wanted to see it, ever since I was a little girl... but not like this.' She clamped her lips together as if she were trying to stop herself from saying something else and then couldn't resist, her blue-green eyes blazing with sparks of defiance as the words seemed to burst out of her. 'As for Lucius Scaevola, I wish he'd never come to Lindum. I wish he'd never set foot inside my brother's tavern. Most of all, I wish I'd never heard his name!'

Chapter Four

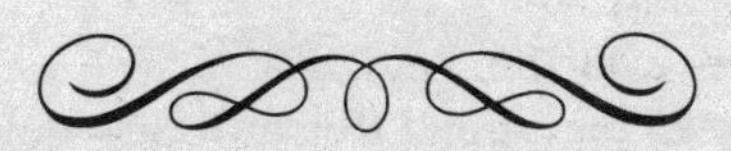

'We're almost there, lady.'

Livia pulled back the window curtain at the sound of Marius's voice. He was walking beside the carriage, looking no different to the way he had earlier, as if the day's march had been nothing more than a light stroll. His uniform still looked pristine, without so much as a speck of dust on it. How was that possible?

'You mean Coria?'

'Take a look.'

He gestured ahead and she craned her head out of the window, surprised to see that they were already entering the outskirts of a small town. There were shops and stalls and taverns as well as several stone villas, more than she would have expected at such a remote outpost.

'Most visitors from the south are surprised.' Marius gave her a knowing look. 'But not everyone here is a legionary.'

'But I thought it was a fortress?'

'It is. Over there.' He pointed down the street towards a tall stone palisade fronted by two massive watchtowers. 'This is just the *vicus*, the town that's grown up around it.'

'What about the great wall? Is it behind the fort?'

'No, lady, we're still two miles from the wall. Coria is a base for the Sixth Legion, four cohorts of it anyway. The forts along the wall are manned by auxiliaries.'

'Auxiliaries?' She didn't understand the distinction. 'What are those?'

'Soldiers who aren't citizens.'

'You mean they aren't Roman?' She looked at him in surprise. 'Then why do they man the wall? Why fight for Rome?'

'To gain their citizenship—' he gave her a strange look as if the answer ought to be obvious '—once they've served their twenty-five years like the rest of us.'

'So they do all the hard work while you sit back here?'

'Not exactly.' His expression slipped into a frown. 'The legion was sent back from Gaul by Emperor Severus to restore those parts of the wall damaged by the northern invasion a few years ago. That means hundreds of men doing building work and providing military support where necessary. Believe me, none of us gets to *sit back* and do nothing.'

'Oh…no, I suppose not.'

She bit her tongue, already regretting the words. It had been an insulting, not to mention revealing, thing to have said, and she didn't want to offend him—or to provoke his suspicions either. After his earlier kindness to Julia she owed him better than that and criticising the Empire wasn't an intelligent thing to do under any circumstances. The way she'd denounced Scaevola earlier had been incriminating enough, but she hadn't been able to contain her anger at her own sense of powerlessness any longer. Still, if Marius repeated the words… Not that she thought he would. As stern as he seemed, there was something inherently trustworthy about him, or at least she thought there was. Then again, she'd been wrong about a man she'd trusted before.

'I'm sorry.' She adopted what she hoped was a suitably apologetic expression. 'I'm just disappointed. I'd hoped I might get to see it today.'

That was true. Despite everything, she was still excited by the thought of catching her first glimpse of the wall and the land beyond it.

'Indeed.' He still sounded offended.

'Can you see it from Coria?'

'No, the landscape's too hilly.'

'Then do you think I might be allowed to visit?'

He gave her a sidelong look, as if surprised by her interest. 'I think that might be up to your husband, lady.'

She grimaced, unwilling to talk about what her new husband would or would not let her do. After her earlier mistake, she felt more nervous than ever about meeting him. Loath as she was to admit it, she had the disturbing suspicion that no other man could possibly measure up to the one she'd *thought* that he was…

A soldier in one of the watchtowers called out a greeting as they entered the gateway and she pulled her head back inside the carriage, smiling at Porcia, though to her surprise, the girl didn't look happy.

'What's the matter? We've arrived safely at last.'

'Yes, but…' Her maid leaned forward, as if she were

afraid of being overheard. 'What about you? What if it all happens again?'

What if...? She felt a ripple of panic start in her chest and begin to spread outwards, coursing through her veins like poison. There was no point in pretending that she didn't understand Porcia's meaning. She'd been thinking the same thing ever since they'd left Lindum, desperately hoping that Tarquinius was only marrying her off to be rid of her this time, without any ulterior motive. Now that she knew who her intended was, however, she had to admit that seemed unlikely. No doubt her brother had big plans for Lucius Scaevola in the future. And if he didn't comply then Tarquinius would have no qualms about blackmailing him as well... Another ripple of panic spread outwards... And since her new husband wouldn't be able to vent his anger on anyone else, it would all fall on her again, just as it had with Julius.

What if it *did* all happen again?

She shook her head helplessly. So much depended on her new husband's character, on him being willing or able to stand up to Tarquinius. Both her and Julia's futures depended on it.

Nervously, she peered out of the window again. They were inside the fort now, rolling down the Via Praetoria between storerooms, barracks and granaries towards the Via Principalis and what looked like the military headquarters, a huge stone building with a column-framed courtyard at the front.

'Are we here, Mama?'

Julia lifted her head from the bench, yawning, as they turned away from the headquarters and rolled to a halt in front of a large villa.

'Yes, love.' She wrapped an arm around her daughter's shoulders, pulling her close. 'We're here.'

'Is this our house?'

'I don't think so.'

'This is the Legionary Legate's house,' Marius interjected, already opening the carriage door. 'My orders were to escort you here.'

'Then I thank you for your escort, Centurion.'

She spoke formally as she took his proffered hand and stepped down, trying to ignore the way her breath caught and then quickened as their fingers touched. Standing so close, her nostrils filled with his scent of leather and sandalwood, she felt as though all her insides were performing a series of unwonted contortions. She could sense his body heat, too, radiating through his mail shirt, though perhaps that was just her own blood heating in response to his proximity. Every part of her skin seemed to be tingling, from the top of her head to the tips of her toes, as if his hands were moving all over her body and not merely grasping her fingers.

She swallowed as her heart seemed to sink and do somersaults at the same time. She'd spent her time in the carriage trying to convince herself that her earlier reaction to him had all been a mistake, a reaction to the tension of the past few days, and yet holding his hand now, the feeling seemed ten times as strong, as if denial had only magnified her body's response. If it were nerves, then it didn't feel like any nerves she recognised. It felt strangely, shockingly, inappropriately pleasurable. How could it *still* when she knew that he *wasn't* the man she'd come to marry?

She peeked up at him, but he was staring straight

ahead at the villa, as if he felt no reaction to her at all. Perhaps he didn't. It was hard to imagine such a powerful emotion being entirely one-sided, but judging by the severity of his expression, it clearly was. Which was a good thing, she told herself. If he felt the same then it would only make things more awkward and her earlier mistake had been bad enough.

She drew her fingers away, pulling her *palla* over her head as he turned to lift Julia down from the carriage, making a small bow as he did so, as if she truly were an empress. She smiled at her daughter's delighted reaction. Even if she never saw him again, which she supposed was quite likely given the size of the fort, she'd remember him for that kindness. The rest of it she would try to forget, not just for her sake, but for that of her new husband. No good could come of dwelling on what-might-have-beens, on what her future might have been if Marius Varro *had* been the man she'd come to marry.

They started up the steps of the villa together, Julia in the middle like a shield keeping them apart. It made Livia no less physically aware of him, but at least it made the cause of her flushed cheeks less obvious. Now if she could just keep her daughter between them while she bade him farewell…

No sooner had the thought entered her head than the little girl tripped, sprawling forward on to the hard granite steps. Instinctively, she sprang forward to catch her, only to find Marius there at the same time, so that they both caught an elbow and lifted her up before she could hurt herself. Livia threw him a grateful look, but he only nodded sternly, waiting for her to move ahead before dropping unobtrusively to one side, though staying close enough to reach them, she noticed, in case Julia stumbled again. For some reason, his presence there made her feel better, as if he were protecting them both.

'Ah, Livia Valeria.' An aristocratic-looking man dressed in a pristine white toga decorated with a purple band appeared in the villa doorway, bowing his head in greeting. 'I'm Fabius Augustus Nerva, Legate Legionary of the Sixth Victorious Legion. Welcome to Coria.'

'Thank you. I'm glad to be here.' She bent her own head in response. As intimidating as the man looked, she was relieved to find that his expression was welcoming. 'This is my daughter, Julia.'

She gestured behind her, better prepared this time for the look of surprise that immediately crossed his features. Obviously he hadn't been expecting a child either.

'I see.' Whatever his private thoughts, he recovered himself quickly. 'Well, we're always looking for new recruits. Have you come to join the legion, young lady?'

'Marius says I'm an empress,' Julia answered seriously.

'*Marius* said that?' The Legate's eyebrows shot upwards as he threw a swift, questioning look at his Centurion. 'Well, in that case I await your commands, but first you'd better come inside. My wife has arranged some refreshments after your long journey. You, too, *Marius*.'

He stepped aside, letting her precede him through the *vestibulum* and into the atrium beyond. It was a large, airy room with a painting of a garden on one wall and an intricate mosaic of two tigers wrestling on the floor, their claws and teeth bared in ferocious combat. Livia bent her head to study it, so impressed by the intricacy of the design that it took her a few moments to notice the pair of sandalled feet standing at the opposite edge.

'Oh!'

She exclaimed in alarm, pressing one hand to her chest as she met the critical stare of another, younger man watching her with arms clasped behind his back. Tall and coldly handsome, he looked to be around twenty years of age with short blond hair, piercing blue eyes and an air of arrogant hauteur that seemed to ooze out of every pore. She didn't need an introduction to know who he was.

'Ah, Lucius.' Nerva gave a strained-looking smile. 'May I present Livia Valeria, your new bride.'

'I'm honoured to meet you, Lucius Scaevola.' She felt vividly aware of the contrast with the first time she'd said those words. They were expected of her, but this time she didn't feel even the tiniest flicker of attraction. Neither, apparently, did he as his gaze flitted over and then past her.

'She's older than I expected.'

He spoke in a tone of contempt to Nerva, as if speaking to her directly was beneath his dignity, and she felt the last of her hopes flitter away, replaced by dismay and indignation. Even if she *was* a few years past the expected age for a bride, he ought not to mention it aloud as if she had neither ears nor feelings.

'Who is *that*?' His gaze homed in on Julia suddenly, his voice turning high-pitched and horrified.

'*That* is my daughter.' She took a step to one side, blocking his view. 'Julia.'

'Is this some kind of joke?' Scaevola drew in a hiss of breath, seeming to rear backwards and upwards at the same time, like a cornered snake rising up on its coils. 'A daughter? I wasn't told anything about a child!'

He whirled away from her towards Nerva. 'Surely I can't be expected to take on another man's whelp? It's preposterous. Just look at her hair! She looks like a Caledonian! A filthy barbarian!'

Livia felt the blood drain from her face, the ball of tension in her chest tightening so fiercely she actually felt winded. She couldn't speak, only stare, stunned into silence by the insult. Red hair had been fashionable in Rome for a time, years before when the sight of tribespeople from the north had been a novelty, but now it was hardly unique. There were plenty of red-headed citizens scattered throughout the Empire, though she'd heard that some Romans still regarded it as a sign of barbarism. Not that she'd ever heard such prejudices expressed quite so blatantly nor so vehemently before. Even Julius had only *looked* his disapproval, but then he'd liked her hair at first. He'd called it her crowning glory before he'd turned it into yet another reason to hate her.

A faint sobbing sound emanating from behind her skirts forced self-pity aside and she curled her hands into fists as a rush of maternal fury overcame shock. Insulting her was one thing. Insulting her daughter was a different matter entirely!

'We're Roman.' She pulled her *palla* back from her head, unveiling her own copper-red curls. If Julia was going to be condemned for her hair colour, then they'd be condemned together. 'Just like you.'

'How dare you!' His expression managed to convey both outrage and horror. 'You're nothing like me!'

'And we deserve your respect!' She tossed her head deliberately so that the long tresses spilled over her shoulders, speaking with a disdain equal to his own. No matter what else, she wasn't going to let Julia see her behave with anything other than dignity.

Scaevola's eyes narrowed to venomous slits before he turned back towards Nerva. 'How could I ever take a pair like that back to Rome? It's unthinkable! I'd be the laughing stock of the Senate.'

'Lucius.' Nerva's voice held a warning note, though the younger man seemed not to notice.

'I won't do it. I'd rather marry a—'

'Sir!'

Livia spun around, as startled as everyone else by Marius's interruption. Despite Nerva's invitation to join them, he'd kept to one side of the atrium, half-hidden in the shadows, though she'd remained acutely aware of his presence. Even without looking she could somehow sense his proximity. If he'd left, she had a feeling she would have known it.

She *hadn't* counted on his coming to her aid, however, and yet that seemed to be exactly what he was doing. He actually looked angry, she noticed with surprise, his jaw a rigidly set line as he eyeballed the other man, though as a centurion he surely had no right to interrupt a tribune. She didn't know much about the Roman army, but she knew that hierarchy was everything. Judging by the way that Scaevola's mouth was hanging open, gaping like a landed fish, he could hardly believe it either.

She held her breath, not knowing whether to feel

grateful or concerned. As much as she appreciated Marius's defending her, she didn't want him to be punished for it. She had enough to worry about already.

'Centurion?' Nerva was the first to recover from his surprise.

'Forgive my interruption, sir.' Marius sounded as if he were speaking through clenched teeth. 'But I believe our guests are tired after their journey.'

'Of course.' To her amazement, instead of issuing a reprimand, Nerva agreed with him. 'We can discuss this another time. Don't you agree, Lucius?'

The Tribune didn't get a chance to answer as a kindly-looking matron emerged through one of the archways at that moment, her genial smile instantly defusing the tension.

'Ah, you must be Livia.' The woman came forward at once, hands outstretched. 'I wondered what was keeping you all out here. I'm so delighted to meet you.'

'This is my wife, Hermenia.' Nerva looked visibly relieved by her arrival. 'She'll show you to your room. Under the circumstances, we thought it might be best if you stayed here as our guest for a few days. Until matters are settled.'

'If they're settled…' Lucius sounded faintly rebellious.

'Thank you.' Livia clasped the woman's hands gratefully, feeling as if she'd just been offered a raft in the middle of a storm-tossed ocean. At that moment anything was better than spending any more time with her intended. Not that running away and hiding was going to solve anything, but it would be a welcome respite.

Then she reached an arm behind her, drawing her

daughter out from her hiding place. 'We'd be happy to, wouldn't we, Julia?'

The older woman's eyes fell on the girl and a look of understanding swept across her features, followed by a genuine-looking smile.

'Then come with me.' She held a hand out to Julia at the same time as she cast a vaguely threatening look towards Scaevola. 'You can have something to eat and then we'll find you a nice cosy bed.'

'Thank you.' Livia glanced towards Nerva. 'I appreciate your hospitality.'

'Think nothing of it. We'll speak properly tomorrow.' He sounded sombre. 'When you're feeling refreshed.'

'Yes.'

She didn't know how else to answer, her gaze darting past him towards Lucius and then Marius. Standing on different sides of the room, the two men looked like complete opposites. She knew what one of them thought of her—he'd made his opinion abundantly obvious—but as for the other…

Marius's expression was stern again, even sterner than it had been on their journey. His anger seemed to have faded and yet there was an air of danger about him, as if he'd only restrained, not overcome, his temper. Even so, she couldn't help but wish that she'd guessed the identity of her new husband correctly the first time. Instead he'd been the one to come to her rescue against her real intended, a man who appeared to be even more loathsome than Julius. She hadn't thought it possible that her second husband could be any worse than her first, but apparently it was.

She dropped her gaze at the thought and fled.

Chapter Five

'I won't do it!' Scaevola's eyes glittered with anger as he stormed up and down the atrium.

'You made an agreement with her brother.' Nerva's usual unruffled demeanour was severely ruffled. 'If you refuse to go through with the marriage then he'll have grounds against you.'

'Better that than dishonour my family.'

'You're the one who's brought dishonour on your family!' Nerva's tone was distinctly unsympathetic. 'Drinking and gambling and who knows what else. Your father would be appalled.'

'He still wouldn't want me to marry a barbarian!'

Marius gritted his teeth at the insult. The combined effort of biting his tongue and restraining his temper was becoming more and more difficult, but unless he wanted to end up demoted, or worse, it was also necessary. His earlier interruption had been bad enough. Arguing with a superior officer was strictly forbidden, even when the officer in question had nothing superior about him. He wasn't exactly sure what had come over him, except that the callous way Scaevola had insulted Livia and her daughter had enraged him to the point that he would gladly have given a year's pay for the chance to beat the living daylights out of him.

In all honesty, he still would. It was bad enough that Livia was going to marry such a man—the very thought of which made him inordinately, inappropriately furious—but from what she'd told him earlier, she was still in mourning for her first husband. What kind of brother would force his sister to marry again while she was grieving? What kind of man would even concoct such a scheme, debt or no debt? Everything about it felt wrong.

'If you're so worried about your family honour, why don't you ask your father to pay the debt?' Nerva fixed Scaevola with a hard stare.

'Because he would refuse.' The Tribune's eyes dropped to his sandals. 'He already told me there'd be no more money before I left Rome.'

'Then as I see it, you've no choice. I suggest that you either apologise to your new bride and hope that she forgives you or prepare to stand trial.'

'Her brother wouldn't dare to accuse me of anything!' Scaevola blustered. 'He knows who I am.'

'I'm sure he does, but do you know who *he* is?' Nerva held up a hand before the youth could answer. 'He's a powerful man in Lindum and you're a long way from Rome. Your family name won't protect you this far away. Now I suggest that you take the night to consider your choices. Try staying sober for once.'

Lucius gave an angry snort, his handsome features contorting with malice as he turned and almost walked into Marius. 'As for you, Centurion, you had no right interrupting me earlier.'

'You're absolutely right, sir.' Marius folded his arms pointedly. 'I didn't.'

'Insolent dog! I ought to have you whipped.'

'If there's any whipping to be done then it will be on *my* authority, not yours!' The last vestiges of Nerva's self-control seemed to snap. 'You deserved to be interrupted. Don't ever insult a lady in my presence again, do you understand?'

'Yes, sir.'

'Now get out. I'm sick of the sight of you.'

Marius lifted his chin, meeting Scaevola's glare with a hard look of his own as the latter stormed out of the room.

'I apologise, sir.' He unfolded his arms again as he turned to face his commander.

'For which part?' Nerva gave him a barbed look. 'The interruption or the insolence afterwards? He's right—you ought to be disciplined.'

'Yes, sir.'

'I ought to have you whipped.'

'Whatever you think best, sir.'

The Legate held his gaze for a long moment before waving a hand dismissively. 'Don't be ridiculous. I'd rather have Scaevola whipped, no matter what his father might say, but what on earth possessed you? I've never seen you behave that way to a senior officer before.'

Marius shrugged his shoulders non-committally. He'd never concealed anything from Nerva before, but he could hardly tell him the truth, that he'd resented the other man's treatment of Livia. Or that, even now, he could hardly stop thinking about her. Even though she'd left, he could still picture every detail of her face: her patchwork of freckles, her sharply curved brows and, most of all, those luminous eyes fringed with dark lashes so long they seemed to caress her rounded cheeks.

When she'd pulled her *palla* back, proudly unveiling the mass of her burnished red curls, he'd found himself half-wanting to cheer, half to bury his face in them. The way she'd stood up to Scaevola had made him want to bury himself in other places, too, not that he ought to think about that. He ought not to think about those places at all. Even if he couldn't seem to help himself. The way that she'd looked and acted had been nothing short of spectacular. He'd never desired a woman more in his life.

He cleared his throat at the thought. 'Scaevola just seems to bring out the worst in me, sir.'

'He does in all of us. We'll be lucky if the fool doesn't start a mutiny. Half the legionaries already want to stab him in the back, or so I've heard.'

'I couldn't comment, sir.'

'No, of course not.' Nerva gave him a penetrating look. 'Although I do expect you to inform me if the situation deteriorates any further.'

'I will, sir.'

'Good. Now tell me about the woman.' Nerva gestured for Marius to follow him into the villa, leading the way past the colonnaded courtyard to his office. 'Not exactly a blushing young bride, is she?'

'No, sir.' The words made him strangely defensive. 'I suppose not.'

'You've had a chance to speak with her. What do you think?'

'I don't dislike her, sir.'

He didn't trust himself to say any more. None of his thoughts were exactly appropriate for sharing. Admittedly, she wasn't young, in marital terms anyway, and she certainly hadn't been blushing that evening. She'd looked more like a ghost when Lucius had insulted her. And he definitely *didn't* dislike her.

'And there's a child...' Nerva closed his office door behind them. 'Well, Scaevola's right about one thing. His father *will* be furious when he finds out.'

'Couldn't you lend Scaevola the money, sir?' It was an indelicate question, but one Marius felt compelled to ask for her sake.

'I've thought about it.' Nerva threw a quick glance at the doorway. 'But it's a considerable amount and, between you and me, his father's a hard enough man to get money out of in person. From this distance, I'd be lucky to see so much as a denarius again. No, the boy's made his own bed. He'll just have to lie in it.'

'What about her, sir?' The mention of bed made Marius's temper rise again.

'What do you mean?' Nerva's brow furrowed. 'She's here willingly, isn't she?'

'I don't think she had much choice in the matter. And even if she did, she might have changed her mind after meeting him.'

'Who could blame her? But she's come too far to change her mind now and the last thing I need is her brother turning up with a grievance.'

'What if—?'

'No.' The Legate put up a hand to forestall him. 'This is Scaevola's problem, not ours. We're supposed to be soldiers, not marriage brokers.'

'Yes, sir.'

Marius straightened his spine at the reminder. That was true. He'd been about to suggest that he escort her back to Lindum and speak with her brother himself, but Nerva was right. It *was* none of his business. Just as the way Scaevola spoke to her was none of his business. Now that he'd delivered her safely to Coria, she had nothing to do with him, no matter how attractive he found her or how much he *didn't* dislike her. He was a soldier first and foremost and he had more important concerns than one woman.

'Have there been any signs of activity over the wall, sir?'

Nerva arched an eyebrow. 'Still worrying?'

'The local tribes are certain that trouble's brewing. I spoke to some Carvetti farmers on the march this morning. They said they haven't had sight or sound of anyone from north of the wall for weeks. It's too quiet.'

'Quiet is good.'

'With respect, sir, not if it's the calm before the storm. With your permission, I'd like to take a patrol north tomorrow.'

'No.' Nerva shook his head firmly. 'Give your men a chance to rest. They work harder than any other century in the legion.'

'Then let me go, sir.'

'On your own? It's far too dangerous.'

'I could ride to some of the other forts to see if they've noticed anything suspicious.'

That was a reasonable request surely. Then he'd be doing his duty and putting some distance between him and Livia at the same time—something which seemed of vital importance suddenly. If he couldn't keep her out of his mind, then he could keep her out of sight instead.

'All right.' Nerva sounded exasperated. 'I don't suppose you'll let the matter drop otherwise, though I very much doubt that the northern tribes will rebel again now we're back up to fighting strength.'

Marius sighed inwardly. For all his many good points, Nerva was still a Roman through and through. That *anyone* would dare to challenge Rome's authority was still a mystery to him. Now that the Legion was back to full force, albeit with half of it still based in Eboracum, he simply assumed that the rebellions of the past few years were over.

'Believe me, sir, nothing would make me happier than being proved wrong, but I still think we need to investigate.'

'As long as you're not looking for problems that don't exist.' Nerva gave him a meaningful look. 'I know you still feel the need to prove yourself.'

He tensed immediately. 'That has nothing to do with it, sir.'

'I'm glad to hear it. Now go and get some rest.'

'Yes, sir.' He paused. 'What about my punishment, sir?'

'I think a reprimand ought to be sufficient for now, but don't let it happen again. Scaevola's a fool, but he has powerful connections. They might not lend him any money, but they have influence and they enjoy using it.'

Marius didn't doubt the last part. Powerful men always did—and they'd enjoy nothing more than destroying the son of a disgraced mutineer.

'I'll keep away from Scaevola, sir.'

'Good. Because if you want to be a senior centurion some day then it would be wise not to make an enemy of him.'

'Yes, sir.'

Marius turned and strode out of the office, unable to shake the feeling that he already had.

Chapter Six

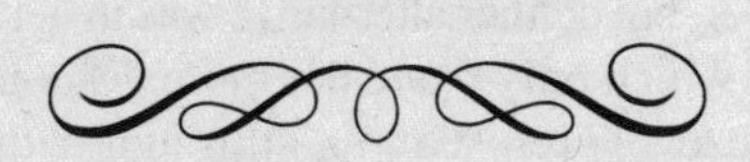

Livia descended the villa steps, inhaling deep gulps of morning air to help clear her head. It was her favourite time of the day, when the air still felt clean and fresh and the sky was a hazy mixture of rainbow colours: yellow and orange and even green in the east where the sun was just rising, pink and purple and pastel blue in the south where the night and dawn met. The north and west were still grey. She knew that she oughtn't to be outside on her own, but she wanted to get a sense of her new surroundings, to feel in control of one part of her life at least, even if she felt completely lost in the rest of it.

She draped a shawl over her hair and kept her head down as she made her way past the camp headquarters and hospital, heading towards the northern rim of the fort. Despite the emotional turmoil of the previous day, she felt surprisingly well-rested. After tucking Julia into bed in the evening, she'd lain down for a few moments beside her, intending simply to nestle, then fallen fast asleep in her clothes.

At least that had stopped her from brooding, though

it hadn't taken long for all her anxieties to come rushing back again once she woke. Her meeting with Scaevola had been nothing short of disastrous. He'd looked at her as if she were some kind of monster, so that now she had no idea if their marriage was even still going ahead.

She didn't know which was worse, the thought of marrying a man like him or of being sent back to her half-brother, but neither alternative was in her control—a thought which only made her more despondent than ever. If Scaevola refused to go through with the marriage, however, then she had no doubt that Tarquinius would find a way to blame her. She was stuck between a rock and a very hard place, but whichever way her future was decided, there was one thing she desperately wanted to do first.

She wanted to see the wall. Marius had said that the landscape was too hilly, but on such a clear morning, surely there was a chance… In any case, if this was her only opportunity, then she had to try.

Fortunately the camp was quiet. It was early enough that most soldiers were either still inside their barrack blocks or eating breakfast on the steps. Those who were outside looked at her curiously as she passed, but she kept going, making her way determinedly towards some steps that led to a walkway around the top of the palisade.

She climbed to the top, looking out over the ditch defences to the landscape beyond. There was something strangely familiar about it, as if part of her had always known what it would look like, though her imagination had failed to do it full justice. It was even more beautiful than her mother had described, with rolling hills and a sky that seemed to stretch on for ever. It gave her an unexpected sense of freedom, ironically, given her current circumstances. Of yearning, too, as if the land itself were calling to her. She tipped her head back, letting her shawl fall around her shoulders as she breathed in the feeling, though to her intense disappointment there was no sign of the wall, no matter how hard she screwed up her eyes.

It was only two miles away, Marius had told her with his customary stern expression. Only two miles. It might as well have been the far ends of the earth.

'Lady?'

A sentry approached her and then halted mid-step, his gaze slipping past her shoulder before he turned and marched away again. Perplexed, she turned around, wondering what had changed his mind, only to find herself face-to-face with Marius Varro.

She gave a small, surprised yelp. She hadn't expected to see him again, but now his unexpected arrival, coming so soon after she'd just been thinking about him, seemed to be doing alarming things to her breathing, not to mention the rest of her.

What was he doing there? There had been no one else with her a moment ago, no sound of anyone behind her either. He seemed to have appeared out of thin air, looking just as she remembered, even wearing the stern expression she'd just been thinking about! Unlike most of the other men in the camp, he was fully dressed, too, looking every inch the imposing Roman soldier. She doubted he ever looked anything else. He seemed like the kind of man who might sleep in his uniform.

'Are you following me?' She felt heat flare in her cheeks, though whether from anger or some other emotion she hardly knew. She seemed to be feeling so many emotions at once.

'Yes.' He made an impatient gesture, as if the question were irrelevant. 'I saw you from the stables. You ought to take more care.'

'Why?' She looked along the walkway in surprise. 'I'm only taking a look around. It's not so high.'

'I didn't mean the ramparts. You're one of only a handful of women in a camp full of soldiers. You shouldn't be out on your own.'

The implication made her cheeks flush an even brighter shade of pink. The fact that it came from him made it feel even more personal. After all, *he* was the one she was standing alone with, the one she'd woken up dreaming about…

She tossed her head, pushing that particular memory aside.

'Do you think so badly of your men, then?'

'No, but they're not all my men. I'm sure Nerva will assign you a guard if you want to look around.'

She shuddered at the thought. Another man to watch her, to follow her every footstep and then report back as if she couldn't be trusted. It would be like living with Julius all over again.

'No!' She shook her head adamantly. 'I'll take my chances. I'd rather be on my own.'

'As you wish.' He scrutinised her face for a few seconds before walking back to the top of the steps and then standing there.

'What are you doing?' She stared after him suspiciously. He looked like one of the sentries.

'Waiting.'

'For what?'

'To escort you back to the villa.'

'I don't need escorting. I remember the way.'

'None the less.'

'I just told you I'd rather be on my own.'

'So you did.'

She glared at him, seized with a combination of irritation and guilt. He'd caught her off guard—again!—and now she was being rude, unfairly so since he hadn't done anything to offend her, not really. On the contrary, since they'd met he'd been thoughtful and protective and sensitive too, in a severe kind of way. Even now he was *still* being thoughtful and protective!

But she *was* angry, not just at him, but at her whole situation. Somehow he made her feel even more powerless than before. It wasn't his fault, but if they'd never met then she would only have had Scaevola and Tarquinius to worry about. Without him she wouldn't have imagined, even for a moment, that her future could have been anything more than a prison.

She heaved a sigh, oppressed by the thought. If only it had been someone else who'd come to greet her! If only it had been someone else who'd defended her the previous evening, too. But it had been *him*, the only man apart from her father who'd ever stood up for her, who'd put a stop to Scaevola's insulting behaviour as if he'd been personally offended. Now the fact that she ought to feel grateful made her even more irritated. But it was only right that she thank him.

'About yesterday evening…' she strove to sound calmer than she felt '…thank you for interrupting when you did. I hope you weren't in any trouble for it.'

'No.'

'Good. I appreciated your help.'

He shrugged his shoulders. 'I only stated the facts. You and your daughter were tired.'

'None the less.'

She repeated his words ironically and saw one side of his mouth twitch upwards. It was the first time she'd seen any hint of a smile from him and it made her feel slightly less irritable.

'Are you going somewhere?' She gestured at his cloak. 'You said you were in the stables.'

'I'm visiting some of the other forts today.'

'Then you shouldn't let me detain you. I'm sure you're eager to be going.'

'It can wait.' He gave her a look that suggested the subject wasn't up for further discussion. 'I'll be here until you're ready, lady.'

She sighed again and leaned forward against the parapet, gazing into the distance, but it was no use. There wasn't even the faintest hint of a wall on the horizon. Meanwhile, Marius's refusal to leave was infuriating. Perhaps he was right and she ought to go back, but she refused to be coerced, even for her own good.

'Have you ever been north of the wall?' She glanced back over her shoulder at him.

'Yes.'

'More than once?'

'More than once.'

'More than ten times?'

His lips twitched again. 'I've lost count, lady.'

'Oh… Have you ever been attacked?'

'Yes.'

She twisted around fully this time. 'Do you agree with Scaevola, then? Do you think that Caledonians are all savages?'

'No. They're not Roman, but that doesn't make them savages.'

She made a sceptical sound in the back of her throat. 'I thought that Rome was always right.'

'Rome isn't perfect, but it's civilisation and order.'

'And conquest and slavery.'

She sank her teeth into her bottom lip, inwardly berating herself for the words. She'd said too much again, just like yesterday, letting her mixed feelings about the Empire get the better of her. It was dangerous to voice such thoughts aloud, but something about this man made her reckless. For some reason, she felt as though she could talk openly to him. Despite his sternness, he didn't seem like the kind of man who would arrest her simply for expressing an opinion.

'Conquest?' His gaze dropped to her mouth as she bit into it, though his expression seemed to become even more serious. 'In terms of conquest, Caledonia has already won. The tribes there are still independent from Rome. Hadrian might have called it a triumph, but the wall marks the limits of Rome's power, not its strength.'

She felt a jolt of surprise. *The limits of Rome's power...* There was something both liberating and dangerous about that idea, although if such cynicism wasn't permitted for a woman, then it certainly wasn't permitted for a centurion, a servant and defender of Rome. Yet he was speaking to her like an equal, like someone he trusted as well…

She looked into his eyes and then wished that she hadn't as the air between them seemed to pulse and vibrate with tension suddenly, as if they were alone together in dangerous territory, in more ways than one.

She felt the fluttering of tiny wings again, only lower down this time, in the very pit of her abdomen.

'How long have you been here?' She changed the subject, trying to break the moment, though her voice sounded oddly breathless.

'Three years.' His voice sounded different, too, rougher and deeper. 'I was among the first of the legion to be sent back from Gaul when Severus became Emperor.'

'Is that where you're from, Gaul?'

'No.' He looked vaguely uncomfortable to be talking about himself. 'I was born in the heart of the Empire, Rome itself. After I joined the army, I spent seven years in Germania before I was sent to Gaul. Then I spent another two years there.'

'So you're almost halfway through your military service already?' The idea seemed incredible. 'You must have enlisted when you were young.'

'I was just past my fourteenth birthday.'

'Fourteen?'

He lifted his shoulders as if the number were of no consequence. 'It's not supposed to happen, but it does.'

'What about your family?'

'I didn't have any. My mother died when I was born and my father when I was thirteen. The family he'd paid to look after me had enough mouths of their own to feed, so I joined the army. There was no other choice.'

'But so young?'

'It's worked in my favour. According to regulations, you can't become a centurion until you're thirty.'

'But you're…' she did the sum quickly '…twenty-six?'

'Not officially.'

He grinned suddenly, revealing a row of gleaming white teeth, and the flutter of wings became a violent flapping sensation. Coming out of the blue, his smile seemed to have a particularly potent effect, as if she'd just drunk a full amphora of wine. When he wasn't frowning, his rugged features became quite devastatingly handsome.

'You must have been promoted very young, too.' She wrapped her arms around her waist, trying to distract herself.

'Not particularly. I'm only in the fourth cohort.'

'Isn't that good?'

'It's not good *enough*. I want to be Senior Centurion of the First Cohort some day. The Primus Pilus.'

'The First?' She was impressed. The Senior Centurion ranked only just below the Tribunes. It was the highest position a legionary could aim for, though something told her that if anyone could achieve such a thing, it was him. 'You're ambitious, then?'

The frown snapped back into place with a vengeance. 'It was my father's rank. He was Senior Centurion of the Eighth Legion.'

'So you want to equal his accomplishment?'

A look of some indefinable emotion flitted across his face, a combination of pain, anger and determination all rolled into one, so intense that she regretted the question almost instantly.

'No.' He looked as though he were wrestling with himself. 'I only want to regain it, to restore my family honour.'

'Oh.'

She sucked the insides of her cheeks, surprised by the depth of emotion behind the words. Some instinct told her not to ask any more. Whatever had happened to his family honour, his feelings about it were clearly still painful and she didn't want to pry. She had no right to ask anyway, still less to offer comfort, no matter how tempted she was to reach out a hand towards him, to stroke the tightly locked muscles of his jaw and soothe away his frown lines... The tension between them was palpable again and pulsing even more strongly, as if her attempts to dispel it had only brought them closer together. Maybe she ought to have gone back to the villa when she'd had the chance, she thought with a gulp, although she *still* didn't want to leave. So much for familiarity breeding contempt. The more time she spent with him, the more she wanted to. The closer she wanted to be...

He cleared his throat, looking visibly relieved when she didn't ask any more questions.

'What of your family?' he asked one of her instead. 'You're from Lindum?'

'Close by, yes.' She grabbed at the words eagerly. 'My father had an estate in the country to the south and I was born and raised there. I had a very happy childhood.'

'Only your childhood?'

She winced. 'My mother died of a fever when I was ten and my father four years later. They were devoted to each other and her loss affected his health. I think the only reason he survived as long as he did was for me. He knew that I'd be alone afterwards.'

'What about your brother?'

'Tarquinius is only my half-brother.'

'Ah.'

He acknowledged the difference in one short word

and she pressed her lips together, trying to dispel the feeling of bitterness. What was she doing anyway? Talking about herself would only bring them closer together and she ought to be putting distance between them instead. This was the point where she really ought to stop talking and leave, but the need to vent her anger at Tarquinius seemed to be stronger than common sense. Besides which, she *wanted* to keep talking to Marius, she realised. Tension aside, he was surprisingly easy to talk to.

'We have different mothers and he hated mine. He called her…' she paused, unwilling to repeat the words out loud '…names. I suppose it was inevitable that the feeling would extend to me. I only met him for the first time when I was thirteen and he made his opinion of me clear straight away.'

'Why did he hate her?'

'What?' She froze at the question.

'You just said he hated your mother. Why?'

'Why?' She swallowed, trying to come up with a convincing-sounding lie and settling on several half-truths instead. 'Maybe because he thought our father was too old to marry again. Maybe because he was worried she only wanted his money. Or maybe because she was a Briton.'

'So I assumed.'

She blinked, taken aback by his matter-of-fact tone. 'You did?'

'Your hair…' He half-raised a hand and then dropped it again. 'It's quite distinctive.'

'Oh.' For a moment, she'd thought he'd been about to touch her. 'Yes. Tarquinius hated that, too.'

'I didn't say I hated it.'

'No...' She was surprised by his defensive reaction. 'I meant that he hated my hair as well as my mother.'

'Ah... Of course.' A muscle in his jaw twitched. 'But he's still your brother, whatever he thinks of your hair. If you don't want to marry Scaevola, then surely you can tell him so?'

'Do you think it's so easy?' She gave an incredulous laugh. 'Yes, I suppose you do. A man is free to choose his own future. A woman doesn't have that luxury. I had no choice with my first marriage, let alone now. I'm under Tarquinius's protection, which means I have to do everything he says. So if you're suggesting that I appeal to his *better* nature, then it's impossible. You can't appeal to a conscience that isn't there!'

She was breathing deeply by the time she finished speaking and for a few seconds there was silence, with only the sound of their combined breathing stirring the air between them.

'I'm sorry. I should have considered.' His voice was gentler when he finally spoke again. 'How old were you when you married?'

'Fourteen. So it seems we have one thing in common.' She gave a brittle laugh at the irony. 'We both started out in the world early.'

Fourteen. So young and afraid and utterly alone. That was what she remembered most of all, being lonely, although at the time Julius had still seemed infinitely preferable to Tarquinius.

'Was he a good husband?'

'Yes, he was very kind.' *To begin with*, she added silently. She didn't want to talk about what had happened later...

'It's not right.' His voice hardened again. 'You shouldn't be forced to re-marry so soon.'

'It's a common enough story. My brother is a man of business. He makes alliances with people who can be useful to him. My first husband was a wine merchant and Scaevola's a tribune. I imagine that Tarquinius thinks he might prove useful one day.'

'He's probably right.'

'So he's sent me here to be married again. Even though neither of us like or want the other. Even though this time…'

'This time?' He prompted her as she stopped mid-sentence.

'This time,' she went on, choosing her words with care, 'I thought that maybe things would be different. I thought…'

She swung towards him impetuously, tempted to tell him all the rest of her hopes, to tell him everything about herself and her heritage, too—the real reason she wanted to see the wall—so quickly that she bumped straight into his chest. At some point he must have moved closer to her, so that now the full length of her body was in contact with his, her breasts pressing against the hard contours of his mail shirt. His arms came up, instinctively it seemed, to steady her, so that he caught her around the midriff, one hand on either side of her waist.

For a moment she forgot to breathe. At the back of her mind she could hear a small voice telling her to move away, but her body didn't appear to be listening. She was standing face-to-face and chest to chest with a man who *wasn't* her intended in almost broad daylight, on a walkway for anyone to see, yet she couldn't seem to do a single thing about it. Her hands were still loose at her sides, but she had to fight the temptation to lift them up around his shoulders, just as she was already lifting her chin, tilting it up so that she could look deep into his eyes, her pulse accelerating at the look of raw desire she saw there.

She licked her lips, the thin sliver of air between them seeming to crackle and spark as if they were in the midst of a lightning storm, making her breasts tighten and her blood heat in response. Still holding her gaze, he slid his hands inside her cloak and she found herself swaying, leaning forward as if he were pulling her towards him by some invisible string, her eyes closing and lips parting as he lowered his head towards hers.

Then he stiffened, yanking his hands away as he took a step backwards. 'Forgive me.'

Forgive him? She opened her eyelids again, though for a moment she found it hard to focus. What had just happened? He'd been about to kiss her, she'd been certain of it, and she'd been going to kiss him back. She'd been ready and eager and *excited.* For the first time in her life she'd been about to kiss a man she actually *wanted* to kiss and then he'd pulled away as if it had all been some terrible mistake.

She felt a rush of shame, mortified as much by his pulling away as by the fact it had happened at all. As if her situation wasn't bad enough already—now he was rejecting her, too!

'It was my fault. I walked into you.' She pulled at the edges of her cloak, wrapping it tightly around herself.

'No, you're grieving for your husband. I should

not…' He cleared his throat awkwardly. 'My apologies, lady… Livia.'

She lifted her eyes again in surprise. It was the first time he'd used her praenomen since they'd arrived in Coria and now it only made her more confused. Never mind the rest of his words! Nothing about her being betrothed to another man, only *you're grieving…*

The idea was so ludicrous that she almost laughed out loud. Grieving for Julius? Maybe she ought to be, but how could she mourn for a man who'd made her life a misery for the last five of their ten years together? Who'd called her a deceiving whore before he'd disinherited both her and their daughter? She'd grieved for the man she'd married a long time ago. She wasn't going to waste so much as a minute grieving for the man he'd become.

For a split second she was tempted to say so, to denounce her former husband out loud, but she'd never told anyone the misery of her first marriage and she wasn't about to start now, especially to a man whose very presence seemed to undermine all her self-possession and who'd just rejected her…

'I have to go.' She darted around him, making for the steps, relieved that this time he didn't insist upon accompanying her. 'Julia must be awake by now. I should go to her.'

Chapter Seven

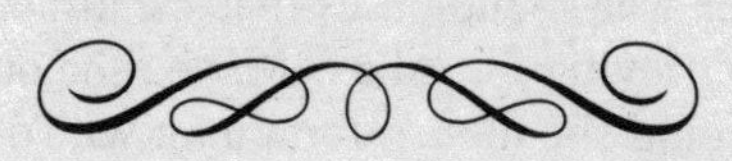

Julia was still fast asleep, Porcia, too, in a small pallet bed on the other side of the room, as Livia stood in the open doorway of their shared *cubicula*, trying to get her thoughts back into some semblance of order. She didn't know what had come over her on the palisade. Her pulse was still racing and not just because of the speed at which she'd fled back through the fort.

It had been an accident, bumping into Marius, yet the memory of it was seared so deep in her mind that she could almost feel the warm, solid pressure of his hands on her waist again, making her knees tremble and her nerve endings tingle anew, as if she had no control over her own body.

They hadn't kissed, but just standing so close to him had provoked a physical reaction she hadn't known she was capable of. *That* side of her marriage had been unpleasant at best and painful at worst, a brief and uncomfortable joining of bodies after which Julius had left her chamber almost immediately. It had brought her joy in the form of Julia, but a guilty part of her had been relieved when he'd turned against her and stopped coming to her bed. That had been the one positive of Tarquinius's interference.

What would going to bed with Marius be like? she wondered. She'd never imagined wanting to share a bed, let alone her body, with any man, but something about him made her curious. No, more than that, positively aroused by the idea. He'd awoken yearnings she hadn't known she possessed and yet it hadn't just been a physical attraction either. Despite her initial irritation and his customary sternness, she'd felt drawn to him as a person, too, genuinely wanting to know more about his past, even wanting to tell him about hers as well. She'd come perilously close to telling him everything, as if he were the kind of man she *could* tell everything to, although she'd settled for a half-truth instead, admitting that her mother was a Briton without specifying which side of the wall she'd come from.

It had been a moment of madness, one that had put them both at risk. They'd been standing on the ramparts in full view of anyone who'd cared to look up, though fortunately they'd been far enough from the barrack blocks that she didn't think anyone had. There had been no sign of the guard when she'd run away either, as if the very sight of Marius had been enough to dismiss him, but it had still been a dangerous thing to do. If anyone had seen them together, it would have looked like a tryst and then Scaevola would *definitely* have refused to marry her, and Tarquinius would have had no compunction about cutting her and Julia off completely—and then where would they be?

If only she'd been the one to put a stop to their kiss! Then she might have maintained some semblance of dignity, but she hadn't. She'd wanted to carry on, to do more than just touch him, to feel his lips moulded against hers and his hands on the rest of her body, so much that for one insane moment she'd risked her whole future and that of her daughter, too.

She must have been mad, but what about Marius? What had *he* wanted? For a few seconds, she'd thought that he'd wanted to kiss her as well. He'd bent his head as if he'd been going to, but then he'd drawn away and apologised, as if it had just been an instinctive reaction that he regretted. He'd even tried to take the blame, apologising again for touching her while she was grieving, as if she *ought* to be grieving, which in other circumstances she supposed she would have agreed with.

She rested her head against the door frame and groaned softly. What must he think of her now, a recent widow wandering around an army camp on her own, betrothed to one man and throwing herself into the arms of another? It was no wonder he'd pulled away. He'd probably been horrified—although he hadn't seemed horrified. His expression had looked torn, as if he'd been genuinely surprised by his own reaction to her, as if, perhaps, he'd been fighting his own inclinations when he'd pulled away. Was that why he'd done it, not from repulsion, but because he'd been trying to do the honourable thing?

There was no way to know and absolutely no way to find out. All she *did* know was that it couldn't happen again. She couldn't afford to get swept up in physical sensations, no matter how pleasurable they promised to be. That was all they were, after all, physical sensations, not emotional ones. She'd only met Marius the day before and surely it was impossible to develop deeper feelings for any man so quickly, no matter how close she might have felt to him.

She *liked* him, that was all, liked his straightforward manner and air of stern dependability. Even his insistence on escorting her back to the villa was appealing in an irritating sort of way. The fact that he'd been prepared to wait, that he hadn't simply ordered her to return, even more so. But the very fact that she liked him was also the reason why she had to avoid him from now on. He wanted to become Senior Centurion and he wouldn't get promoted by being seen alone with his senior officer's new bride. As for her, she was there to marry Scaevola and that was what she had to do, for Julia's sake, no matter what her own personal desires. She had to build a secure future for her daughter, even if it meant sacrificing her own.

Besides, it was enough, she told herself, the love that she felt for her daughter. It was the reason why she'd submitted to another unwanted, arranged marriage in the first place, putting aside her own hopes and dreams. She'd hoped, as she'd almost told Marius on the walkway, that she might one day build a different kind of relationship with a man, a new husband of her own choosing, a man she could be herself with, her *real* self, without judgement or condemnation. But who was to say that Marius wouldn't behave the same way as Scaevola if he ever discovered the whole truth about her, if he discovered that her mother wasn't just Briton, but Caledonian, too? Not to mention the rest of it. What made *him* any different to any other man? He was a Roman from Rome itself! What made him special except for a *feeling*?

'Ah, there you are.' Hermenia bustled up behind her, bearing a cup filled with what looked and smelled like warm milk. 'You must be famished, my dear. You were fast asleep when I came to find you last night and I didn't want to wake you. The pair of you looked so cosy.'

'I'm sorry. I meant to come back and say goodnight, but...'

'Nonsense, it's a horrendous journey. I ought to know—I've made it often enough. Here...' Hermenia passed her the milk '...I've flavoured it with honey for sweetness. Now I'm afraid that you have to pay for your accommodation here by spending all of your free time with me. I'm so pleased to have another woman to talk to and your daughter is perfectly adorable. I have two sons, both of them grown now, but between you and me I always wanted a girl. I should warn you, I intend to spoil her terribly.'

'I think she'd like that.' Livia smiled at the thought. It would make a nice change for Julia to be spoiled by anybody. 'Aren't there any other women in the fort?'

'Not many.' Hermenia sighed. 'The new Emperor's changed the rules about soldiers being allowed to marry, but it's still early days and a lot of the officers' wives prefer to stay in Eboracum.'

'Didn't you want to stay there, too?'

'Not a bit.' The older woman shook her head vehemently. 'I've been at Nerva's side for twenty-five years and I intend to stay there to the end. A few discomforts don't bother me, not that there are many now that repairs to the villa are finished, but not everyone's cut out to be a military wife.'

'I'm not sure I am either.'

'Well, *I* am sure. I knew the moment I saw you that you weren't like the rest.'

Livia took a sip of milk to hide her expression.

Hermenia's warm tone made it sound like a compliment, but she'd spent so much of her life *not* belonging that she couldn't help but wonder if there was another meaning behind the words.

'By the by—' Hermenia gave her a shrewd look '—I noticed that you went out for a walk this morning.'

'Ye-es.' She forced herself to sound casual, though the memory of her *walk* sent a sharp thrill shooting down her spine. Foolishly she'd assumed that no one would have noticed her absence. Now she didn't know what to do with her expression. 'I wanted a look around.'

'Alone?'

'Yes.' She took another sip of milk, bracing herself to mention Marius's name. If she didn't mention him, then it would be more incriminating if Hermenia found out about their meeting from someone else, though she was sure the guilt must be obvious on her face.

'I met Centurion Varro on the ramparts. He told me I shouldn't be out on my own.'

'He's right. At that time in the morning, half the men aren't even dressed.' The older woman chuckled. 'You might have seen more than you bargained for.'

'I just wanted some time on my own to think.'

'Of course.' Hermenia put a hand on her arm. 'It's just lucky that it was Marius who found you. He's a good man and an excellent soldier. My husband trusts him more than anyone else in the Legion, but then they go back a long way. He's known Marius since he was a boy.'

'Yes, he told me he joined the army at fourteen.'

'Marius told you that?' Hermenia looked surprised. 'Well, it's true, although I admit I didn't approve of

Nerva turning a blind eye to his age at the time. But it was what the boy wanted and, in all honesty, there was nowhere else for him to go. After what happened to his father he didn't have many choices. Nerva always felt bad about that, not that he could have done any more to help than he did, but it was still a terrible thing.'

'What happened to his father?' Livia lifted her eyebrows in surprise. Marius had mentioned his father being a senior centurion, but what was so bad about that? Although he'd said something about family honour, too...

Hermenia's expression seemed to waver for a moment and then settle again. 'Something that's better left in the past. Nothing for you to worry about anyway, but he and my husband were great friends. That's why Nerva sponsored Marius when he enlisted. He felt responsible for him in a way. It's why he's always kept a close eye on him, too, not that he needs it any more.'

'Yes. He seems very...' she sought for a suitably bland word, not wanting to say anything that might arouse suspicion '...competent.'

'He is.' Hermenia gave her a nudge with her elbow. 'Handsome, too.'

'I suppose so.' She drained the last of her milk in a hurry. 'Although he looks very stern.'

'He has a lot to be stern about.' The elbow nudged outwards again. 'But he's certainly more of a man than Scaevola. Not as well connected obviously, but superior in other ways that matter. If I were twenty years younger... Come now, you've been married before. You know what I mean.'

'No.' Livia felt herself blushing. She *didn't* know what the other woman meant, not exactly, although since meeting Marius she was beginning to get a clearer idea.

'Ah.' Hermenia's eyes filled with sympathy. 'Your first marriage wasn't a happy one, then?'

'I...' She hesitated, instinctively about to deny it, and then shook her head. 'No.'

'Oh, my dear... Well, try not to worry about Scaevola. Yesterday was bound to be difficult for both of you. You'd never met before and he's...'

'An arrogant, opinionated boy?'

'Ye-es.' Hermenia made a face although she didn't deny it. 'He has a high opinion of himself, it's true, but I'm sure tonight will be different.'

'Tonight?'

'Nerva's inviting him for dinner. I'm sure you'll get along better now that you've both had a chance to sleep on it.'

'Oh.' She didn't think any such thing. Instead she felt a definite sinking feeling.

'In the meantime, we'll have a pleasant day together. I'm sure you'd like a bath and a change of clothes. Then I can show you around properly.'

'Yes, thank you, I'd like that very much.' She forced herself to smile. After all, perhaps Hermenia was right and she'd simply got off to a bad start with Scaevola. She ought at least to give him a second chance.

'Good.' Hermenia looked relieved. 'Then it's all settled. I'm sure by tonight he'll be a whole different man.'

Livia clamped her lips together. If Scaevola was going to be a whole different man, then she knew *exactly* which one she'd want him to be.

Chapter Eight

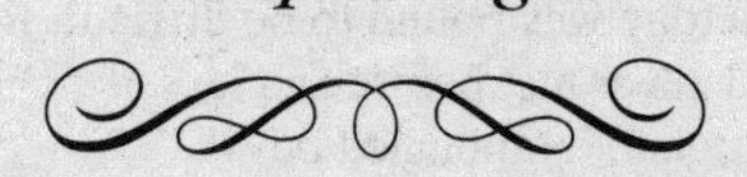

Marius dismounted from his horse outside the villa, dust-covered and in dire need of a bath. He'd ridden a third of the way along the wall and back that day, trying to find out if his suspicions had any basis, but no one had seen any sign of activity to the north—a fact that was worrying enough in itself. More than anything, he wanted to take off his armour and relax in the caldarium, but he had a report to make first. He only wished that he could make it somewhere else.

According to Pulex, Nerva was busy entertaining Scaevola and his new bride and he would have preferred to walk to the furthest end of the wall than intrude upon *that* particular occasion. No matter how hard he'd ridden, pushing both himself and his horse to their limits, he'd been unable to get Livia out of his mind.

The way she'd looked standing on the palisade that morning, her red curls blazing in the light of dawn, was seared into his mind's eye, eclipsing all else. As for his body… His blood seemed to turn into a fiery torrent every time he thought of her, which was far too often for comfort, both figuratively and literally. He'd spent half of his time reliving the moment when he'd circled his hands around her waist and pulled her against him, savouring the memory of her soft curves. The experience had been more than a little unnerving, as if he'd been riding through a mist all day, his mind only half on a task that ought to occupy his full attention.

At intervals, he'd tried to persuade himself that nothing had really happened between them. Yes, he'd held her in his arms, but only because she'd walked into him—even if the length of time it had taken for him to release her again belied that argument. Deep down, however, he knew that something *had* happened, something he'd been trying to resist and deny ever since he'd first laid eyes on her. There had been a moment of mutual recognition, of shared desire, one that he'd only just been able to stop from turning into something else, though it had taken all his self-control to do so. He'd felt an attraction to her from the start, but she was there to marry Scaevola, a tribune, not a lowly centurion like him. He'd heard stories of high-ranking ladies who liked to dally with soldiers, but she didn't seem like that type…

Worse than that, she was newly widowed. She'd told him that it was barely two months since her husband's funeral, which meant that she was surely still grieving. Her reluctance to marry again had been obvious on their journey to Coria and no matter what the attraction between them—if it really *had* been attraction and not wishful thinking on his part—she was clearly still vulnerable. Only a cur would take advantage of that.

Or a man like Scaevola.

He gave a message to one of the servants, fervently

hoping that Nerva would come out to the atrium to speak with him, dismayed to find himself summoned to the dining room instead.

He muttered an oath, unstrapping his armour and putting it aside. At the end of a long day it felt ten times as heavy as it had at the start, though he would gladly have worn it a whole other day just for the chance to turn round and leave again. Instead he followed the smell of incense and cooked food through the villa, clenching his jaw as he entered the *triclinium*.

By the look of things, the banquet was already nearing its end. The two couples were reclining on couches around a low central table laden with a dessert course of pickled fruits, pear tarts, honey cakes and stuffed dates. He was vaguely aware of it all looking and smelling delicious, but the very thought of eating made him feel nauseated, his stomach lurching into his hobnailed boots at the sight of Livia.

She was dressed in an orange tunic pinned at the shoulder with a bronze brooch that both complemented and emphasised the copper shade of her hair, piled high on her head in what looked like a hundred tightly coiled ringlets. Bronze earrings, a bronze necklace and bronze bracelets completed the effect, as if she were determined to make the colour as conspicuous as possible. He didn't know which he admired more, the spirit of defiance or the stunning result, though he had a feeling that both would be wasted on Scaevola.

'Marius!'

Hermenia waved a greeting and he allowed himself a tight smile. Nerva's wife was one of his favourite people in the entire Roman army. Her warm manner and innate common sense made her a surrogate mother to the younger recruits and an object of respect for the older. He knew that any one of his men, himself included, would lay down his life to defend her if necessary, though he also knew that she herself was more than competent with a sword. She had more sensitivity than her open demeanour suggested, too. In all the long years that he'd known her, he'd never once heard her criticise or condemn his father—which was more than could be said for most of the officers.

'Apologies for the interruption, but I came to make my report.' He bowed to both ladies and then tore his eyes away quickly from Livia. She'd looked up briefly when he'd entered, shifting to an upright position before dropping her gaze to the floor, a faint blush suffusing her cheeks, though her expression itself seemed oddly empty, as if she were wearing a mask.

'The report can wait until tomorrow.' Nerva gestured to a spare couch, his face noticeably flushed with wine. 'Sit down and join us.'

'Thank you, sir, but it's been a long day…'

'Just one, Marius. Come, it's a celebration. You can't refuse a drink.'

'Let him go if he wishes.' Hermenia put a restraining hand on her husband's arm, but he only shook his head more insistently.

'No, he works too hard. Sit down, Centurion. That's an order.'

'As you wish, sir.'

Marius sat on the edge of the couch, swallowing another, more violent oath and regretting that he'd come anywhere near the villa. He ought to have known from experience that Nerva enjoyed his wine far too much to want to deal with official business in the evenings.

He'd clearly drunk enough to forget his own advice from the previous day as well. If he'd been sober then he would never have asked him to sit in the same room as Scaevola.

'Here.' Nerva passed him a cup of wine before refilling and raising his own. 'To Lucius and Livia. May their marriage be as long and happy as mine has been.'

Marius raised the cup to his mouth and then lowered it again untouched. Livia seemed reluctant to drink, too, he noticed, her cup barely skimming her lips, though Scaevola drained his in a few short gulps. Seated on adjacent couches, neither of them looked very happy about it. The bride's spine was as straight as a javelin, while the groom was sprawled in an inelegant heap.

He narrowed his eyes suspiciously. If he wasn't mistaken, the boy was even more intoxicated than Nerva.

'So what have you discovered on your travels?' The Legate leaned back against his couch, regarding him through half-closed eyelids. 'Are we about to be invaded by Caledonian warriors?'

'Preposterous!' Lucius snorted. 'They wouldn't stand a chance!'

'It's no laughing matter.' Hermenia admonished him. 'They've overrun the wall before—recently, too. It's best to be cautious.'

'You're right, of course.' Nerva smiled indulgently. 'But any further assaults on the wall are highly unlikely. The tribes took advantage of the Legion's absence in Gaul, but now that we're back they'd be fools to attack again.'

'The wall's still vulnerable in places, sir.'

'But we have plenty of men to defend it. Besides,

where's your proof, Marius? Have you seen *anything* to support your theory?'

'No, sir. Nothing. That's the problem.'

'You mean you're worrying about *nothing*?' Lucius laughed scornfully.

'Yes.' Marius didn't bother to look at him. 'Something just feels wrong.'

Nerva sighed sceptically. 'Look, I know you've been here longer than the rest of us, but perhaps you've simply got used to fighting. Trust me, the rebellion's over. It's probably just quiet because the tribes have learned their lesson.'

'Or perhaps they're regrouping, sir. They know that once the wall is fully repaired they'll have lost their advantage. If they're planning an assault, it will be soon. Spring's here and the weather's already warming up.'

'All right.' Nerva pressed two fingers against the bridge of his nose and squeezed. 'Supposing you're right, what exactly do you suggest I do about it?'

'As I said last night, sir, with your permission, I'd like to lead a patrol north to investigate.'

'Isn't that dangerous?'

The voice was oddly high-pitched—so different from her usual tone that for a moment he didn't recognise it as Livia's. It was the first time that she'd spoken since his arrival and all eyes turned towards her at once.

'Only for most soldiers.' Nerva chuckled. 'Marius here is an exception.'

Scaevola gave another snort and the Legate's eyebrows arched upwards interrogatively.

'Unless you'd prefer to go, Lucius? Your father told

me you needed military experience. This would be a perfect opportunity.'

'Me?'

Marius bit back a smile, gratified to see the look of horror on the younger man's face. It would serve him right if he were sent north, though not the men he commanded. They deserved better than an arrogant youth. Even the tribes deserved better. If there wasn't a rebellion already, then there would be by the time Scaevola had finished.

Marius stole another furtive glance towards Livia, just in time to catch the flash of concern in her eyes before she dropped them again. Was she worried about him? The thought made him feel even closer to her and he looked away again. That was the last thing he needed.

'I thought not.' Nerva's tone was mocking. 'Besides, I wouldn't do that to you on the eve of your wedding.'

Marius's amusement fled at once. The *eve* of their wedding? Meaning that the wedding was going to take place tomorrow? He wondered what Nerva had said to persuade Scaevola to go ahead with it. Probably just the blunt truth, that he faced imprisonment otherwise, but confronted with the reality, he realised that he'd been hoping Scaevola would refuse anyway, that he'd object and leave Livia free. Not that her freedom would make any difference to *him*, he reminded himself. He had nothing to offer beyond a small room in a barrack block and a centurion's pay, but at least she wouldn't have to marry against her will.

'Perhaps I *should* lead a patrol.' Scaevola's tone was sullen. 'Then I could teach those red-headed barbarians a lesson.'

A heavy silence descended over the room. Marius looked quickly towards Livia, but her expression seemed even more frozen than before.

'Lucius!' Nerva's voice had lost all trace of mockery. 'There are ladies present.'

'Forgive me.' Scaevola looked pointedly towards Hermenia. 'I forgot.'

'Of course you did.' The Legate's wife got to her feet haughtily. 'But it's getting late. I believe *we* ladies ought to retire.'

'Good idea. I've no desire to continue mixing with people who look like savages either.'

'I am not a savage!' Livia's voice echoed loudly around the room, vibrating with emotion. *'My daughter is not a savage!'*

'Of course not.' Hermenia reached a hand across the table towards her. 'She's the sweetest child I ever laid eyes on.'

'You keep her, then.' Lucius swayed as he sat up, pointing one finger accusingly towards Livia. 'Your brother ought to cover more than my debts if he wants me to take the pair of you. I ought to be *paid*, too!'

Marius was out of his seat and on his feet before the other man had finished speaking, closing the space between them in two strides, but Livia was there before him, lifting the amphora of wine from the table and depositing the contents over Scaevola's head. For a few seconds, the Tribune's face took on a look of open-mouthed incredulity before he shot to his feet, dripping purple liquid.

'You did that deliberately!' Scaevola's face was mottled with anger, almost the same shade as the wine. 'You all saw it!'

'I dropped it.' After her outburst, Livia sounded almost unnaturally calm.

'You did not!'

'Of course she did.' Hermenia went to stand beside her. 'I saw it fall.'

'I won't be insulted like this! If you won't punish her, then I will!'

'Lucius!' Nerva sounded completely sober now. 'We'll speak in my office. Marius?' He gave him a pointed look as he passed by. 'Stay here.'

'And I'll find a fresh tunic.' Hermenia followed after them, turning at the last moment to murmur a low 'Brava, Livia' over her shoulder.

Marius stared after them, slowly uncurling his fists and flexing his fingers, stunned by the realisation of what he'd almost done. He'd crossed the room with every intention of striking a senior officer, an act of disobedience that even Nerva wouldn't have been able to ignore. It would have been a brief victory, a momentary satisfaction that would have destroyed his career and ended all chances of promotion, earning him a flogging at the very least.

He would have ended up just like his father.

Slowly, he turned his head towards Livia. In the light of a flickering oil lamp, her hair seemed to glow even brighter than before, vibrant and mesmerising. She was standing perfectly still, her eyes fixed on the opposite wall, though judging by her glazed expression, he doubted that she could see anything. If she hadn't acted first, then he would have lost everything. He would have ruined his career—*his life*—for a woman he'd met only the day before, a woman who was going to marry another man, a woman whom, at that moment, he wanted nothing more than to haul into his arms.

The best thing he could do for them both was to leave. Leave and take a patrol north and only come back once she was married. With any luck, Scaevola would have been transferred to another fort by then, taking her with him, or if not then perhaps he could request to be posted elsewhere himself. Anything to make sure that he'd never see her again, to make doubly sure they wouldn't ever be alone together. As they were now.

He flexed his shoulders, trying to relieve some of the feeling of tension. Leaving was the best thing he could do, but Nerva had told him to stay where he was—and even if he hadn't, he had a feeling that his feet wouldn't take him anywhere. If his eyes wouldn't obey when he told them to look away, then what hope did he have of commanding the rest of his body? Besides, he couldn't go, not now… It would feel like abandonment and, for whatever reason, he couldn't abandon her.

'Livia?'

He used his Centurion's voice, one that never failed to attract attention, and she spun around, catching her breath as if she were coming out of a trance.

'Marius.' Her expression looked haunted somehow. 'Why couldn't it have been you?'

He knitted his brows. What did she mean, that she wished she'd poured her wine over his head instead? That would have had fewer consequences, he supposed, though he wasn't exactly thrilled by the idea. Considering that he'd been ready to risk his career for her, it seemed somewhat churlish, too.

'Not that.' She shook her head, as if she had guessed

what he was thinking. 'I mean, why couldn't you have been the one I was supposed to marry? I thought that you were when we met. I wish it had been true.'

He didn't answer, using every ounce of self-discipline he possessed to stop himself from crossing the room and going to her. The words made his pulse quicken, but what could he say? That he wished it, too?

Did he?

The idea took him by surprise. Marriage had no place in his carefully planned future. He'd always considered the army his life and yet the thought of marrying *her* made all his other ambitions seem less important suddenly. But it was impossible. What good was wishing in the face of hard reality? Even if her marriage to Scaevola didn't go ahead, he could never offer for her. For one thing, her brother would never consider him a good enough match and, for another, he doubted that she'd want to ally herself to a man with his family history. Who *would* want to share his family dishonour?

'I'm sorry.' Her expression turned apologetic as the silence lengthened between them. 'I shouldn't have said that. What must you think of me?'

'I think…' he spoke slowly, trying to work out his feelings as he did so, '…that I'm grateful to you.'

'Grateful? For what?'

'Because if you hadn't poured that wine over him, I would have rammed his teeth into the back of his skull.'

'You would?' Her eyes widened with a look of surprise, quickly followed by a hint of laughter. 'I think I might have enjoyed that.'

'Except that I would have been in prison by now.'

'Oh.' She turned serious again. 'Then I'm glad that I did it, whatever the consequences.'

Her gaze flickered towards the door, as if she expected those same consequences to rush through at any moment, and he curled his hands into fists again. Somewhere Nerva and Scaevola were discussing that very subject. No doubt Scaevola was still furious. He wouldn't forget such an insult, nor leave it unpunished either, though whether he'd take his revenge before or after the wedding was another question.

As much as he hated to admit it, she was right to be anxious. And once she was married to Scaevola there would be nothing he could do to protect her. She'd be completely at the other man's mercy.

Somehow he found himself standing in front of her. 'Isn't there any way...?'

'No.' She shook her head even before he finished the question. 'There's no way out. I told you, my brother has arranged a marriage he thinks will be useful to him. I don't have a choice.'

'But if you told him how Scaevola insulted you?'

'Scaevola didn't say anything that Tarquinius wouldn't agree with.' She gave a brittle-looking smile. 'They're similar in a lot of ways. In any case, I can't go back to Lindum, not unless Scaevola himself breaks the arrangement, and even then...'

'Then?'

Her expression looked haunted again. 'Then I don't know what would happen. Tarquinius might not take us back. He might say it was all my fault. I'm trapped.'

She twisted away from him, but he put an arm out instinctively, her final word ringing in his ears. *Trapped.* Just like him, she was at the mercy of powerful men who thought they could treat people however they wanted, as if human beings were just pawns in a game in which they decided the rules. He'd spent thirteen years of his life pushing against the bars of his own cage. He couldn't bear the thought of abandoning her in hers.

'Livia.' He murmured her name and she stopped moving at once. Her orange tunic was lower cut than the one she'd been wearing the day before so that he could see the curve of her breasts above the fabric, rising and falling erratically, barely a hair's breadth away from his arm.

'If there were something I could do…' His voice seemed to have gravel in it.

She looked up at that, her lips parting slightly as her breathing seemed to accelerate even faster. 'You could kiss me.'

He held himself completely still for a moment, wondering if he'd misheard her. Then she took hold of his outstretched hand, enveloping it between both of hers before lifting it to her cheek.

'Unless you think I'm a red-haired savage as well?'

'You know that I don't.' Her cheek felt as smooth as the silk she was wearing. 'I think you're the most beautiful woman I've ever seen anywhere in the Empire, but you're marrying another man.'

'Who might come back at any moment.' She rubbed her cheek against his hand briefly before pulling it away. 'You're right. I just wanted to know how it would feel.'

'My hand?'

'No.' Dark lashes fluttered over luminous blue-green eyes. 'I wanted to know how it would feel to be kissed by someone I *wanted* to kiss… Just once.'

Somewhere in his mind he registered a dull sense of surprise at what the words suggested about her first marriage, but he didn't bother to dwell on it. He didn't need any further encouragement either. He reached for her instead, cupping the sides of her face in both hands as he lowered his mouth towards hers, kissing her with an intensity that seemed only to build in strength. Her lips were soft and warm and tasted faintly of wine, intoxicating in more ways than one and arousing beyond measure.

He deepened the kiss, sliding his tongue along the seam of her mouth before slipping inside. She let out a faint gasp, her body stiffening in surprise, before she looped her arms up around his neck and lifted her own tongue to meet his. Emboldened, he pushed his hands through her hair, teasing his way through the curls before sliding them over her shoulders, past the rounded curves of her breasts and down to her waist, pulling her towards him so that their bodies were pressed tight, even tighter than they had been that morning, only now with no armour between them.

He moaned against her mouth and she broke the kiss, tipping her head back with an echoing murmur of pleasure, and he sank his mouth against the smooth line of her throat, inhaling the faint verbena scent of her skin. He felt his groin tighten even more in response. He wanted her. At that moment, he wanted her so badly that he was prepared to risk everything to have her. He'd never wanted any woman so much. Her hands moved over his shoulder blades and he pressed his lips against the mounds of her breasts, feeling almost ferocious with need. So did she, if the sharp stab of her nails against the back of his neck was anything to go by…

The sound of a muffled exclamation brought them both back to reality with a jolt.

'Ah, Marius, Livia, there you are!'

Hermenia stood in the doorway, her raised voice making it obvious she wasn't really talking to them, the horrified look in her eyes belying her cheerful-sounding tone.

Marius heeded the warning instantly, dropping his hands to his sides and moving away at the sound of approaching footsteps. Livia moved, too, snatching up a cup of wine from the table and gulping the contents with a speed that would have put most of his legionaries to shame.

He felt a spasm of dread. Had she drunk more than he'd realised, after all? Was *that* the reason why she'd asked him to kiss her?

No. The swift glance she gave him just before Nerva rounded the corner of the dining room assured him of that fact. She was sober.

'Good. You're still here.' Nerva gave Marius a stern look.

'Yes, but it's too late to talk tonight.' Hermenia seemed to have recovered from her shock sufficiently to take charge of the situation. 'Marius has been riding all day. Surely you can discuss matters tomorrow?'

'Now would be better.'

'It's been a trying evening.' The martial gleam in her eye didn't brook any argument. 'I think we'd all appreciate a good night's sleep.'

Nerva frowned, but didn't argue any further, and Marius found himself exhaling with relief. There was no sign of Scaevola for some reason, but he didn't feel calm enough to speak with his commanding officer just yet. Livia was still too close, looking more enticing than ever with her swollen lips and flushed cheeks, tempting him to throw caution to the winds all over again.

He took a deep breath to steady himself. What the hell was wrong with him? He seemed to lose his mind every time she was close. If he threw caution to the winds, then it would only destroy both of their lives. They were both of them trapped.

In which case, the sooner he requested a transfer to another fort, the better. Only not tonight. Tonight he had to get out of there—as quickly as possible.

'I *am* tired, sir.' He made a formal bow, retreating behind his customary stern facade as he strode quickly towards the door. 'Goodnight, ladies.'

Chapter Nine

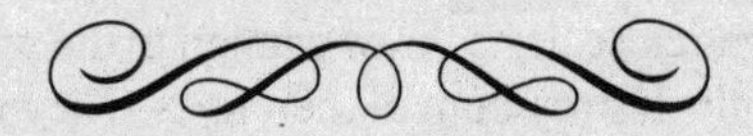

'Where's Scaevola?' It was Hermenia who asked the question.

Livia lifted her head, belatedly realising that her intended was nowhere to be seen. She supposed that she really ought to be the one asking about his whereabouts, but then *she* didn't care. All she cared about, she realised, was the man who'd just left.

'I've ordered him to go and sleep off the wine.' Nerva was still scowling.

'Ah.' Hermenia's gaze flickered towards her. 'Well, perhaps that's for the best.'

'I've also persuaded him that what happened tonight was an accident. He's agreed for the wedding to go ahead tomorrow.'

'Tomorrow?' Livia felt as though she'd just been handed a death sentence.

'Yes.' The Legate at least had the decency to look uncomfortable. 'I'm sure he'll apologise for what he said.'

Livia stared at him in silent horror. She was sure of no such thing. On the contrary, she was quite positive that Scaevola would find all kinds of ways to vent his resentment at being forced to marry her, to punish her for looking like a 'barbarian', never mind for pouring an amphora of wine over his head. The vengeful glint in his eye had been unmistakable.

She swallowed nervously. How much more would he punish her if—*when*—Tarquinius told him the whole truth? It was vaguely ironic how close Scaevola had come to it himself, accusing her of looking like a savage—an insult to her mother's people that still made her furious—when in fact she had even more in common with the Caledonians.

'Very well.' She tried to keep her voice from shaking. 'Then I ought to get some sleep.'

'I'll help you get ready for bed.'

Hermenia took her arm and she felt her nerves tighten. The last thing she wanted was to talk about the scene the other woman had just witnessed, but it seemed there was no escaping it. She had no way to defend or justify her behaviour either. She could barely explain it herself. Only it had felt like something that had been going to happen, that she'd *wanted* to happen, ever since she'd first set eyes upon Marius. There had been an inevitability, even a kind of rightness to kissing him, no matter what anyone else might think.

'I know what you're going to say.' She spoke in an undertone as they walked down the corridor.

'Do you?' To her surprise, Hermenia didn't immediately berate her. 'Because I don't.'

'It won't happen again.'

'I should hope not if you're marrying Scaevola tomorrow.'

'If?' A rush of anger overtook her. 'It's not as *if* I

have a choice. *If* there was any other way, then believe me, I'd take it!'

The older woman was silent and Livia bit her tongue, regretting her temper.

'I'm sorry, but Scaevola isn't the only one who's being controlled by my brother. I wasn't offered a choice about this marriage either.'

'I know.' Hermenia wrapped an arm around her shoulders. 'Don't you have any money of your own? A way to be independent?'

'No. My father left me some, but it went to Julius on our marriage.'

'But surely your husband left you provided for?'

'No, he left Julia and me with nothing, not even a place to live. He wanted to leave us dependent on my brother, I think. It was a kind of revenge.'

She dropped her gaze, letting Hermenia draw her own conclusions about his reasons for doing so. After what she'd just seen, she'd probably think the worst.

'Was he cruel to you?'

She looked up again, surprised by the note of sympathy in the other woman's voice.

'No… Yes… I mean, no, not at first, but he changed. He was much older than I was and he came to regret marrying me.' She put up a hand before Hermenia could protest. 'He said so.'

'Well, I'm sure it wasn't because of anything you did. Some people just aren't suited.'

'Maybe not, but now I have to do it all over again because if I don't we'll be destitute.' She shook her head. 'I'd hoped that Scaevola would be a different kind of man, but he's even worse than Julius.'

'Whereas Marius…?'

'Marius…' She repeated his name softly, letting it hang in the air between them. 'He *is* different, but I know it's no use thinking that.'

'Good. Because for both your sakes…'

'I know.'

She felt as if there were a lead weight in her chest. But at least she *did* know the truth, that no matter how attracted she was to Marius, no good could come of it. If it had been Scaevola who'd caught them, then there definitely wouldn't have been a wedding going ahead tomorrow and as for Marius—what would have happened to him? A flogging? Demotion? She didn't want to be responsible for either.

'I won't say anything.' Hermenia squeezed her shoulders one last time before releasing her. 'Believe me, if there was something I could do…'

Livia forced a smile, hearing the echo of Marius's words earlier. 'You've been kind enough already. Thank you.'

She closed the chamber door behind her. Just like that morning, Julia and Porcia were both already asleep and she leaned back against the wall, letting herself slide gently to the floor.

How could she have let it happen, endangering her whole future just for the sake of one kiss? Hadn't she told herself that very morning to keep away from him? She felt as if she'd actually run mad for a few minutes, but everything had seemed to hit her at once—the possibility of a Caledonian rebellion, the idea of Marius leading a dangerous patrol, the secret of her own divided loyalties, not to mention her anger at Tarquinius and Scaevola. She'd been so confused and frustrated that she'd shamelessly *asked* him to kiss her! But then she'd only intended it to be brief—a single, fleeting kiss that no one else would have witnessed. She hadn't been remotely prepared for the tumult of emotion that had followed.

She pressed her fingers to her mouth, the memory of it still making her lips tingle. Marius had kissed her with an urgency that had awoken something inside her she hadn't known existed. She'd felt urgent, too. She'd wanted—no, *needed*—it to be everything, a whole lifetime of sensations crammed into a few moments. Maybe it had been the risk of discovery or maybe just the desperate situation in which they'd found themselves, but she'd surrendered all of her inhibitions, kissing him with all the passion she'd kept pent up inside through the miserable long years of her marriage.

It had felt more real, more powerful and profound than any kiss she'd ever shared with her husband, as if the rest of the world had fallen away and there had only been her and Marius and a feeling of intense, spine-tingling, light-headed pleasure. She had no idea how long it had lasted, but it hadn't felt like anywhere near enough. She wasn't sure that it could *ever* have been long enough. Even now, despite everything, she wanted more.

But Hermenia was right. It was too dangerous for it ever to happen again. The moment was gone and she had that at least, the memory of one real kiss to sustain her in the future. No matter what her life with Scaevola was going to be like, and she didn't anticipate a happy one, at least she had one moment of real intimacy—she wasn't going to call it love—to remember.

Marius stormed back to the barracks, barging his way through the door that led to his private quarters and slamming it heavily behind him. The mist that he'd been riding through all day had turned into a fog, thick and impenetrable, so that he had no idea what to think, still less what to do. All he knew was what he wanted and *that* was utterly and completely forbidden.

He picked up a flagon of wine and drank a few cupfuls in quick succession. He rarely drank to excess, but tonight oblivion seemed particularly tempting.

'How did it go, sir?' Pulex opened the door behind him and stuck his head inside.

'What?'

It took him a few moments to comprehend what his Optio was asking and then the question struck him as hilarious. What could he say? That he'd achieved almost nothing during his long ride—he certainly hadn't discovered anything new—and then he'd done his best to destroy his career by kissing the soon-to-be-wife of a senior officer? He doubted that Pulex would see the funny side.

'Not very well.' He focused on the relevant part of his answer. 'The other forts all say the same thing. They've had no sight or sound of anyone for weeks.'

'What does Nerva think?'

'He has other things on his mind.'

'You mean Scaevola?' Pulex rolled his eyes. 'I noticed he was drunk again.'

'You've seen him? Where?' Marius paused with his cup halfway to his lips. He'd overheard Nerva saying that he'd ordered Scaevola to bed on his way out of the villa.

'In Arvina's barracks, gambling.'

'Damn it.' He put his cup down again.

'I'd leave him to it if I were you, sir.' Pulex looked faintly alarmed. 'He's an angry drunk.'

Marius made a face. That was undeniably true. Scaevola was surly enough when he hadn't had an amphora of wine poured over his head. Tonight he'd be positively savage. He was also the very last person in the legion he wanted to see again, but if the Tribune was disobeying orders then Nerva would want to know and he had a duty to report it. On the other hand, he had absolutely no intention of returning to the villa. If he saw Livia again, then he had no idea what might happen.

No, he glowered to himself as he threw his cloak back over his shoulders, that wasn't true. He knew exactly what *might* happen. That was the problem.

Which meant that he had to confront Scaevola himself.

There were four barrack blocks between his and Arvina's, giving him sufficient time during the walk to fully appreciate the folly of what he was doing. He was going to order a senior officer to bed. If Scaevola hadn't been his enemy before, he certainly would be after this.

He set his jaw grimly, offering curt nods in response to the hails of various legionaries as he passed, making his way determinedly towards Arvina's block, Pulex trailing a reluctant path behind. Just as his Optio had said, Scaevola was gambling inside, sitting on a stool in one corner of the Centurion's quarters, flanked by two of the Seventh Cohort's officers.

'Marius!' Arvina, a round-faced Centurion with a shock of spiky blond hair, greeted him cheerfully as he entered. 'Come and have a game.'

'Yes, come in.' The other Centurion, Drusus, winked at him. 'We've just switched to tabula. Scaevola thinks his luck's about to change.'

Marius took in the scene with one glance. Scaevola was too drunk to notice the conspiratorial looks of the other officers and he knew there was no love lost there either. In one short month at the fort, the Tribune had managed to offend and alienate nearly all of his comrades. Arvina and Drusus were merely taking revenge in the only way that they could. He couldn't blame them even if he did have to put a stop to it...

'He's played enough.' He jerked his head at Scaevola.

'I'll say when I've played enough.' The Tribune's expression was beyond sullen now, positively burning with hatred. 'You might be Nerva's pet at headquarters, but I outrank you here, Varro.'

Pet? His temper flared at the insult. The man really was asking to be taught a lesson the hard way.

'Perhaps you're right.' Arvina seemed to notice the tension in the room suddenly, looking between them with a newly wary expression. 'It's getting late.'

'No. I want to play a round with Marius.' Scaevola jerked his chin up belligerently. 'If he'll lower himself to gamble, that is.'

'You don't seem to have anything left to stake.' Marius folded his arms with a look of contempt.

'Maybe not, but I have some*one*. Nerva might be blind, but I've seen the way you look at her.'

'Her?' Only years of practice enabled him to keep his expression neutral.

'Livia Valeria. Or are you going to pretend that you don't want her?'

He clenched his jaw at the challenge. Apparently the Tribune was more observant than he'd thought.

'You're not denying it.' Scaevola's expression turned

leering. 'Why don't you just admit it? Admit that you want her!'

'I didn't say that, but she deserves better than to be part of some game. She's a woman, not a pile of coins.'

'She's *my* woman.' Scaevola leaned forward abruptly. 'Unless you win the game, that is. What do you say, Varro—why don't we make this interesting?'

Chapter Ten

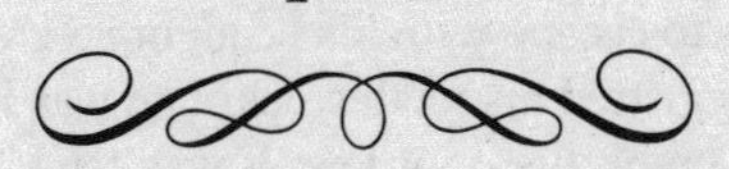

'What do you mean?'

Marius held his breath as the already taut atmosphere of the room became even more strained. Had Scaevola really just suggested what he thought he'd just suggested, staking his prospective bride in a game of tabula? Incredibly enough, that seemed to be exactly what he was saying, offering him the chance that he'd wished for—the chance to save her from a marriage she didn't want.

'I mean, let's play for some real stakes.' Scaevola's voice taunted him. 'How much are you willing to risk for her?'

'You've had too much wine.' Marius resisted the temptation to take advantage of the other man's drunkenness. Although, on the other hand, he wasn't exactly sober himself. It would be a fair game in that regard… *if* he took up the offer…

'What's she worth to you?' Scaevola ignored the accusation. 'Five thousand denarii? Ten thousand? You have the money, I know that. You don't spend it on drinking or women.'

'I've no intention of gambling it away either.'

'Not even when the prize is so appealing?' Scaevola's expression turned scathing. 'Of course, I forgot you're the model soldier, just like your father. Oops.' He put a hand to his mouth in mock horror. 'I forgot—he left the army in disgrace, didn't he? Stripped of his command and dishonourably discharged, although he was lucky to escape with his head, or so I've heard.'

Marius gritted his teeth so hard he was half-afraid he might crack his own jaw. It was true, his father *had* escaped charges of treason with his life, thanks largely to Nerva's intervention, but he'd been a broken man afterwards. He'd barely made it home, dying of fever a mere month after he'd returned, using his last breath to tell his thirteen-year-old son the truth about the charges laid against him.

'I think it's time to call it a night.' Arvina tried intervening again.

'Pity.' Scaevola's eyes kindled maliciously. 'I thought you had more backbone, Varro. I thought you might actually appreciate the chance to win her. I suppose I can see the appeal myself in a rustic kind of way, even if she does look like a savage. I wonder if she acts like one in bed, too?' He grinned. 'But then I suppose I'll find out after we're married. After I've dealt with her behaviour tonight, of course. I haven't thought of a punishment yet, but—'

'How much?' Marius slammed his fist on to the tabula board.

'I knew it!' Scaevola cackled. 'I knew that you wanted to bed her.'

'Not to bed her. To win her. That's what you said.'

He fixed the other man with a challenging stare. 'That means if I win, she's mine completely.'

'What?' Scaevola's voice faltered. 'No, that wasn't what I meant.'

'How much do you owe her brother?'

'Too much to risk losing her in a game.'

This time it was Marius's turn to look scathing. 'I thought you had more backbone, too. Or are you so scared of a tavern owner from Lindum?'

As he'd anticipated, Scaevola's temper flared instantly.

'Twenty thousand denarii!'

'That's ridiculous!' Arvina pushed his stool back and stood up. 'Marius, don't do it.'

'I have five hundred here…' he took a leather pouch from his belt and placed it on the table '…and nine thousand in the legion strong room.'

'Not enough.' Scaevola jutted his chin out, though his gaze dropped to the money pouch acquisitively.

'But enough to pay back a big chunk of the debt. Probably enough to buy your way out of the marriage.'

'There still needs to be more.' Scaevola's gaze wavered for a moment before settling on his sword hilt. 'Your *gladius*. I want that.'

For a moment Marius thought about walking away. His father's sword was his most treasured possession, made of the finest Spanish steel and with both sets of their initials carved into the hilt. It was the last thing his father had given him on his deathbed and he'd worn it every day since, to the point where it felt like an extension of his own body. Losing it would be like losing a limb. Losing it to Scaevola would be unbearable.

But if he refused to gamble, then he'd be sacrificing

his one chance to save Livia. If any woman was worth gambling for, then surely it was her… The memory of their kiss was enough to decide him.

'Done.' He drew the weapon from its scabbard and laid it on the floor between them. 'But if I win, whatever agreement you made with her brother is void.'

Scaevola's gaze flickered uncomfortably. 'As long as you explain that to Nerva.'

Marius sat down with a snort of contempt. For all his bravado, it seemed the Tribune was no more than a frightened boy, unwilling to accept the consequences of his behaviour. No wonder he'd got himself into such a mess.

'There's no going back, Varro.' Scaevola scooped up the pair of dice.

'For you either.' Marius arched an eyebrow, watching as the dice clattered on to the board. That was well and truly that, he thought with a sense of foreboding; the die was cast. Win or lose, there was no going back now.

They played for a few minutes in silence, Arvina and Drusus going to stand with Pulex in the doorway as if determined to distance themselves as far away from the game as possible. Marius couldn't blame them. Whoever won, there was going to be hell to pay. If he lost, then Nerva would surely notice the absence of his father's sword and ask him about it, and if he won…his pulse raced at the idea…if he won, he'd have to explain why Scaevola's planned marriage wasn't going ahead. He could hardly be punished since the game was fair and legitimate, but the Legate wouldn't be pleased.

'Ha!' Scaevola broke the silence finally, his face

lighting up with glee as he threw yet another set of doubles. 'You're losing, Varro.'

Marius frowned at the board. He couldn't deny it. Scaevola was definitely in the lead, though he wasn't going to give up quite so easily.

'I haven't lost anything yet.' As if to prove it, he threw a pair of fives and Scaevola's exultant expression turned surly again.

'You still haven't brought all of your pieces on to the board.'

'Neither have you.' Marius glared across the table. 'Why don't you concentrate on your own game and let me worry about mine?'

They continued in even deeper silence, the tension disturbed only by the scuffing sound of Arvina's boots as he paced up and down behind them. Marius didn't think he'd ever played a game so seriously in his life. Scaevola had sobered up noticeably, too, though his skin was still stained a faint shade of purple. It gave him a slightly unreal appearance, as if they were playing in a dream.

If it *was* a dream, however, he thought it must be a nightmare, one in which he felt completely out of his depth. Scaevola was clearly an experienced player while he was more than a little out of practice. He tried not to dwell upon that fact, trying to hold his nerve as he moved his pieces steadily around the board, occasionally catching the other man out, occasionally being captured himself. Even so, after ten minutes, he had the vague and somewhat startling impression that he was gradually winning. Every roll seemed to be exactly the one that he needed until, at last, he heard Scaevola suck in a sharp breath.

'You need a pair of sixes to win.' The taunt held more than a trace of fear.

Marius didn't answer as he picked up the dice, rolling them around in his hand for a few seconds as he willed them to fall favourably. Two sixes was a tall order, but if he rolled any lower then both of his last pieces would be exposed, and at this point in the game, that could scupper his entire chances of winning. Scaevola's pieces were perfectly positioned for a counter-attack. In which case, he told himself, he had no choice but to roll high. There was such a thing as beginner's luck, wasn't there?

He let his hand hover over the board for a second and then dropped the dice, his throat constricting as time seemed to slow and they rolled gradually to a standstill. Then he stared in amazement, only the pressure of Arvina's hand on his shoulder telling him he wasn't imagining things.

'Marius wins!' The other Centurion sounded almost as shocked as he felt.

'You cheated!' Scaevola shot to his feet, overturning the table and almost himself as he did so. 'Those dice are weighted.'

'They're my dice,' Drusus interjected.

'He still cheated. You all saw it!'

'All we saw was Marius winning.' To Arvina's credit, he didn't hesitate to stand up for him. 'There was no cheating.'

'You're all in this together! I'll see you all disciplined.' Scaevola's face turned an even more vivid shade of purple. 'It's my word against yours.'

'That's four against one.' Drusus came to stand at

Marius's other shoulder. 'We'll vouch for you if you need us to, Varro.'

Marius stood up at last, his senses still reeling from shock and relief. He'd been so close to losing and yet somehow he'd managed to throw exactly the right combination, winning the game and Livia, too. He felt the same as he did after a battle, as if his emotions had all been put on hold and he was struggling to come back to reality.

'I'm sure that won't be necessary.' He faced Scaevola over the upturned table. 'A man of honour wouldn't go back on his word.'

'I made a promise to her brother.' Scaevola's lips were almost white now. 'I owe him money. If I don't marry her, he'll take the case to the Governor. I could be imprisoned. You don't understand, Varro—I *have* to marry her.'

'So that you can punish her?' Marius repeated his earlier threat with a steely expression.

'I won't, I promise.' Scaevola was close to begging now. 'I won't lay a finger on her. You have my word.'

'I don't believe you.'

The Tribune's face blazed with a sudden burst of hatred. 'If you do this, then I'll destroy you. My family won't let me rot in a prison cell for long. I'll be back and I'll make what happened to your father seem like a stroll along the Tiber. I'm not bluffing, Varro. Either forget this game ever happened or I'll ruin your career.'

Briefly Marius considered the threat. Money and possessions were one thing—his career another. He'd spent half of his lifetime following one distinct path and purpose with only one aim in mind. Was he really prepared to risk his ambition, his honour, the promotion that would finally redeem his family name, all for a woman?

Yes. He'd known that at the start of the game, though his reasons for doing so were somehow less clear. Still, his moment of misgiving was just that, a moment. He believed Scaevola's threats, but if he'd needed any further proof that he was doing the right thing, this was it. He wasn't just saving her from an unwanted marriage. He was saving her from a monster.

'Then there's nothing more to say.'

He picked up his sword and slid it back into its scabbard, relieved to feel its solid weight against his hip again. Somehow he'd kept his money, his prized sword, and won himself a wife into the bargain.

A wife?

The realisation sank slowly into his consciousness. All the wine he'd consumed had prevented him from realising the full implications before, but now the truth hit him like a hammer in the chest. He hadn't just been playing for Livia's freedom, although that had been his main concern. He'd been playing for a wife. She'd already told him that her brother would probably refuse to take her back if she didn't marry Scaevola, which meant that he had no choice but to do the honourable thing and offer her an alternative.

Would she want him? He frowned. That was something he probably ought to have considered before risking his money and career on a game. After all, he was only an obscure centurion, not to mention one with a disgraced family name—the details of which he was now going to have to tell her. She'd said that she preferred him an hour ago, but what if that was only in comparison to Scaevola? What if his family history changed her mind? Would she *still* prefer him to Scaevola? Or had he just blighted his career for nothing?

There was only one way to find out. He had to go and tell her everything and then offer her the choice. When dawn came he'd go and speak to Nerva, ask him permission to make a formal offer for her hand. Perhaps by then it might have started to feel real for him, too.

Chapter Eleven

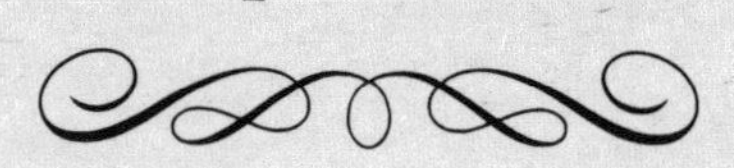

Livia opened her eyes reluctantly, roused by the light touch of a hand on her shoulder. After a restless night, she felt as though she'd only just got to sleep and the last thing she wanted was to be dragged awake again.

'Wake up.' Hermenia's voice was insistent. 'It's important.'

'What's happened?' She heaved herself up on her elbows, turning quickly towards Julia on the other side of the room, but the little girl was sleeping peacefully. 'Is something wrong?'

'Not exactly.' Hermenia was still in her night *tunica*. 'Nerva told me to fetch you. He needs to speak with you.'

'Oh...just a moment.'

Livia climbed out of bed and pulled a shawl over her *tunica*, seized with a dull sense of dread. Was it about her and Marius? She glanced at Hermenia nervously, wondering if she'd felt compelled to tell her husband what she'd seen, after all. She couldn't imagine what else it could be, but whatever it was, it had to be important. Judging by the faint glow emanating from the sky above the courtyard, it was only just past dawn, and there was no sight or sound of activity anywhere else in the villa.

She followed Hermenia into Nerva's office, unsurprised to find Marius already standing in front of the Legate's desk. He wasn't wearing his armour, for once, though he looked no less imposing, his arms folded behind his back as if he were on trial. Was he? Her heart plummeted to the soles of her thin leather slippers. It was hard to tell which of the two men looked the most sombre. It *must* be a trial. Hermenia must have told and now they'd both been summoned for punishment. The only consolation was that there was no sign of Scaevola.

'My apologies for waking you so early—' Nerva's expression was unreadable '—but Marius has something he needs to say.'

'Oh.' It wasn't exactly the condemnation she'd been expecting.

'Perhaps in the courtyard?' The Legate gestured towards the door. 'The two of you have a lot to talk about.'

She turned towards Marius in consternation as he took hold of her arm and led her outside. There was no softness in his touch, although it wasn't exactly rough either. Instead it felt strangely official, as if he were a guard leading a prisoner, and yet she still couldn't stop her body from reacting to the heat of his fingers against her skin.

'Marius? What's going on?'

She raised a hand to her arm, rubbing it lightly over the place where his fingers had been as he released her and folded his arms behind his back again. He still looked sombre and she glanced around as if the scene itself might reveal something, but it was too dark to make out much of the courtyard. A pair of torches illuminated the colonnade behind, but all she could see of the garden were decorative *oscillae* twirling in the trees around them, silver discs reflecting the last of the fading starlight. They looked eerily beautiful and mysterious sparkling in the darkness—almost as much as the situation she found herself in.

'I played a game of tabula with Scaevola last night.'

'You...played a game?'

She repeated the words slowly. There was no preamble, no apology for waking her, no mention of their kiss, just a bizarre statement of fact about a game. The words were as incongruous as they were surprising. She hadn't thought that he was on good enough terms with Scaevola to play games with him, especially after the events of the previous evening, but what did tabula have to do with their situation? What did it have to do with *anything*? It didn't even begin to explain why Nerva had sent them off alone together.

Alone. The thought made her pulse start to quiver. They ought not to be alone together. It was too dangerous. Hermenia had said as much, so why had she allowed it? She opened her mouth to ask, but he spoke first.

'I won.'

'What?'

'The game. I won.'

'Oh.' She stared at him blankly. Did he expect her to congratulate him? 'And you woke me to tell me that?'

'No.' His expression shifted to one she hadn't seen there before, as if he were uncertain of himself. He seemed to be having trouble finding words. 'There's more...about Scaevola.'

'Has something happened to him?' She felt a fleeting, *very fleeting*, moment of concern. If he was hurt in some way then it would explain his absence. Although it might also postpone their wedding, she thought hopefully.

'Not physically, but, yes, in a manner of speaking. He ran out of money.'

'You mean he was gambling?'

He inclined his head and she rolled her eyes scornfully. Of course he'd been gambling and now he'd run out of funds again, just as he had in Lindum. She was amazed he'd had anything left to play with in the first place. Then she tensed as another thought struck her. Was *that* why Marius was there? Because Scaevola owed him money? Had he come to ask *her* to pay the debt? Her mouth turned dry at the thought. Surely that couldn't be the reason he'd come to wake her and yet… what else could be so important?

She pulled her shoulders back, bracing herself for the worst. 'If he's indebted to you, then I'm afraid I can't help. I don't have any money of my own.'

He drew his brows together so sharply they met in a hard line in the middle. 'I'm not here for money, Livia. Is that what you think of me?' His gaze dropped to her mouth. 'After last night?'

She tensed again as the low, intimate tone of his voice sent a frisson of excitement racing through her body, though she forced herself to ignore it. They shouldn't talk about last night.

'No. You're right—I shouldn't have said that. I just thought…' She licked her lips, trying to put her confusion into words. 'I *don't* think of you like that, but why are you here, Marius? What's so important about a game? Did Scaevola lose so much?'

'Yes, but it's not about money…'

'Then what?'

He muttered an expletive before answering. 'He staked you.'

'What?' Her body seemed to go into shock, though it took her brain a few seconds to catch up with the words.

'He had no money left, so he staked you.'

'In a game of tabula?'

'Yes.'

'You're saying that he offered me as a prize?'

'Yes.'

'And that you won?'

'Yes.'

'So you won…me?'

The word fell like a stone into a river between them, a heavy splash followed by a series of small, yet equally powerful shock waves. Neither of them moved or made a sound, as if all of the air had been sucked out of the room suddenly. Which was impossible, she thought, since they were in a courtyard. It wasn't even a room. There was no roof. There was air around and above them…

But Marius was still speaking, she realised, only she couldn't make out the words. His lips appeared to be moving, but there was no sound, at least none that she could hear. She felt as if she were inside a bubble, isolated from everything except the vibrations of her own heartbeat, thudding against her chest like a drum. And then the shock waves ceased and the air seemed to pop suddenly and sound came back in a roaring torrent, bringing with it a tumult of anger and disappointment.

This time, she felt as if there was too much noise around her, as if every thought in her head were shouting and clamouring for attention all at once. Scaevola had staked her. That idea was outrageous enough, but what exactly did it mean? Since he couldn't *not* marry her without facing some kind of retribution from Tarquinius, he couldn't have staked her personally—which meant that it had to be something else that Marius had won, something that Scaevola himself didn't want, but that other men might.

There was only one thing she could think of.

She clutched a hand to her belly, feeling as if she were about to start retching. Was this Scaevola's idea of punishment for her pouring wine over his head? Or was it simply a glimpse of her future, being used as payment for her husband's gambling debts? Either way, how could he demean her like this, whoring her out as if she were his possession to do with as he pleased? How could he still expect her to marry him after this? Even if he didn't want her himself, how could he stoop so low? Worse still, how could Marius agree to it?

'Livia?'

Marius reached out a hand towards her, but she staggered backwards, horrified by the thought that he'd actually colluded in the game. He'd played *for* her, treating her just as callously as Tarquinius and Scaevola had ever done! She would never have believed it of him, not unless the words had come from his own lips, which they just had. Were all men the same, then? Whatever their outward behaviour might suggest, were they all equally monsters underneath?

Or was it because of their kiss? She lifted a hand to her mouth. The memory of that encounter had been one that she'd wanted to savour, to remember during the lonely years to come, but perhaps he'd taken it to mean more. Perhaps he'd thought that she *wanted* to sleep with him!

If she'd ever been tempted by the idea, she wasn't any more. Every moment she'd spent with him felt jaded. Foolishly, she'd thought that he was different, that there had been some kind of special bond between them, but now she realised that it had only ever been physical. He'd gambled for her body, that was all.

She lifted her hands, making a barrier between them.

'Let me get this straight. You won me in a game of tabula from the man my brother sent me to marry?'

He nodded stiffly. 'I was trying to help.'

'Help?' If there had been any kind of weapon nearby, she would have attacked him with it. There were only stones at her feet and she wondered how much damage she could inflict by hurling them.

'You said you didn't want to marry Scaevola.'

'And you think that gives you the right to gamble on me?' She took an angry step towards him, lifting a finger and jabbing it into his chest. 'Do you think I'll just do what I'm told because the two of you played a *game*?'

'No.' He didn't flinch. 'I intended to give you a choice.'

'A *choice*?' Somehow the words only made her angrier. 'Before or after my marriage? Or doesn't Scaevola care who his *barbarian* wife sleeps with?'

A hand shot up and circled her wrist as she made

to jab him again, his face registering a series of emotions, starting with shock and culminating in anger.

'I intended to give you a choice about marrying *me*.'

'Marrying…you?'

'Yes.' He let go of her wrist again, though her arm stayed where it was as if frozen. 'That's why I'm here. I came to ask you to marry me.'

Her mouth fell open, though she had no idea what to say. She hadn't been *asked* anything for as long as she could remember. She'd only been told what to do for the past ten years. The idea of being asked to make any decision at all seemed incredible. Being asked whether she wanted to marry him rendered her utterly speechless.

Even when they'd kissed, the thought of marrying him had never occurred to her. She might have wished that he'd been the man she'd come to marry, but the possibility had seemed as remote as the stars. She'd been a legal possession of her brother and an integral part of the business arrangement he'd made with Scaevola. There had been no question of her having a choice.

But if Scaevola really *had* gambled her, then surely it meant that his agreement with Tarquinius was no longer valid? Nerva's sending them outside to discuss matters suggested that he thought so, too. Tarquinius might dispute it, given that she was still legally under his care until a marriage took place, but then Tarquinius wasn't there. Marius was.

'So when you said that Scaevola staked me, you meant *all* of me?'

'Yes.' His voice was clipped, as if he were angry.

'I thought…'

'I know what you thought.' He was definitely angry. 'But as I said, I wanted to help. You said that you couldn't go back to your brother and that you had no money to be independent. You also said that you didn't want to marry Scaevola. If you've changed your mind about either of those things, then you're free to do as you please. I'm only offering you an alternative. It might not be the same as freedom, but it's the best I can offer.'

She stared at him in wonderment. He could hardly have looked or sounded any less like a suitor. In fact, it was hard to believe he was the same man who'd kissed her so passionately the night before. His expression was almost fierce, his dark eyes gleaming like obsidian stones in the half-darkness, as if she really *had* offended him this time, which given the nature of her assumption was a reasonable response.

She seemed to have made a habit of mistaking and misjudging him. But then the very last thing she'd expected was for him to propose! True, there had been an undeniable physical attraction between them from the start and she believed that he was honourable enough to want to rescue her—and surely he'd played the game of his own free will!—but neither of them had ever mentioned feelings.

Her heart seemed to stall in her chest. She knew why she preferred him to Scaevola, but why did *he* want to marry *her*? It made no sense. He'd said that he wanted to be Senior Centurion. Winning her away from a tribune could only damage his career prospects, so why had he gambled? Was it because he'd felt honour-bound after their kiss—the kiss that she'd asked for? Had she trapped him somehow? Or was it possible that he might care for her, too?

On the other hand, what did it matter *why* he was asking her to marry him? The reasons were surely irrelevant. All that mattered was that he was prepared to save her from a life with Scaevola. Even if he was acting out of a sense of honour, how could she say no? She ought to grasp at the opportunity. Still, she wanted to know…

'How much did you bet?'

She asked the question lightly, hoping that the amount he'd risked would tell her something about his feelings, but his frown only deepened.

'It doesn't matter. I won.'

'I'd still like to know.'

'Some money…and this.' He gestured towards his *gladius*. 'It belonged to my father.'

'Oh… May I?' He nodded and she reached out, curling her fingers gently around the hilt. 'It looks valuable.'

'It is.' He cleared his throat. 'It's also the sword of a man who brought dishonour on his family, who was accused of cowardice, disobeying orders and inciting mutiny. Before you make a decision, you ought to know that Varro isn't a name most people would choose to associate themselves with.'

She lifted her head to look at him, her fingers tightening around the hilt. He was telling her something painful, she realised, something important about himself before she gave him an answer. He was telling her about his family history under the assumption that there was nothing out of the ordinary about hers. Ironically, he was giving *her* a chance to say no. Surely she owed him the same? It was only fair that she told him about her mother, too.

'In that case, there's something I ought to tell you as well.'

'I can't offer you riches, Livia.' He seemed to not hear her. 'But I'll be a good husband. A good father, too.'

She caught her breath at the words. *A good father.* Wasn't that what she'd wanted most when she'd come north, a good father for her daughter? Providing a stable home for Julia was the most important thing of all. How could she risk telling Marius anything that might jeopardise that? After all, he was a Roman soldier facing a potential Caledonian rebellion. What if she told him about her heritage and he was horrified?

No, she decided, now was hardly the time to complicate matters with the truth. Besides, he hadn't seemed to care about her being half-Briton, and as for her mother's tribe and the rest of it…well, she could tell him all that after they were married…when she was ready…or perhaps never… Marius didn't seem like the kind of man who'd tolerate blackmail, but surely there'd be no reason for Tarquinius to blackmail a centurion either. Her secret would be safe. Even if it felt wrong not to tell Marius, as if she were misjudging him again.

Yet, ironically, she *wanted* to tell him the truth. She wasn't ashamed of her mother or her heritage. No matter how often Tarquinius had denounced her, she was still proud of her mother, a woman whose warmth and vibrancy had shone like a beacon in her early life. She could never be ashamed of anything connected with her. She *wanted* to tell Marius about her, to be as honest with him as he was being with her, but the habit of secrecy was so strong that she didn't know where to start.

'If you need time to consider…'

He seemed to interpret her silence as a refusal, starting to move backwards, but she tightened her grip on his *gladius* convulsively, stopping him from leaving.

'No. There's nothing to consider. I don't care about your name, Marius. I don't care about your father's dishonour. If you'll have me, then I'd be honoured to marry you.'

Chapter Twelve

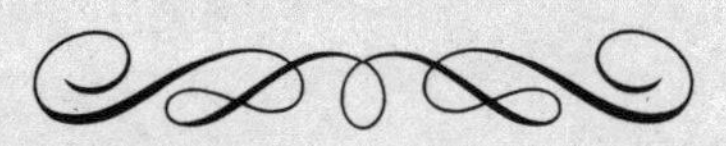

The door to Nerva's office was open. Which was a good thing, Marius thought, since his senses were so addled he might otherwise have walked straight into it. He'd just asked Livia to marry him and she'd accepted, though her exact words had taken him by surprise. She'd be honoured to marry him? *Honoured?* No one had been *honoured* to be connected with him since… ever. The very word sounded bizarre. He'd wanted to catch her up in his arms right then and there, but he'd felt as stunned as if he'd just been hit over the head.

So had she, apparently. He'd started his proposal off badly, almost disastrously, leading her to think first that he wanted money, then that he only wanted to sleep with her, though when he'd finally told her the truth she'd seemed equally shocked. It had taken her a few minutes to answer, long enough for him to wonder if he'd made a terrible mistake after all.

Then she'd said yes, though there hadn't been time for him to say anything in response. Or if there had been, he'd been too dumbstruck to use it. He had a vague memory of Hermenia entering the courtyard a few seconds later, of Livia saying something that had made her smile, albeit somewhat over-brightly, and then of the two women leaving together.

At the last moment, Livia had looked back over her shoulder and he'd immediately regretted not having seized the opportunity to kiss her again. If his thoughts hadn't been in so much turmoil, then he would have. He would have sealed their betrothal with a kiss like the one they'd shared the previous night, a real kiss, not a chaste peck on the cheek, only this time one that didn't have to be clandestine. Because she was going to be his wife.

He felt a soaring sense of elation. She'd chosen him. *Him*, despite what he'd told her about his father, despite the fact that he had no money and probably not much of a future now either—not that the last part was necessarily true. He hadn't surrendered his ambition. He still intended to win his promotion, even if he'd probably just made it a hundred times harder for himself with Scaevola as an enemy, only now he was going to achieve it with a wife at his side.

Livia. A woman he liked and admired, whom he'd desired from the first moment he'd seen her, who preferred *him* to a tribune. Despite everything, he couldn't stop himself from smiling.

'Sir.' He walked up to the Legate's desk with a spring in his step.

'You're looking pleased with yourself.' Nerva's voice was the one he normally reserved for formal occasions, distant and impersonal. 'Can I assume that you were successful in your suit?'

'Yes, sir. She's agreed to marry me, sir.'

'I see.' The Legate slammed the tablet of wax he

was holding down with a thud. 'So, to be clear, after I dismissed you both last night, you and Scaevola took it into your heads to start gambling?'

'It wasn't intentional, but, yes, sir, something like that.'

'I've just spoken to Pulex. His story matches yours.'

'Didn't you believe me, sir?'

'Of course I believed you,' Nerva snapped, 'but if I'm going to make a report—and I'm going to have to make a report—I need to have witnesses. Fortunately, Pulex confirms everything you said when you dragged me out of bed so early this morning. No doubt Arvina and Drusus will do the same. I only have one question.'

'Yes, sir?'

'What the hell were you thinking, gambling over a woman?'

Marius gave a small shrug. At that moment, it was just about the only answer he could think of. 'I believe we'd both drunk a fair amount, sir. The game got out of hand.'

'I'd have to agree. You bet everything you owned on a game of chance! Do I need to tell you how reckless that was?'

'No, sir.'

'Or how impulsive?'

'No, sir.'

'Or how much like your father?'

Marius jutted his chin out. 'I'm not my father…sir.'

'No? You know, there are times when I look at you and it's like I'm looking at him again. You're so similar. He was my dear friend and a good man, but he had a temper and he flouted authority. I don't want you to make the same mistakes.'

'I've no intention of doing so, sir.'

'Pulex says you gambled your sword. *His* sword.'

'As you said, sir, I was being reckless. My stake wasn't high enough and it's the most valuable item I own.'

'The most precious, too, I'll wager.' Nerva's eyes narrowed. 'You told me once that you carry it as a reminder so that you never forget your purpose in life—to redeem your family honour. That was what you wanted most, or so you told me.'

'It still is.'

'Yet you risked your sword, the very symbol of your family honour, in a game of chance? Why? Are you in love with her?'

Marius clamped his brows together, his mind instinctively shying away from the idea. Love wasn't an emotion he recognised, not any more. He had personal attachments—to Nerva, to Hermenia, even to Pulex. He cared about them all, but love? No, he hadn't loved anyone since his father, and as for his father…

He felt a familiar tightness in his throat. What did it matter what he'd felt for his father? If his father had loved him, then he wouldn't have behaved in the way that he had. He wouldn't have put himself and his opinions ahead of family honour. He wouldn't have come home in disgrace and then simply wasted away, leaving his son all alone in the world.

No, he could honestly say that love hadn't entered into his thoughts at all, although he could see why Nerva might think so. In some ways it was the only answer that made sense. Why *had* he been prepared to gamble so much if he wasn't in love with Livia? *Could* he be in love with her? Was he capable of it? The very idea made him uncomfortable. His love for his father had brought him only pain and betrayal. What if the same thing happened with Livia?

'Tell me the truth, Marius.' Nerva steepled his fingers beneath his chin. 'You haven't been yourself since she arrived and now this.'

'I only want to help her, sir.' The answer rang true to his own ears, even if it didn't seem quite enough either. 'She doesn't want to marry Scaevola.'

'That doesn't mean you have to marry her yourself instead! If that's all you're worried about, then send her back to her brother. Don't shackle yourself.'

'It's not shackling.' He resented the word. 'But she can't go back to Lindum. She already told me as much. There's no other choice.'

'So you're really prepared to marry a woman whose dowry's already been spent by another man?'

'Yes, sir, I am.'

Nerva sighed heavily. 'What makes you responsible for her, Marius?'

'I don't know,' he answered honestly. 'It's just a matter of honour.'

'Honour...' Nerva ran a hand through his hair with a grunt. 'Perhaps I should have expected something like this eventually, but you've always been a model soldier... But are you sure this isn't just about revenge?'

'Sir?'

'About getting back at the class of men who condemned your father? Scaevola's one of them, after all.'

Marius took a moment to answer, offended by the suggestion, as if that were all his behaviour was, a rebellion against Rome, against Scaevola and all the other Tribunes who'd condemned his father. No. Even if he didn't know what his feelings for Livia were, they were more than that.

'It has nothing to do with revenge, sir.'

Nerva made a sceptical expression. 'Very well, if you're certain this is what you want?'

He nodded. He was certain.

'All right, on your head be it. Hermenia made all the wedding arrangements for this evening so the ceremony can still go ahead. In the meantime, I suggest you start packing.'

'Packing?'

'Yes. I've told Pulex to take over your duties for the foreseeable future.'

Marius felt a painful lurch in his chest. 'You're relieving me of my command?'

'Don't be ridiculous.' Nerva picked up his wax tablet again. 'I'm simply giving you what you've wanted these past few weeks, a transfer to the wall. You want to find out what's going on over there? Well, this is your chance.'

'Thank you, sir.' His spirits lifted again. 'But I don't understand. Why are you sending me now?'

'Why?' Nerva peered at him over the edge of the tablet. 'Because after the ceremony, I think it's a good idea for you and your new wife to get out of Coria and as far away from Lucius Scaevola as quickly as possible.'

Livia was already dressed and eating breakfast with Hermenia, Julia perched on her lap, when Marius entered the *triclinium*, his earlier elation somewhat muted.

'Is everything all right?' She sat bolt upright when she saw him, her face expectant and slightly anxious.

'It's all settled. With your permission, we'll be married tonight.'

'So soon?' Her eyes widened a fraction, though other than that he couldn't judge her response.

'Would you prefer to delay?'

'No.' She hesitated for another moment and then shook her head emphatically. 'The sooner the better.'

'Good.'

He drew in a breath, wondering how to tell her about his new posting. It was something he ought to have expected, an understandable response from Nerva, though he only hoped Livia would understand that, as well as the rest of what he was about to ask her.

'Under the circumstances, Nerva thinks it would be best if we left Coria for a while. He's posting me to Cilurnum, one of the forts along the wall.'

'Because of Scaevola?'

He nodded. 'Just until his temper's cooled and the situation with your brother is resolved. Things might get unpleasant.'

'Probably.' Her face clouded at the mention of her brother and then cleared again suddenly. 'So I'll get to see the wall after all?'

'It appears so.'

'Do you hear that, Julia?' Her smile widened as she looked down into her daughter's face and then back up at him. 'When do we leave?'

He cleared his throat slightly louder than was necessary and threw an imploring look towards Hermenia.

'Well now—' the older woman took the cue at once '—I think we've eaten enough, don't you, little one?

Let's go and find you something to wear for the ceremony tonight.'

'What is it? What's wrong?' Livia frowned as Julia jumped down from her lap and Hermenia bustled her quickly out of the room.

He cleared his throat a second time. Apparently there was no easy way to say it…

'It would be better if the child stayed here.'

'What?' She jumped to her feet, her expression turning rigid with a look of horror. 'No! She's my daughter. She comes with me.'

'Ordinarily I would agree…'

'Even Tarquinius didn't try to separate us!'

'I'm not trying to separate you, but it would be safer if she stayed here.'

The look of horror receded slightly, replaced by one of understanding. 'You mean you really think there might be a Caledonian rebellion?'

'I do. I hope that I'm wrong, but I don't think I am. Given a choice, I wouldn't risk taking either of you, but I have orders from Nerva. We both have to go. Besides, if you stay here, I wouldn't put it past Scaevola to try something.'

'For how long?'

'A month at the most.'

'A *month*?'

'I know it might seem like a long time…'

'It *is* a long time!' Blue-green eyes flashed and then faded again. 'I can't just abandon her here.'

'You won't be. Nerva's already agreed that she can stay with him and Hermenia. They'll take good care of her.'

She gave him a long, penetrating look. 'Do you *truly* think she'll be safer here with Hermenia?'

'Yes. For what it's worth, I don't think she could have a better protector in the whole Roman army.'

'Do you promise?'

He held her gaze solemnly. 'I do.'

'All right.' She bit her lip, her gaze drifting towards the door as if her thoughts were already elsewhere. 'In that case, I need to go and explain to her.'

'Of course.' He raised a hand, staying her for a moment. 'Then perhaps afterwards you'd like to visit the market with me? Both of you, that is.'

'You want to go shopping?' She stared at him as if he'd just gone mad.

'Not for myself, but you need some warmer clothes.' He gestured vaguely in the direction of her gown, though he kept his gaze fixed on her face. Getting distracted by her body at that moment definitely wasn't a good idea. Now that they were free to be alone together, their relationship seemed to have shifted, as if they were back at the beginning again with a whole new set of problems. He was separating her from her daughter, for a start. As marriages went, it wasn't the best of beginnings.

'Oh.' She glanced downwards as if she had no idea what she was wearing. 'But it's getting warmer, surely?'

'The seasons here aren't as predictable as in the south. It can be spring today and winter again tomorrow and the wall is exposed to all the elements. You'll need a warm cloak and some sturdier boots.'

Her expression wavered uncertainly. 'I don't have any money...'

'But I do and I'd be happy to buy whatever you need.'

'Very well.' She gave a strained-looking smile. 'In that case, we'd be glad to accompany you. Just give me an hour to talk to Julia first.'

'Take as long as you need.'

'Thank you.' She made for the door and then stopped. 'So the ceremony will be…?'

'Tonight. Then we'll leave for Cilurnum first thing in the morning.'

Chapter Thirteen

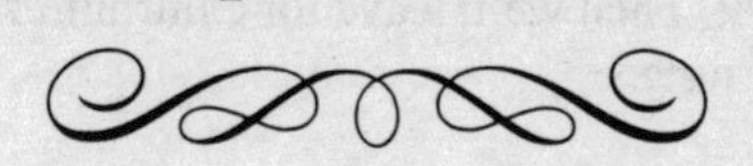

'What do you think, Empress? Would you like a new cloak, too?' Marius bent his head towards Julia as they walked out of the fortress gates towards the *vicus*, smiling when she nodded enthusiastically.

'Yes, please! Can I have a doll as well?'

'Julia!' Livia admonished her.

'Anything you want. You're the Empress.'

'You shouldn't have promised her that,' she remonstrated with him as the little girl skipped ahead with Porcia. 'Now she'll choose the biggest doll she can find.'

'Then she can have it. This is a special day, after all.' He glanced sideways, as if to see her reaction to the statement. 'She ought to get some kind of a present to celebrate.'

Celebrate. Livia forced a smile, the word hovering in the air as they made their way towards the market, a brightly coloured collection of shops and stalls bordering both sides of the street, stocked high with breads, meats, fish, clothes and anything else an army garrison might require. A group of boys called to Marius as they passed, inviting him to play some kind of ball game with them, but instead of looking angry at their familiarity as she might have expected, he only grinned and shook his head back.

Despite his *celebratory* mood, she felt a new sense of awkwardness in his company. Underneath his outward appearance she was certain he felt it, too. The atmosphere of tension between them was stronger than ever, as if they were both struggling to adjust to their new relationship. They were even walking an arm's length apart like strangers. Whatever else his proposal had done, it hadn't brought them any closer together. Quite the opposite, it seemed to have pushed them further apart. She still had no idea either why he'd proposed or how he felt towards her—and apparently he had no intention of talking about it.

Now, confusingly, he was talking about their wedding as a cause for celebration, but she couldn't celebrate. Instead, she felt oppressed by the one-sidedness of it. He'd risked so much—his money, his sword, probably even his career—while she was only using him to escape Scaevola.

No, she frowned at the thought, that wasn't true. She wasn't using him, at least not in any calculated manner, and she couldn't deny her physical attraction to him, but was he really a man she could spend the rest of her life with? After all, she barely knew him, not really, and she hadn't exactly been honest with him either. Although there was still time, she reminded herself, if she wanted to risk telling him everything…

'A wedding present, you mean?' She pushed the thought aside.

'In part, and because she's been through a lot. It

must have been a difficult few months for both of you.' He looked sombrely at her. 'I won't try to replace her father, Livia, but I'll do my best for her. You have my word on it.'

'Oh…thank you.' She swallowed the lump that arose in her throat suddenly, touched as much by the words as by the poignant idea they evoked, that of a little girl grieving for her father, no matter how far from the truth it was. *Thank you* sounded inadequate somehow, but then what more could she say, that Julia had hardly known her father? That he'd accused her of belonging to someone else? She could hardly tell him that without also explaining why…

She kept her gaze fixed determinedly ahead on her daughter. After a few tears that morning, Julia had adapted quickly to the idea of staying with, and no doubt being spoiled by, Hermenia for a month. That was one consolation at least and the older woman had seemed almost as excited.

'Do you think you'll be happy here?' Livia had wrapped Julia up in her arms and squeezed tight.

Her daughter had made an indistinct sound and wriggled. No wonder, she'd thought, feeling foolish. It was far too big a question for a four-year-old to answer. Children lived in the present, not the future. She only wished that she could do the same, though it was too big a question even for her.

Hermenia had been kind, too, patting her hand as she'd tried to reassure her. 'Marius isn't the most communicative of men, but he's a good one none the less. You're far better off with him than Scaevola, only don't tell Nerva I said so.'

'Is your husband very angry?'

The other woman's expression had spoken volumes. 'It's put him in an awkward position. If your brother brings a case against Scaevola, then his father will want to know what happened. My husband will have a lot of explaining to do.'

'But can't he simply tell him the truth? Scaevola's a grown man. Surely Nerva can't be held accountable for his actions?'

'He's a grown man who's been raised to see himself as superior to the rest of us. His father is just an older, marginally wiser version. Trust me, whatever the truth, he'll blame everyone else before his son. My husband in particular.'

'And Marius?'

'Probably.'

'Oh.' Her conscience had stabbed her anew. 'Does Marius know how important his father is?'

'He couldn't not. Lucius makes certain that everyone does.'

'But then I don't understand.' She'd put her head in her hands, stricken with guilt. 'Why did Marius gamble on me? Why did he ask me to marry him? If it causes so much trouble, why is Nerva even permitting it?'

'Because Marius insisted that the marriage go ahead, after he spoke to you, that is. He obviously cares for you and he won the game fair and square.' Hermenia had smiled indulgently. 'But I'm sure it'll all blow over soon enough, don't worry.'

Livia had smiled uncertainly, desperately hoping that was true. And the fact that Hermenia thought he cared for her was encouraging... In the meantime, unlikely as it seemed, she and Marius were going shopping. She needed supplies for their journey to the wall and he was going to pay for them. Yet another one-sided arrangement. As if she didn't have enough to feel guilty about.

Her gaze fell on a fishmonger's stall and she had a sudden burst of inspiration.

'Perhaps I could cook dinner for us tonight?' She spun towards him enthusiastically.

'You can cook?' He sounded surprised.

'Yes, my mother taught me. I used to cook for my father all the time. I'm out of practice, but I haven't forgotten how. I enjoy it.'

'Then why are you out of practice?' Dark eyes regarded her questioningly. 'Didn't you cook for your husband?'

'No-o.' She dropped her gaze quickly. 'Julius said it wasn't appropriate for someone in my position. He said they weren't the skills of a lady.'

'Ah. Fortunately, they're just the sort of skills needed for a soldier's wife, although not perhaps on her wedding day. I'm sure Hermenia will be planning some kind of dinner even if we have to keep it quiet from Scaevola.'

'Oh… Yes, of course.'

Her momentary disappointment was quickly replaced by panic. In the impulse of the moment she'd forgotten that it was their wedding meal they'd be eating tonight—which meant that tonight was also their wedding night! Why on earth had she just offered to cook? She doubted that she'd be able to eat a mouthful. She'd barely been able to eat breakfast.

'He must have been an important man, your husband.' Marius's tone shifted subtly.

'I suppose so, in Lindum anyway. He was a wine

merchant. He and Tarquinius were business associates and friends until…' She faltered, biting her lip before she gave too much away.

'Until?'

'Until they weren't.'

'I see.' He didn't push the subject. 'He came from a good family, too, I presume?'

'Mmm.' She made a pretence of examining some bread loaves. She definitely didn't want to talk about that. Julius had considered his family one of the oldest and most distinguished in the city, until she'd come along, that was.

'Do you want some bread?' He stopped beside her, looking faintly surprised. No wonder, she realised, when the Legate's villa was so amply stocked with its own provisions.

'No, I was just…' she racked her brains, failing to think up a suitable excuse '…looking.'

'Ah.' He sounded unconvinced as they continued on to a stall selling furs and woollen garments. 'Now, this is more like it.' He picked up a cloak and held it against her. 'How about this one?'

'Red?' She regarded it dubiously and then gestured at her hair. 'You don't think I'll look a little too bright?'

'No, I think it'll suit you.' His gaze flickered with a look of something like appreciation, his dark eyes seeming to turn even darker despite the bright sunshine. 'You'll look like a legionary, too.'

'So I'll fit in with the crowd?' The idea struck her as both funny and sad at the same time.

'Not unless I make you wear a helmet, which I won't. I want to see your hair, not hide it.'

She felt a warm, fuzzy feeling that seemed to start

in her chest and then spread outwards, suffusing her whole upper body in a vivid pink glow.

'Well, it certainly looks warm.' As if that would explain why she suddenly looked like a beetroot!

She lifted a hand, hoping the movement might distract him. 'It feels lovely and soft, too. Can I try it on?'

'Of course.'

He opened it up for her, unwrapping the long folds and then draping them gently about her shoulders. She tensed as his fingers brushed lightly against her back, the warmth of them seeming to penetrate all the way through the fleece to her skin. Then he tugged the ends of the cloak together under her chin and she felt as though he were gathering her into his arms, just as he had the night before. The thought made her temperature soar even higher, as if she were wearing ten layers of wool rather than one.

'What do you think?'

What did she think? Her heart was pounding so rapidly she found it hard to concentrate on the question. He was standing only a few inches away, towering above her so that, unless she wanted to stare at his chest, she had to tilt her chin up to look at him. When she did their eyes locked and she felt a familiar spark pass between them, one that seemed to render her completely speechless and immobile at the same time. *What did she think?* She was thinking that he felt strong and safe and honourable and that she wanted nothing more than for him to take the cloak off again, preferably along with the rest of her clothes, too.

'Mama?'

Julia's voice interrupted her daydream and she dropped her chin quickly. 'Yes, dear?'

'It's pretty. Can I have one, too?'

'Of course you can, Empress, one just like your mama's.' Marius crouched down beside the girl. 'Or would you like me to show you some others?'

'Yes, please.'

'All right.' He scooped her up in his arms, allowing her to survey the selection from above. 'Now tell me, which one do you like?'

'The green.'

Livia smiled, the fuzzy glow seeming to increase tenfold as he put Julia down again and picked up a smaller, forest-green version of her new cloak. It was strange how different he seemed, so much more relaxed and easy-going around children, revealing the softness behind his stern facade. If nothing else, he'd be a good father, she was sure of it.

'How's that, Empress?'

Julia nodded and he jerked his head towards Porcia. 'You, too. I don't want any of you catching a chill.'

'Thank you.' The maid beamed as she picked up a blue version. 'It's beautiful.'

'Good. Then we're all happy.' He turned away to hand a few coins to the shopkeeper before clapping his hands together decisively and winking at Livia.

'Now, I believe there was mention of a doll?'

'Over here!' Julia grabbed one of each of their hands, leading them across the street towards a stall selling an impressive array of toys and trinkets.

'This might take a while.' Livia took a step closer towards him as Julia broke away, jumping up and down with excitement at the range of choices before her. 'That was very kind. You know, it's been a long time since I've seen either of them so happy.'

'I'm glad.'

'Thank you.' She put a hand on his arm in a gesture of gratitude and felt the muscles immediately contract beneath her touch, so violently that she started to pull away again.

'Wait.' His spare hand came up to stop the movement, forcing her fingers back down on to his arm before resting gently over them.

Neither of them spoke then for a few seconds. Instead they stood side by side, watching Julia without looking at each other, though Livia was intently aware of the still spasming muscles beneath her fingertips. Suddenly she wished there was some space between them again. Surely the intense physical attraction she felt for him—that he seemed to feel for her, too—must be obvious to everyone around them.

'I'm truly sorry about separating the pair of you.' His voice sounded deeper than ever when he spoke, so deep that she felt the vibrations all through her body. 'I know it must be hard to leave her.'

'It is.' She swallowed as his fingers tightened around hers. 'We've never been apart before. I hate the very idea of it, but her safety is more important, and at least she's excited about spending some time with Hermenia. Porcia's staying, too.'

'You're not bringing your maid?'

'Not if you think it might be dangerous and it's more important for Julia to have familiar faces around her.'

He twisted towards her with a look of concern. 'You'll be safe in the fort. There'll be plenty of soldiers there to protect you, but you know I'd leave you here, too, if I could.'

That time she laughed outright. 'I'm not sure that's

the most complimentary thing you could say on our wedding day.'

'I didn't mean it like that.' He looked faintly sheepish.

'I know. You meant for my protection, too.'

'Yes.'

'This one!' Julia whirled around suddenly, holding up a wooden doll only a few inches shorter than she was.

'I hate to say *I told you so*.' Livia lifted her eyebrows.

'But you will?' Marius laughed and released her hand slowly, as if he were reluctant to do so. 'I suppose I asked for that. This might take some haggling.'

She bent down as he walked across to the stall-owner, putting on a suitably admiring expression as Julia showed off her new doll.

'I'm going to call her Flavia. Isn't she pretty, Mama?'

'She is.'

'The man said I might like her because she has hair like me.'

Livia reached a hand out to stroke the doll's bright red woollen hair. The stall-owner was right, though it could hardly have looked any more Caledonian. The thought made her vaguely uncomfortable. What if somebody here guessed their identity?

'Livia?' Marius had finished haggling and was looking at her with concern. 'Are you all right?'

'Yes.' She sucked the insides of her cheeks, trying to control her expression. 'I was just thinking about…' her gaze fell on a neighbouring stall '…boots. You said I needed new ones.'

'So I did.' He sounded dubious, as if he weren't completely convinced by her explanation.

'What about these?' Quickly, she picked up a pair of sturdy-looking, brown-leather ankle boots. Julius would have been horrified. 'They look practical.'

'Not practical enough.' He pointed to the undersoles. 'No hobnails.'

She blinked in surprise. 'Are you expecting me to do marches?'

'No, although I'm sure you'd be perfectly capable. Here.' He passed her a pair of even sturdier-looking ones. 'Try these.'

'They're man's boots!'

'Does it matter?'

She stared at him thoughtfully for a few seconds and then shrugged. 'No, I suppose not.'

'Then try them on.'

She sat down on the stool provided, unfastening her everyday sandals as Julia settled down beside her, playing with her new doll.

'Here.' Marius crouched down on his haunches in front of her, too. 'Let me help.'

He reached for her foot, cupping the back of her heel in one hand as he lifted the boot in the other and then slid it inside. She wriggled her toes, trying to concentrate on her purpose and not the sudden profusion of knots in her abdomen.

'How does that feel?' He fastened the buckle and then looked up, green eyes hooded, and all the knots seemed to twist and tighten, forming one giant skein that would surely never unravel.

'Good.' Her voice sounded strange even to her own ears.

'And the other.'

This time she held her breath, trying her hardest not

to react as he lifted her other foot. It was no use. Her toes caught on the leather and she leaned forward at the same moment as he shifted towards her, bringing their faces within an inch of each other, so close that their noses were almost touching. She could feel the warm caress of his breath on her cheek and see every fleck of stubble across his chin. He needed a shave, she noticed, although she liked the effect, too. She wanted to reach out and stroke it, to feel its roughness against her own skin.

'Can I have a wooden horse, too?' Julia darted into the edge of her vision, pointing back to the toy stall where she'd just noticed a row of carved wooden animals.

'No!' Livia twisted her head sharply, simultaneously relieved and disappointed by the interruption. 'You have enough already.'

'Except boots. You need some of those, too.' Marius *didn't* turn his head as he spoke. She could still feel his gaze on her face, making her heart beat so rapidly she felt almost dizzy.

'You're spending too much.' She forced herself to meet his gaze again. 'I can't repay you.'

'I don't want you to. Considering that I'm taking her mother away for a month, I think it's the least I can do for her. I want you both to be happy, Livia.'

'I know.'

She felt a renewed stab of guilt. She believed him. He really did want them both to be happy. It was what she wanted, too, to be happy with a husband she liked and respected and could feel close to, not to mention one who would be a good father to her daughter, but she still felt ungrateful to be keeping secrets from him.

How could she ever *truly* be close to him while she was doing that? How could she ever truly be happy?

'Try to walk in them.'

He sat back on his heels as she stood up, testing the leather.

'They're a perfect fit.' She tugged her *stola* up, showing the boots off to Julia. 'What do you think?'

The little girl scrunched up her face. 'They're not very pretty.'

She looked down with a laugh. That was undeniably true. They were a strange kind of wedding present, yet they made her happier than any gift she'd ever received before. 'You're right, but some things are more important. They're actually quite comfortable.'

'Then we'll take them.' Marius was looking up at her with a strange expression in his eyes, one that made her want to sink down into his arms. 'Now is there anything else you want? Anything you need to do before the wedding?'

She hesitated, looking between him and Julia. Her daughter was smiling, looking happy, truly happy for the first time in as long as she could remember. More than that, *she* was aware of a burgeoning feeling of happiness, too. She was being selfish, but if she told him the truth then it might jeopardise all that. How could she risk it?

'No, there's nothing else.' She swallowed the guilt, looking him straight in the eye. 'I'm ready.'

Chapter Fourteen

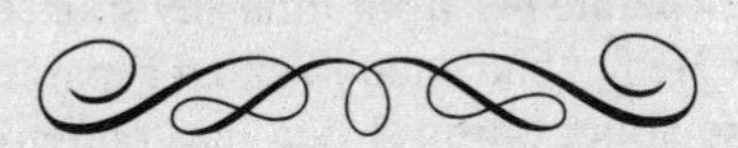

The sky was a slate-coloured grey, heavy with rain that threatened to pour over their heads at any moment as Marius tucked the last of his equipment inside his goatskin saddlebag. There were only ten of them riding north that morning, a single *contubernia* of his finest soldiers to accompany them, but he'd made sure that every man was armed and armoured to the hilt. Ordinarily he would have made the journey on his own, but today he wasn't taking any chances. There were still breaches in the wall defences and if Nerva insisted on him taking his new wife with him then he wasn't going to do it without a heavily equipped escort.

His new wife.

He looked across to where she was standing to one side, gazing forlornly back at the Legate's villa as if she'd left a part of herself behind. Which in one sense, he supposed, she had. He hadn't witnessed her farewell to Julia, but her face had been paler than usual and her eyes distinctly red-rimmed and swollen when she'd appeared in the *vestibulum* that morning.

After their brief wedding ceremony the evening

before—so brief and so sparsely attended that it was hard to believe something so monumental had actually taken place—they'd dispensed with the usual formalities so that she could spend her last evening with her daughter. He'd even insisted on her sleeping in Nerva's villa, claiming that he needed to arrange matters for their departure, though truthfully because he hadn't wanted to separate her from Julia any sooner than was necessary. He felt bad enough about separating them; even worse about taking Livia into potentially dangerous enemy territory. Letting them spend their last night together was the least he could do.

It wasn't quite the way he'd thought to spend his wedding night, alone on a pallet bed in his barracks trying not to think about how heart-stoppingly radiant Livia had looked in a plain white wedding gown tied with the traditional woollen belt and a deep yellow *flammeum* crowning her glorious curls, but the last thing he'd wanted was a bride wishing she were somewhere else. Besides, they hadn't discussed that aspect of marriage yet and, much as he was looking forward to it, he didn't want to rush her either. Not that she'd seemed so averse to him yesterday. On the contrary, if they hadn't been in public, in the middle of a market in broad daylight with her four-year-old daughter at their side…

He clamped down on the memory before he got carried away and went to stand beside her, speaking gently. 'It's time to go.'

'Yes.' She dragged her gaze away from the villa, pressing her lips together as if she were trying not to cry. 'How far away is Cilurnum?'

'Just a couple of miles. We'll be there before noon.'

He hesitated, wondering whether or not to address what was obviously upsetting her and then deciding to go ahead. 'You won't be far away.'

'I know.' A look of anxiety touched her eyes. 'It's just hard. What if she has a fall? What if she catches a chill?'

'Then Hermenia will send word and I'll bring you back.' He reached out and took one of her hands, folding both of his own around it. 'I promise, Livia. You can come back whenever you need to.'

'Thank you.'

Their eyes met and he felt the familiar urge to envelop her tightly in his arms, but he couldn't, not yet anyway. Their trip to the market had gone some way to restoring the closeness between them, but he didn't want to jeopardise it again so soon.

'We should be going.' He took a firm step backwards, releasing her hand again.

'Yes.' Her voice sounded faintly unsteady as she plucked at the folds of her cloak. 'You were right about this. I'd be freezing without it.'

'Here.' He tugged the hood up over her head, settling it gently over her hair. 'In case it rains.'

'In case?' She looked pointedly skyward.

'*When* it rains. Welcome to north Britannia.'

'I don't mind the weather.' She walked alongside him to where the horses were waiting, grasping hold of the bridle and pulling herself up into the saddle before he could so much as offer to help. 'If it didn't rain so much then the scenery would look different and I love it too much to object.'

'You do?' He lifted an eyebrow, surprised as much

by the easy way in which she'd mounted her steed as by the words themselves.

'Yes.' She seemed equally surprised by the question. 'Don't you?'

'I do. Only a lot of visitors find it too empty and weather-beaten. I thought you might prefer the area around Lindum.'

'No.' She shook her head almost fiercely. 'This is just how I imagined it would be.'

Imagined? He wrinkled his brow at the wistful note in her voice. She sounded as if she'd spent a lot of time imagining it, as if it were more than just common interest. A vague memory came back to him from their very first day together. *I've always wanted to see it...* She'd been talking about Hadrian's Wall—the same wall she'd asked if she could see from Coria, that she'd seemed so excited about when he'd told her they were going to Cilurnum yesterday...

'This way.' He mounted his own horse and led their small procession out through the gates, impressed by her skill in the saddle as she guided the horse with a mere tap on the shoulder.

'I told you I grew up in the country.' She must have noticed him looking because she gave a small smile. 'I rode most days when I was a girl. I always enjoyed it, but my husband...'

'Didn't approve?' He finished the last sentence for her. He was starting to wonder if there was anything her husband *had* approved of.

'He preferred a carriage, but I've always loved riding.' She leaned forward, patting her horse's neck as if to prove it.

'Then you'll be pleased to know that Cilurnum is a cavalry regiment.'

She sat up straight again. 'But I thought you said all the forts on the wall were manned by auxiliaries?'

'They are. These are auxiliary cavalry soldiers.'

'I didn't know there was such a thing.' She sighed. 'I'm starting to think I have a lot to learn about the Roman army.'

'I feel the same way at times. Most of the forts along the wall are manned by infantry regiments, but a few are mixed and four of them are cavalry only. They're organised differently to the legion. For a start, they're called *alae* and they're divided into *turmas*, not centuries. Each *turma* has thirty-two riders.'

'As opposed to eighty soldiers in a century?'

He nodded approvingly. 'You're learning.'

'So what's the difference between an auxiliary and a legionary? Apart from auxiliaries not being Roman citizens?'

'They get less pay and less training, but there are some advantages. Fewer rules, for a start, and not so much hard labour. It's a better life in some ways.'

'You sound as if you want to join.'

'Some days I think so, too, but it doesn't work that way. Every so often, a decurion gets promoted to the legion, but not the other way round.'

'So how many men are there in Cilurnum altogether?'

'About five hundred riders, give or take.'

'Just in one fort? That seems like a lot.'

'It's a long wall.'

'So why are we going there? I mean, I know *why*

we're going, but I mean why *there* in particular? Why to a cavalry regiment when you're an infantry centurion?'

'Because Nerva's finally given permission for me to take a patrol north and we can cover more ground on horseback.'

'What?' Her voice sounded higher-pitched all of a sudden. 'He said it was too dangerous!'

'If I were on my own then he'd probably be right, but I'll have men with me.'

'But what if *you're* right and the tribes are planning a rebellion?'

'Then we'll find out once and for all.' He felt stirred by the note of concern in her voice. 'I'll take care, don't worry.'

She fell silent for a few moments after that, though he could still see her chewing her lip. 'So it's not a punishment, then?'

'What do you mean?'

'For marrying me and causing problems with Scaevola's father.'

'You mean is Nerva sending me north to be killed as some kind of punishment for our marriage?' He chuckled at the idea. 'No. He doesn't think there's any danger, remember? I doubt he would have given me permission if we hadn't got married, but now it's a good excuse for him to keep me out of Scaevola's eyeline. I'm glad of it.'

'You are?'

'Yes. I told you, if a rebellion's coming then we need to be ready. The more I can find out, the more lives can be saved.'

'But will you be safe with auxiliaries? You just said they weren't as well-trained as Roman legionnaires.'

'Ah, but cavalry are the exception to that rule, in this case especially. The Ala II Asturum were formed in Hiberia originally and they're some of the best soldiers in the army. Their senior officer is a decurion called Ario. He's from the Parisi tribe and…'

'Parisi?'

'Yes.' He was taken aback by the stricken note in her voice. 'Why?'

'You mean he's a Briton?'

'Yes, a lot of local tribesmen join the army. Once they serve their twenty-five years they become Roman citizens.'

'And then what? Rome gives them back the patch of the land they were born on?'

This time he twisted around in his saddle to look at her. She looked *and* sounded angry, as if she were angry about Rome itself. He found himself remembering something else she'd said on the palisade two mornings ago, something about Rome being all conquest and slavery. Strange how sometimes she spoke as if she disapproved of—no, more than that, actually *disliked*—the Empire, as if she somehow wasn't a part of it.

'Rome gives its protection, too. We defend the tribes on this side of the wall from those on the north.'

'Doesn't it occur to you that maybe the tribes are capable of taking care of themselves?'

'Many of them are glad to come under Roman rule.'

'Many doesn't mean *all*.' She glared at him. 'Besides, who's to say the tribes on the north side aren't simply trying to reclaim territory that was once theirs? It was a *Roman* who decided where the wall ought to go and he did it in a straight line. He took no account of tribal boundaries.'

'You seem to know a lot about it. More than most Romans.'

'I've heard stories.' Her strident tone faltered. 'I told you, my mother was a Briton.'

'So you did, though you didn't say which tribe she was from.'

There was a significant pause before she answered. 'Carvetti.'

'From around here?' His unease receded slightly. At least that explained her strange desire to see the wall, although something about that pause was mildly disquieting…

'My father's father came from Italia.' She sounded defensive now. 'Only he liked it in Britannia. He never wanted to go back.'

'I can understand that.'

'You can? Don't *you* want to go back to Rome?'

'No,' he answered without hesitation, though honestly he'd never considered the question before. When he *did* stop to think, however, he realised he was telling the truth. 'There's nothing there for me now. Nearly everyone who knew my father disowned us.'

'I'm sorry.' She tipped her head to one side inquisitively. 'You never told me what it was about, the mutiny.'

'What does it matter? He rebelled against Rome.'

'But surely his motives make a difference? Just because he mutinied doesn't mean he was in the wrong.'

'He was. A soldier ought to follow orders, no matter what he thinks of them.' He felt himself scowling and made a conscious effort to unclench his jaw. 'In any case, I can't imagine ever going back to Rome. The legion is my family now. I—*we*,' he corrected himself, 'have to follow wherever it leads.'

She was silent for a moment before nodding her head almost imperceptibly. 'Then it's a good thing I have strong boots.'

Chapter Fifteen

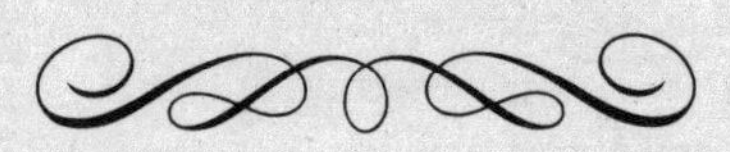

After the first half-hour, Marius moved to the front of their small column and Livia was able to study his back at leisure, as if that might tell her something about the man she'd recently married. She had no idea who he was, not really, and their wedding night certainly hadn't revealed anything new, primarily because they'd spent it apart.

Grateful though she'd been for the extra time with Julia, she'd felt strangely, irrationally slighted, too. She'd thought that he was attracted to her, but perhaps she'd been mistaken about quite how much. Either that or she'd simply projected her own desires on to him. As mortifying as the idea was, perhaps he hadn't *wanted* to spend the night with her. Common sense told her that it was only him being thoughtful again, but common sense seemed to hold no sway over her emotions. Now she was even more afraid that he'd married her out of a sense of honour. Which made her keeping secrets from him ten times worse.

As for those secrets, she'd already decided to tell him the truth—just as soon as they had some time alone together in Cilurnum. She'd spent most of the previous night unable to sleep for thinking about it, Julia clasped tight in her arms, until finally her conscience had got the better of her. No matter what the risk to her and her daughter's future, she owed him the truth. She ought to have told him before they'd married—she had no excuse for that except that events had moved so quickly—but since she hadn't, she had to do it as soon as possible and definitely before anything physical happened between them, *if* anything physical were going to happen between them, that was.

An opportunity had just presented itself when he'd asked about her mother's tribe and she'd lied. Although she could hardly have told him now in the middle of their journey with eight guards on either side of them. She needed to sit him down, to look him calmly in the eye and tell him everything. If he was the man she thought, *hoped*, he was then he would understand. If not…

She pushed a lock of wet hair from her eyes, trying not to think about that. She'd deal with that if and when it happened. In any case, now definitely wasn't the time for *that* conversation, not when she must look so utterly and thoroughly bedraggled. They all did, all except Marius. Somehow he was still managing to look the very epitome of a Roman soldier, his armour still polished and gleaming, despite the weather. How did he do that?

She was so engrossed in admiring the broad contours of his back that she didn't notice it at first, a dark line emerging out of the grey drizzle on the horizon ahead of them. Then she thought it must be some kind of low-lying cloud, rising and falling as it followed the rolling undulations of the landscape, clinging to the ground like some kind of petrified wave. It was a few seconds before she felt a dawning suspicion, accompanied by a sharp jolt in her chest.

'There it is.' She was only certain when Marius dropped back to her side. 'Hadrian's Wall.'

She pulled on her reins, holding her horse steady as she stared into the distance, too overcome with emotion to speak. As if on schedule, the drizzle ceased and a few shafts of sunlight broke through the clouds, bathing the scene in a vibrant golden glow that looked nothing short of spectacular. There it really was, the boundary between the *civilised* Roman world and the *barbarian* wilderness beyond—her mother's homeland. Her heart ached with the beauty of it. She felt tears well in her eyes and tipped her head back, letting the feeling soak in. She was here. She'd made it at last and with Marius at her side. For some reason, his presence seemed strangely fitting.

'It's quite impressive the first time you see it.' He spoke softly, as if reluctant to intrude upon her silence.

'It is.' She blinked the tears back, unable to keep the wonder out of her voice. 'My mother told me stories, but I never imagined anything like this…' She twisted her neck back and forth, following the line into the distance. 'It goes up and down. Somehow I imagined it was a flat line.'

'It follows the shape of the land. This area is actually flatter than most, perfect for cavalry.'

'Why are there so many towers?'

'There's a mile-castle every mile and two turrets between each of those. That way if there's an attack, the soldiers on guard can communicate with flags or beacons. They can get a message from one end of the wall to the other in less than an hour.'

'Is that Cilurnum?'

There was really no need for her to ask. The road they were riding along led directly towards a long, rectangular-shaped fort with a huge double gateway at the front and more towers at each corner.

'That's it.' He nudged his horse forward again, leading them over a narrow strip of land like a bridge over what looked like a deep, man-made ditch.

'What's that?' She pointed downwards.

'The *vallum*. There are ditches on both sides of the wall.'

'To defend it from attack?'

'Yes.'

'Oh.' She pursed her lips, resisting the urge to ask why the south side would need protecting if its inhabitants were, as he claimed, so in favour of Roman rule. But she'd already given away too many of her thoughts on that subject earlier, too upset about leaving Julia to mind her tongue and be cautious, and the last thing she wanted was for him to guess her secret before she had a chance to tell him.

One side of the gateway creaked open as they approached and they rode into a smaller, more compact version of Coria, though this time they took an immediate left turn away from the Via Principalis towards some stables.

'Varro!' A giant of a man with a thick, bushy beard and piercing blue eyes came striding towards them as they came to a halt. 'I didn't expect to see you again so soon. Have you missed my company so much?'

'Ario.' Marius dismounted quickly to greet him. 'Has your beard really grown so much in two days? There are more knots in it every time I see you.'

To her surprise, the two men embraced like old friends before Marius held an arm out towards her.

'May I present my wife, Livia Valeria.'

'Wife?' Ario didn't make any attempt to conceal his surprise. 'Have you been keeping secrets from me, old friend?'

'I'll explain later. Livia, this is Ario, the man I told you about.'

'Nothing unsuitable for a lady's ears, I hope.' Ario winked at her and she had to stifle a laugh. Apparently Marius was right about the lack of discipline amongst auxiliary troops. The Decurion was nothing like any Roman soldier she'd ever come across, though the speculative way he was looking at her hair made her uneasy, too.

'Ario.' She inclined her head, lips still twitching, before turning back to her husband. 'Is this where you came two days ago?'

'One of the places. I have to visit Ario whenever I can.' Marius grinned. 'He gets grumpy otherwise. You know we met on the very first day I arrived at the wall. He fell off his horse at my feet.'

'Fell?' Ario shoved him hard in the ribs. 'I was being chased by a war party of Caledonian warriors, as I recall. They shot my horse out from under me and I rolled to a stop in front of this man. Still, under the circumstances, I was glad to meet him. He saved my life that day.'

'And now I'm stuck with him as a friend.'

'That insult works both ways.' Ario gave another,

even harder shove. 'So how long are you here for this time?'

'A few weeks, perhaps. You and I have an expedition to lead.'

'Over the wall?' The Decurion's expression turned serious at once. 'It's about time. Nerva's finally taking the threat seriously, then?'

'Not exactly. He just wants me out of Coria for a while.'

'Ah.' Ario's gaze settled on Livia appraisingly. 'In that case, you and I had better talk. But first, let me show you to your quarters. I have just the place for you two to stay.'

'In a moment. I think my wife would like to visit the wall first.'

'Really?' Livia looked up eagerly.

'Really.' Marius twisted his head slightly towards Ario though he kept his eyes fixed on hers. 'We won't be long.'

He gestured towards a side tower and then let her precede him up the stone steps on to the wall itself. She drew in a few deep breaths, bracing herself for her first view of the north, though she made sure to turn around first, looking southward so that the direction of her interest wouldn't be too obvious. To her surprise, the walkway was only a few feet wide, though the parapet wall was taller than she was, albeit with gaps at regular intervals to look through. She peered through one at last and then bit her lip to stop herself from exclaiming aloud.

The land beyond was everything she'd imagined and more, wild and sweeping and vast, making her chest ache again with a sense of belonging she hadn't felt since childhood. *Belonging?* The idea surprised her, but then why not? Surely this, if anywhere, was where she belonged, here on the line between the two worlds, half-Roman, half-Caledonian, neither belonging to nor accepted by either and yet inherently a part of both. Maybe here on the border she could finally be herself.

'It's beautiful.' The words emerged as a whisper.

'It is.' Marius's voice came from just behind her shoulder. 'Even more so to the west. The wall follows a natural ridge of cliffs and crags, so it looks even more impressive. You can see for miles.'

'You sound as if you like it.'

'I do. It's beautiful on both sides of the wall, but...'

'But?' She risked a quick glance behind her, surprised to find him gazing into the distance with a look that seemed to mirror her own admiration. 'But what?'

'But...' his brow furrowed slightly '...when I look to the north, I can feel the beauty somehow, down deep in my gut. When I look to the south I see roads and forts and ditches and *order*. There's a beauty in them, too, but they take something away from the land as well. All of our forts and towns are built on the same patterns. All of our lives are ordered the same way. Sometimes I think we have too many rules. Over there, there's a sense of freedom.'

'You think the northern tribes are free?'

'Probably not, but maybe more than we are. We're all slaves of Rome in a way.'

She studied his face curiously. The subject of slavery wasn't one she wanted to discuss, not yet anyway, but it was strange how a man who could say that soldiers ought to follow orders without question could at other times sound so subversive. Apparently there was a rebellious edge to him when it came to Roman order after all, on every subject except for his father. On that, he seemed completely intractable.

'Thank you for bringing me here.'

He gave an ironical smile. 'You should really thank Scaevola. He's the real reason we're here.'

'I doubt he'd appreciate my gratitude.'

'Perhaps not. In that case, you're welcome. You said you'd always wanted to see it the first day we met.'

'Yes.' She was surprised that he'd remembered, though she supposed her behaviour must have made it obvious, too. 'And I appreciate you letting me on the walkway.'

'It's a pre-emptive gesture.' He grinned. 'I thought that if I didn't do it now then I'd only have to come searching for you in the morning.'

She bit her lip at the insinuation. 'I've caused you a lot of problems, haven't I?'

'I wouldn't say that. I just never thought that my life could change so much in one week.'

'I want you to be happy, too.' She said the words impulsively. 'I'll do my best to make you happy.'

'Well, in that case…' He lifted a finger, nudging her gently under the chin. 'If we're both trying to make the other happy…what can go wrong?'

What could go wrong? *If only he knew.*

She averted her gaze, turning back towards the stairwell. 'We should go. Ario must be waiting.'

'As you wish.' He offered her an arm, leading her back down in silence.

'Not a bad view, eh?' The Decurion was leaning against the tower wall with his arms folded when they emerged.

'It's beautiful.' She smiled in response.

'Wait until the weather warms up. Then you can see fish jumping in the river.'

'River?'

'It's on the eastern side. The wall goes right over it. You'll be able to watch your husband swimming in the summer, though I should warn you, it's not a pretty sight.' He guffawed loudly. 'Though I suppose you know that already.'

'It's still better than looking at you.'

Marius gave the other man a hard shove as she felt her cheeks redden, embarrassed and surprised again by the drastic change in her husband's demeanour. He seemed far more relaxed here than in Coria, ironically given that Ario seemed to take the threat of a rebellion as seriously as he did. The thought was more than a little alarming. Until now, she'd clung to the hope that Marius was overreacting, as Nerva had suggested. Here on the wall there seemed to be a different opinion.

'Here we are.' Ario led them into the middle of the fort and up some steps into a small villa. 'Consider this your new home. We patched up the damage to the walls after the last Caledonian raid, though I'm afraid most of the furniture was destroyed.'

'But isn't this your house?' She looked around in surprise.

'I live in barracks with my men. Officially this is the Camp Commander's villa, but with all the commotion in Gaul it's been empty for years. It's a bit run-down, but you're welcome to use it.'

Livia wandered through the villa, exploring every nook and cranny with wide eyes. The atrium led into a corridor with two rooms on either side, beyond which was a small enclosed courtyard with half-a-dozen larger rooms around it. Ario was right—the house showed distinct signs of neglect, with stucco peeling off the walls in places and dust on every visible surface, though there was little enough furniture for it to land on. Still, it was the perfect size for a family such as theirs, even if, she quickly reminded herself, it was only temporary. It was highly unlikely that Julia would ever visit Cilurnum at all, let alone live there, but it still wouldn't hurt to prepare a room for her, just in case. Somehow it felt like exactly what Ario had just called it, a home. She fell in love with it at once.

'We don't have any servants, I'm afraid.' Ario sounded apologetic when she finally returned to the atrium. 'We do all our own cooking and cleaning around here, but I can send a few men over to tidy up.'

'There's no need.' She swept off her cloak and rubbed her hands together briskly, eager to get started. 'In fact, I'd prefer to do it on my own. I'd like to cook, too, if I can get supplies from somewhere?'

'Cook? If you're hungry…'

'Not particularly.' She laughed at his bemused expression. 'I just want to cook.'

'Then I'll tell the quartermaster to give you whatever you need.' He turned towards Marius with a raised eyebrow. 'I thought Roman ladies lay around on couches all day?'

'Some of them do—' her husband's dark eyes regarded her approvingly '—just not this one.'

She smiled inwardly at the words. From Julius they would have been an insult. From Marius, they sounded like the most heady of compliments. Not that she wanted him to know how much they'd pleased her, as she put her hands on her hips indignantly.

'Of course, if you stand there gawping then I'll find you both jobs to do!'

'Now *that* sounds like a wife!' Ario bellowed with laughter while Marius held up his hands.

'Then we'll get out of your way. I'll be back tonight, but if you need anything…'

'I'll find someone. Don't worry.' She gave him a genuinely happy smile. 'I'm going to enjoy myself.'

Chapter Sixteen

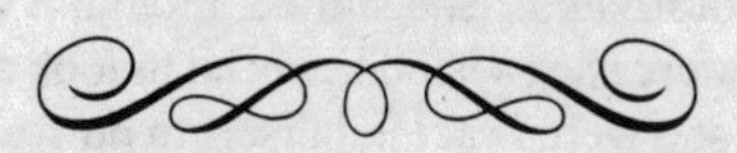

Marius was halfway through the atrium when he stopped to sniff the air. Something inside the villa smelled wonderful. Not only that, but the whole place seemed to have been transformed during the course of the afternoon, every surface polished and every floor scrubbed until it gleamed. While he'd been outlining his plans for an expedition north, inspecting equipment and preparing Ario's men for what they might find, it seemed his wife had been equally busy.

'Livia?'

He called her name as he removed his mail shirt, draping it over one of the few remaining chairs before following his nose to the courtyard. There she was, her new red cloak pushed back over her shoulders as she crouched beside a small firepit in the centre, stirring a heavy pot that hung from a hook attached to a tripod of three metal poles. She clearly hadn't noticed him arrive, so he was able to examine her face in profile for a few moments, her small brow wrinkled in concentration as she lifted the spoon, blew on its contents and then lifted it to her lips.

The effect on his body was instantaneous. He'd never been so jealous of a spoon in his whole life.

'Smells good.' He sat down on the low wall that ran along the perimeter of the courtyard, resting one forearm on his leg to hide the evidence of his sudden and surprisingly potent arousal. 'Fit for the Emperor himself.'

'He's not invited.' She smiled, though it was a few seconds before she twisted her head to look at him, almost as if she were bracing herself to do so. 'It's mutton stew, one of my father's favourites.'

'I'm sorry if I kept you waiting.'

'You haven't, but it's ready now if you're hungry?'

'Famished. You know there are ovens on the east wall of the fort. You can use them.'

'I know. The quartermaster told me, but I wanted to cook here. My mother used to say a house wasn't a home until you'd cooked in it.'

Home. The word gave him an almost visceral jolt. He hadn't had a home, tents and barrack blocks excepted, for twelve years. His last home had been with the family his father had paid to take care of him while he was away fighting and then after, when he'd known that he wouldn't recover…

He pushed the memory away quickly. 'So what do you think of it? The house, I mean?'

'It's perfect.' She gave a contented-sounding sigh. 'I can't believe no one's lived here for so long.'

'Ario doesn't like living apart from his men. He expects them to follow him because he's their comrade and a good leader, not just because of his rank.'

'You mean he's still more Briton than Roman?' She peered up at him from under her lashes.

'I suppose so.' He ceded the point. 'In any case, consider this your home for the time being. You can do whatever you like with the place.'

'*Our* home.' She dipped a ladle into the pot and doled out two bowlfuls. 'Not just mine.'

'Ours, then.' He tried to catch her eye as she passed him the bowl, but she kept hers cast downwards as if she were deliberately avoiding looking at him. There was an edginess to her movements, too, he noticed, as if she were nervous about something.

'Do you want to eat inside?' She gestured towards one of the rooms as his stomach growled with anticipation. 'There aren't any tables, but we could put some chairs together to make one.'

'No. I'm comfortable here.' He patted the space on the wall beside him. 'Join me?'

'Yes. Oh!' She sat down and then sprang up again almost instantly, picking up a basket of bread and placing it on the wall between them, along with two cups and an amphora. 'I forgot these.'

Marius lifted an eyebrow. 'The quartermaster was generous.'

'His name is Trenus and he was. He said we ought to drink a toast to our marriage.' She lifted the amphora with a smile. 'Care for some? I promise not to spill any this time.'

'Yes, please. It's been a long day.'

'Ye-es, I suppose so.'

The words only seemed to make her more anxious somehow as she poured two cupfuls and then sat down again, arranging her skirts with more precision than was necessary, her fingers twitching over the fabric as if she couldn't bear to keep still.

'Ario seems friendly.' There appeared to be a deliberate lightness to her tone as well. 'Did you really save his life?'

'Possibly, although I doubt it. He's been in tougher situations than that and survived. I just happened to be there at the right time.'

He frowned as she picked up her bowl and started to fidget with the spoon. Something was definitely bothering her. Strange when she'd seemed all right—happy, even—when he'd left earlier. Had something happened in the meantime? In the fading twilight, with the only illumination coming from the fading campfire and their two oil lamps, it was hard to make out her features distinctly, making him wish they'd gone inside after all. It would be pitch-black soon, as darkness descended over their first real night as a married couple… His mind hit a stone wall.

Was *that* what was bothering her? Was *that* why she was acting so strangely—because she was nervous about going to bed with him? Or, worse still, didn't she want to? They hadn't kissed, had barely even touched since the wedding and they'd never discussed the subject, although he'd thought they'd been getting closer again. Now, as much as he wanted to carry her off to bed, quite desperately in fact, he wasn't going to force his attentions on her just because they were married. He couldn't presume to know anything about her feelings and apparently she wasn't going to tell him anything about them either, not when she was making small talk about Ario.

The thought was enough to put him off his dinner, but she seemed to be watching expectantly, waiting for him to start eating.

Reluctantly, he took a mouthful of stew and then groaned. He didn't think he'd ever tasted anything so mouth-wateringly succulent in his whole life. It was all he could do not to lift the bowl to his lips and guzzle the rest.

'It tastes even better than it smells.' He scooped up a few more mouthfuls eagerly.

Her smile held a hint of pride. 'Try dipping the bread.'

Obediently, he tore off a piece and dunked. It tasted even better. 'This is delicious. If we weren't already married, I'd ask you again just for your cooking. Your husband was a fool.'

Her smile faded instantly and he put the bread down again, afraid that he'd said the wrong thing.

'Forgive me, I shouldn't have said that. I know that you're still grieving…'

'I'm not.' She jerked her chin up abruptly. 'That is, I did grieve for him, but a long time ago. Not any more.'

He frowned slightly. 'I thought you said he only died two months ago?'

'He did, but our marriage was over years before that.' She swallowed, as if the words were hard for her to say. 'You should know that he thought I was unfaithful. He thought that Julia wasn't his daughter. That's why he disinherited us both.'

'I see.'

'Aren't you going to ask if it was true?' Dark eyelashes quivered though she kept her chin firmly in the air.

'No.' He held on to her gaze intently. 'I think that would be an insult to both of us.'

The eyelashes fluttered more rapidly, as if she were

taken aback by his answer. 'But don't you want to know *why* he thought so?'

'Not if you don't want to tell me.' He paused. 'Did you love him?'

'No.' Her voice sounded strained. 'I tried to, but… no. In the end I disliked him intensely, though I know that's a terrible thing to say about my own husband.'

'That depends on the husband.' He felt an inappropriate sense of elation at the words and then frowned again. 'You told me once that he was a good man.'

'He was, or at least he was kind to me at first. We lived as brother and sister for the first few years, but then I got older and we had Julia and things changed. He let other people change his mind about me. He became angry and cruel.'

'Did he hurt you?' He tried to control his own anger.

'Not physically, but he made my life miserable. That's why I was so scared of marrying Scaevola, of living with a man like that again.'

'Well, you don't have to be scared any more. And you don't need to worry about being disinherited again either. I have a good amount saved in the legion stronghold at Coria. It's not a fortune, but it's enough for you and Julia to be independent. I've left instructions in case anything happens to me.'

She shook her head slightly. 'You shouldn't say that.'

'It's just a precaution. Speaking of which, I'll make sure there's a guard stationed in the atrium at night from tomorrow, just for while I'm away.'

'What?'

'I don't like the idea of your being alone here without even a maid.'

'Not that. You mean you're leaving so soon?'

'At first light. Under the circumstances, it's better to go sooner than later.'

'With how many men?'

'Four *turmae*. That's more than a hundred riders, Ario included, and we're only going to take a look around. There won't be any fighting if we can help it.'

'Just don't take any unnecessary risks.'

'I've no intention of doing so, especially now.' He reached a hand out, rubbing his knuckles gently across her cheek as she drew in a ragged-sounding breath.

'I'll hold you to that.'

'What about you?' He skimmed his thumb lightly across the bridge of her nose. 'Will you be all right?'

'Yes. There's lots to be done here. Don't think about me.'

He turned his hand over and drew a red tendril away from her face. How could he say that he couldn't help but think about her, that ever since they'd met he'd done little else? Her round face looked even more beautiful in the moonlight, her earlier nervousness replaced with concern. She looked as if she truly cared about whether or not he came back. How ironic that now, for the first time in all the weeks he'd been asking Nerva to let him lead a patrol, he didn't want to go. He wanted to stay with her. His groin stirred again at the thought. At that moment, he wanted nothing more than to lean in and kiss her so thoroughly that she wouldn't have either the time or leisure to become nervous about sleeping with him. In fact, if it was speed he wanted, then that shouldn't be a problem. He already felt close to bursting.

Not that he wanted their first encounter to be in a courtyard, he admonished himself. He'd rather carry her to bed first and start their marriage properly. There would be time for more imaginative ideas later. They'd have to find more furniture from somewhere...

He slid his hand down and around the back of her neck and then stopped, struck by the distinct feeling that something wasn't right. She already seemed nervous again—tense, even—the muscles in her neck palpitating beneath his fingertips. Was it the marriage bed itself she felt tense about? Or the idea of him in it? From what she'd just told him, her married life had been a long way from happy. He'd stopped her from explaining the reasons why her husband had accused her of infidelity, but perhaps he shouldn't have. Now, too late, he had the distinct suspicion that she'd *wanted* to tell him, as if she'd *needed* to almost, as if, even though she wasn't grieving, she was still recovering from the after-effects of her marriage. Perhaps she needed time to recover from those. Which meant that he couldn't rush her, no matter how much he wanted to.

He wondered if it were too late to visit the *frigidarium...*

'Marius?' She looked strangely resolute all of a sudden. 'There's something I need to tell you...'

'There's only one bed.'

They weren't the words she'd intended to say. They weren't even the words she was thinking of, though she supposed some part of her brain must have been thinking about bed—how could it not when he'd been looking at her so intently?—but they definitely weren't part of the speech she'd been planning.

She'd spent the afternoon preparing both the house and herself, reciting the words over and over in her mind until she knew them by heart. She'd made a promising start, she'd thought, telling him the truth about her marriage to Julius, but it was still only a small part of the whole story. Ironically, he'd stopped her from telling the rest, saying he only wanted to know if she wanted to tell him. Now she almost felt angry. Why did he have to be so honourable all of the time? Why couldn't he just demand to know the truth?

'Ah.' He looked faintly surprised by her statement, too. 'Ario did say there wasn't much furniture.'

'Yes.' She swallowed, wondering what on earth had possessed her to start a conversation about their sleeping arrangements now. With one bed, it wasn't as if they had many options, but if they were going to share it then she *definitely* had to speak up first!

'It's not very big.' Her nerve failed her again. 'But I've made it up ready…for you.'

'*Just* for me?' His eyes seemed even darker than the dusk around them. 'No, you take it. I'm used to sleeping on the floor.'

'No.' She shook her head adamantly. Coward as she was, she wasn't going to make him suffer for it. 'I can't let you do that, especially if you're riding north in the morning.'

'I insist.'

She chewed her lip. Clearly he wasn't going to back down. In which case, she'd have to try something else. Another lie to make matters worse… She stood up and stretched her arms out to the sides, feigning a yawn. 'In that case, we ought to share it. It's big enough and we're both tired. I know I am.' Another yawn for good measure. 'I'm sure I could sleep for a week.'

'Is that so?' There was a cynical edge to his voice suddenly.

'Yes. I'll just clean up first.'

'Can I help?'

'No.' She picked up a jug of water and doused the fire, avoiding his gaze as studiously as she had when he'd first arrived and she'd been building herself up to her speech. 'It won't take me long. You go ahead.'

'Very well.' He picked up a lantern in one hand and his wine in the other. 'Which room?'

'That one.' She pointed quickly over her shoulder, waiting for him to close the door before smacking a hand to her forehead and rebuking herself for cowardice. *Why* hadn't she told him? It had been the perfect opportunity. They'd been alone with no danger of interruptions, for once, and he'd been in a relaxed mood, one she'd done her best to bolster with food and wine. There had even been a feeling of intimacy sitting on the wall beside him, close enough that all her nerve endings had seemed to positively throb with awareness. There had been a strange look on his face, too, when she'd admitted that she hadn't loved Julius, one almost like relief, as if he'd been pleased by the fact. She *should* have told him everything right then, but she'd shied away at the last moment, telling herself the timing still wasn't right. After all, he was leaving at first light, so he'd said, heading into enemy territory for who knew how long, and she hadn't wanted him to leave on an argument.

She washed the bowls out, gratified to find his was empty, and then made her way through to the *cubicula*. It wasn't the biggest, but it was the most habitable of all the bedrooms, with a tattered-looking chair, a scratched chest and a medium-sized bed pushed up against the wall. With any luck, Marius would be in there already. If he was already asleep, then she'd only have to crawl in beside him…

She stopped in the doorway. Not only was he *not* in bed asleep, but he was sitting wide awake and half-naked on the edge, the muscles of his torso rippling as he bent over to pull off his boots, the light from her wobbling lantern making his skin seem to gleam in the shadows. Somehow, incredibly, his chest looked even broader without armour, almost alarmingly well defined, as if it were made of pure sculpted muscle. Slowly, she curled her fingers into her palms, resisting the impulse to reach over and find out.

She cleared her throat instead, gesturing at the bed matter-of-factly. 'I got some clean blankets from the quartermaster.'

'So I see.' He glanced upwards, his eyes hooded, before turning his attention back to his boots.

'I couldn't find a brazier.' She felt the need to keep talking. 'But there's a wolfskin in case it gets too cold.'

'We won't freeze.' He picked up his cup and drained the remainder of his wine in one swallow.

'No… I suppose not.'

She put her head down and made her way quickly across to the chest, extinguishing her lantern and removing her cloak as she went. In all honesty, cold was the last thing she was worried about. She had no idea what the real temperature was. The thought of sharing a bed with him made her feel as though she were standing next to a bonfire.

She removed her hairpins and dragged a comb through her curls, trying to make them look neater, though long experience told her that was impossible. The copper ringlets simply refused to lie flat, tumbling about her shoulders in rampant disarray. If anything, her attempts at control only made them look wilder. Defeated, she put the comb down again and darted across to the bed, taking advantage of Marius's distraction while he unfastened the string of his *braccae* to remove her *stola* and wriggle quickly under the blankets, sliding to the furthest side as close to the wall as possible.

'Is that enough room for you?' She rolled on to her shoulder, her back towards him, acutely aware that she was wearing only a thin linen *tunica*.

'Too much.' The bed dipped as he climbed in beside her. 'You need some space, too.'

'I'm all right.'

'No.' His voice sounded as stern as it had the first time they'd met. 'You're not.'

She gasped as a hand wrapped around her waist, tugging her back towards him.

'I don't want you to be crushed against the wall.'

She swallowed, trying to ignore the ripple of desire that coursed through her body even after he pulled his hand away again, glad that she was facing in the opposite direction so that he couldn't see her face. The bed was barely big enough for two people, but if she were going to be crushed by anything then she'd prefer it to be his chest. Its hard contours had pressed briefly against her back before he shifted away and she felt somewhat deprived without it.

'Yes.' Her voice sounded like somebody else's. 'How early did you say you were leaving again?'

'Early. I'll try not to wake you.'

'I don't mind.'

She closed her eyes as he extinguished his own lantern, willing herself to sleep, though it was hard to concentrate on anything, even sleep, knowing he was so close beside her. She stretched her legs after a few minutes, trying to get more comfortable. If she could just relax, then maybe she could sleep, unlikely as the possibility seemed. Was *he* asleep? She held her breath, listening to the sound of his breathing, though it was impossible to tell. She hadn't shared a bed with a man for five years, not since before Julia was born, and Julius had never slept in her room in any case. What *did* a sleeping man sound like? She felt as jittery and apprehensive as a virgin bride in bed for the first time with her new husband, although apparently hers had absolutely no intention of touching her.

Why *didn't* he touch her? The irrational thought entered her head and refused to go away. She didn't want him to touch her, not tonight anyway, but *why* didn't he? They were lying in bed together as man and wife, almost completely naked in her case, and in his…well, she wasn't sure about his, but she'd heard the rustle of some kind of fabric before he'd climbed in. *She* wanted to touch *him*, but she had her own private reasons for not doing so. What were his? Had he felt so rebuffed simply because she'd said she was tired?

She felt a shudder of ignominy. What if he simply *wasn't* that attracted to her? What if she'd been imagining things all along? After all, *he'd* been the one who'd pulled away that first morning on the ramparts and *she'd* been the one who'd asked him to kiss her after she'd poured wine over Scaevola's head. That was still their one and only kiss after more than a day of marriage! Shaming as the realisation was, it was yet another area in which their relationship was alarmingly one-sided. What if he didn't really want her at all? What if…?

The pressure of his hand on her hip stopped the thought in its tracks.

'Livia?' His lips were close to her ear, warming it with his breath. If she wasn't mistaken, he was inhaling the scent of her hair. She'd washed it in rose-petal water for their wedding—would the scent still cling to it? She hoped so…

'Yes?' she answered before she could think better of it, holding her breath while his fingers slid gently along the curve of her thigh and then around, coming to rest between her legs.

'When I get back…'

He didn't finish the sentence, his lips drifting along the side of her throat as his hand continued its slow progress between her legs, upwards this time.

When I get back… She arched herself backwards, moulding herself into the curve of his arms as the words sent a frisson of anticipation rippling along every nerve ending. They sounded like a promise, a vow, filling her mind with ideas…

His hand and his lips stopped and she waited, every part of her straining towards him, though he didn't move. He seemed to be waiting, too, though for what she had no idea. For her to touch him? But a wife couldn't simply touch her husband, could she? She'd never even considered the idea with Julius and yet somehow her situation with Marius seemed completely different. Why *couldn't* she touch him? Even if she shouldn't…

She ignored the last thought, unable to resist any longer, twisting around and coiling an arm around his neck as he lifted himself on to one arm and leaned over her, covering her body with his. She pushed upwards to meet it, pressing her breasts into his chest as he lowered his head towards hers, making a guttural sound that might have been her name or a groan, she didn't care which, but which she answered with her mouth, finding his instinctively in the darkness.

Their second kiss was just as all-consuming as the first, everything she remembered and more. She opened her lips eagerly and his tongue plundered inside, exploring every last part of her mouth as if he were still hungry after their meal, filling her body with an aching fervour that seemed to build in her abdomen and radiate outwards. He wanted her. The thought brought with it a heady combination of triumph and vindication. Their bodies were pressed so closely together that his ardour was more than abundantly obvious. Quite powerfully so, she realised, somewhat alarmed by the pressure of his manhood between her legs. He definitely wasn't wearing any undergarments.

She ought to put a stop to it, a small voice at the back of her mind still argued. Or at the very least she ought to tell him everything about herself first. It was wrong not to, but she didn't seem able to stop, swept along on a raging tide of excitement and desire. She'd tell him later, she answered the voice guiltily, afterwards. Right now, all she wanted, needed, *had to* know was what the feeling in her abdomen and lower now, too, between her thighs, was building towards.

The hand between her legs moved upwards again, slowly and deliberately towards her centre, his fingers teasing the folds of her skin, and then all she could feel was stunned. What was he doing? She opened her mouth to ask, but his own closed over it with renewed pressure and she forgot the question almost at once.

After a few moments, he tore his lips away again, trailing a path over her collarbone and then lower, over the mounds of her breasts towards her nipples. She felt a jolt of surprise as his tongue found one and suckled, tracing circles around it before taking it fully into his mouth while his fingers continued to play with her.

She tipped her head back, gripping the bed beneath them in shock as a spasm of some powerful reflex shot down her spine and into the very core of her body, making all the tension there release suddenly, pulsing through every limb with a force that made her shake all over, as if she were in the grip of some fever. She'd never conceived that such a feeling was possible, as if her insides were somehow rearranging themselves all at once.

'Marius!' She gasped his name, clutching her arms around his shoulders again to steady herself. If she didn't, she had a feeling she might lose herself somehow.

He lifted his head and placed his lips tenderly against hers for a moment, nuzzling them gently this time.

'Get some rest.' She had the vague impression he was smiling.

'But…' But she was halfway to sleep already, the trembling sensation gradually fading away, replaced by a feeling of satiated exhaustion.

'When I get back…'

Chapter Seventeen

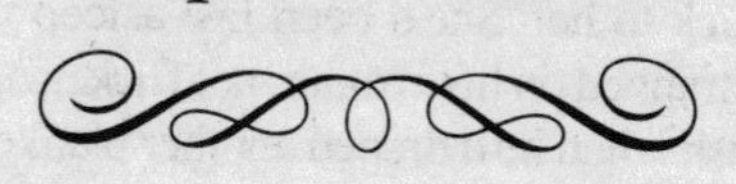

When I get back...

Marius twisted in his saddle, looking back towards Cilurnum's gate in the silvery wolf-light of dawn and wishing he were riding back inside, back to the sleeping woman he'd left sprawled across a warm bed in a posture of what looked like languorous contentment. Instead he was riding north at his own request to find an enemy probably intent on killing him. If ever he'd needed proof of his own stupidity, this was it. Two nights and he still hadn't consummated their marriage! Not that dwelling on the fact was going to make the tightness in his *braccae* go away…

He turned around again, facing the wilderness ahead. That was what most of his legionaries called it, a *barbarian* wilderness, many of whom resented their posting to this far-flung border of the Empire, disliking the cold, the damp and the desolate hills that seemed to roll on as far as the eye could see. He didn't see anything barbaric about it. He loved the ruggedness of the northern landscape, the absence of turrets and palisades and trenches, the lack of rules and constraints. There were only a few Roman forts left beyond the wall, abandoned ruins mostly, but since none of them was visible from his current vantage point astride a grey stallion, there was nothing to spoil the natural beauty of the view.

Because it *was* beautiful, he thought with admiration—although still not as much as the woman he'd left behind. He scowled, seemingly unable to stop his thoughts from drifting back to her. She'd been fast asleep when he'd risen and strapped on his armour, not flickering so much as an eyelash when he'd draped another blanket over her shoulders.

At least *she* ought to be well-rested that morning, which was more than could be said for him. He would have done better sleeping on the wall itself. He wasn't accustomed to sharing a bed in the first place and the physical tension between them had made things even more strained. And *that* was a monumental understatement. The way her curls had tumbled forward in a glorious cascade when she'd dragged a comb through them had driven him half-mad with desire. Then when she'd peeled her *stola* over her shoulders, wriggling out of the garment when she'd thought he hadn't been looking, making the shadowy curve of her breasts beneath her *tunica* clearly, tantalisingly visible, his body had reacted almost painfully. She'd looked stunningly gorgeous and infinitely desirable, so much that the mere memory of it made him shift uncomfortably in the saddle.

He'd pulled her towards him simply to give her some room, although the moment he'd touched her he'd known it had been a mistake. He certainly hadn't intended to take things as far as he had, especially after her somewhat over-emphatic and vaguely insulting pretence of tiredness. After *that* performance, he hadn't intended to touch her at all, let alone to kiss her, but once his fingers had encountered the smooth curve of her waist he hadn't been able to resist.

Her eager response had taken him completely by surprise and yet somehow—even now he wasn't sure how—he'd forced himself to hold back. Despite the contradictory signals she'd seemed to be sending him, she'd been tense and vulnerable that evening and he'd still had no idea what about. He hadn't wanted to take advantage of her and he'd needed to prove that to both of them, though the feeling of wetness between her legs had driven him to the very brink of control, so that it had taken all his self-restraint not to plunge deep inside her. So he'd focused on her pleasure instead, surprised by how well he'd succeeded. Her response had both aroused and frustrated him in equal measure, making the room seem to fairly crackle with tension for the whole rest of the night. The warm cocoon of their body heat had eventually lulled him into a fitful slumber, though it hadn't been anywhere near enough, and even then he'd dreamed of her...

For some inexplicable reason, however, it hadn't been her body that he'd dreamed of. It hadn't even been the way that she'd moaned his name after she'd climaxed, though that had been particularly memorable. No, he'd dreamed of the bright gleam of her eyes when she spoke, the small dimple in her left cheek when she smiled, the patchwork of freckles across her nose and cheeks and, most of all, the way she'd looked standing on the wall the day before, poised and graceful and somehow contented-looking. Now he could hardly wait to get back to her and not just because he wanted to bed her, but because he wanted to just *be* with her, even if simply to gaze at her...

What the hell did that mean?

'So what are we looking for exactly?' Ario cantered up beside him and Marius shook his head, glad of the distraction.

'I can't say *exactly*. What I want is to find some sign of life carrying on as normal.'

'All right.' The Decurion snorted cynically. 'That's what you want, but what do you *think* we'll find?'

'I think we'll find a gathering of warriors, or some sign of them. I think the tribes are joining together to launch another attack on the wall. And I think there may be more of them than we're prepared for.'

'You think a lot.' Ario sounded neither conspicuously alarmed nor unduly surprised. 'So essentially we're looking for an army?'

'Something like that.' Marius gave him a sidelong look. 'You know everyone in Coria still thinks I'm being alarmist.'

'That's because Coria isn't on the wall. If it was, Nerva might sit up and take more notice. Not that it's a criticism of him personally.' Ario raised a hand before Marius could interrupt. 'I know the two of you are close. All I'm saying is that it's easy to be complacent when you're not in the vanguard.'

'So you believe me?'

'Yes. I think something strange is going on and it's safer to believe you than not. I hate surprises.'

Marius grunted and then pulled on his reins, steadying his mount as a bird burst out of the undergrowth ahead of them.

'You know you're not bad with a horse.' Ario gave him an approving nod. 'For an infantryman.'

'I appreciate your qualifying the statement,' Marius answered drily. 'My father taught me when I was a boy.'

He regretted the words the second they were out of his mouth. In thirteen years, barely a day had gone by when he wasn't reminded of his father's dishonour in one way or another, but the number of times he'd spoken about him out loud could be counted on the fingers of one hand. Yet since he'd told Livia about him—as part of what now struck him as a particularly unromantic proposal—he felt as if an old injury had reopened. Her comments about his father's motives for mutinying yesterday had only rubbed salt in the wound. Now the memory of his childhood riding lessons made his chest heave with an emotion he thought he'd put behind him a long time ago.

'Varro?' Ario was looking at him quizzically, he realised, and he straightened his shoulders, once again bemoaning his lack of sleep, just in time to see something move in the woodland ahead.

'Hold!' He raised a hand, bringing the *turmae* to a halt.

'What is it?' Ario spoke in an undertone.

'Something moving. Over there in the trees.'

'An animal maybe?'

'Maybe.' Although if it *had* been an animal, it was something large. A stag or a bear maybe. Far more likely for it to have been a man.

'Keep half of your men here. I'll go ahead with the rest on foot.'

Ario looked dubious. 'It might be a trap.'

Marius nodded sternly. If he'd seen what he thought he'd just seen, it probably was a trap. They were following the rutted remains of the old Roman road where it passed along the edge of some woodland, an almost perfect spot for an ambush, and the northern tribes were skilled at laying those. It was a large part of the reason why the Roman army had never fully conquered Caledonia. Still, it would be surprising if the tribes attacked so soon, in full daylight and against cavalry to boot. If they did, then it meant they were either very confident or desperate to prevent them from going any further and finding something. But it was still better to hunt them down in the trees than follow the road into a trap.

'We need to find out. Wait here. We'll march on and draw them out if they're there. You come and help if necessary.'

To his relief, Ario didn't argue, quickly dividing his men and holding half of them back while he gave the order to dismount and led the rest straight towards the trees.

The attack came even sooner than he expected, a volley of arrows hissing out of the undergrowth before they'd gone barely fifty paces.

'Shield wall! *Testudo!*' Marius bellowed, digging his shield into the dirt and crouching behind it as more arrows whistled overhead. The rest of Ario's men did likewise, forming an impenetrable line of shields in front, around and even above their heads as another volley of missiles slammed into them.

A moment later a horde of warriors emerged from the woodland, seemingly all at once, roaring a bloodthirsty battle cry as they charged towards them almost completely naked, wearing only short *braccae* and copper bands around their necks and arms, with no armour except their leather shields.

Marius braced himself as the cry built to an almost deafening fever pitch and the combined force of a hundred bodies hurled themselves into the shield wall, forcing them back a few steps. He yelled orders at his men, bellowing at them to hold the line as he strained his feet in the dirt, pushing back against the press of warriors with all his strength.

There was a momentary lull and he took advantage of it, jabbing his sword between a narrow gap in the shields and thrusting it at the first warrior he saw. He heard a grunt of pain, followed by a bellow of anger, and thrust again, lunging forward in a ferocious counterattack, heartened to find the two men on either side of him doing the same.

'We need prisoners!' he shouted over the din.

'Tell them that!' Ario's voice rose to meet his and he peered out, just in time to see the cavalry thunder past them and start to encircle the warriors.

Then there was only the sound of combat, every voice drowned out by the clash of weapons and the heavy thud of sword upon shield. Marius felt a fresh burst of energy, swiping and smashing his sword over the top of the shield wall, parrying away spears and axes that tried to find their way through the gaps.

Then it was over. The rebels must have realised their mistake as the horses reared and pounded the earth around them, fleeing back to the safety of the trees even faster than they'd burst out of them before. Only one straggler slipped on the mud as he ran, dropping his axe as he struggled to regain his footing.

Marius was after him in a heartbeat, tossing his shield to one side as he ran forward and grabbed hold of the warrior's arm before he could reach his axe again.

Then he raised his sword, about to land a blow with the hilt and knock him unconscious when he saw the age of the face looking back. It was that of a boy, not a man, in his late teens perhaps, but still young enough to make him spin the blade around, pressing it up against his throat instead.

'Yield.' He ground out one of the few Caledonian words he knew, relieved when the boy lifted both of his hands in the air in surrender.

It was enough. He had a prisoner.

Whatever the commotion was, it was coming from the direction of the gates. Livia stood on the top step of the quartermaster's storeroom, looking out over the top of the clustered auxiliaries, trying to catch a glimpse of the returning soldiers. They were back sooner, far sooner than expected—so soon that having slept for most of the morning, she'd barely had a chance to get dressed. Was their early return a good or a bad thing? she wondered. She wouldn't know for sure until she found Marius.

She stretched up on her tiptoes, heart beating frantically in her chest as she sought for him, torn between gut-wrenching anxiety, guilt and a new sense of trepidation. After the unexpected, and frankly breathtaking, intimacy of their night together, she felt almost shy at the thought of seeing him again, though not enough to stop her from wanting to repeat the experience as soon as possible. *If* he wanted to… She still wasn't sure about that. As much as she'd enjoyed what had happened, it had been as one-sided as the rest of their relationship. He hadn't joined with her. Hadn't he wanted to? Although that was a good thing, she chided herself, since she *still* hadn't told him the truth about her past! This time she was determined not to be a coward again…

But where was he? There was a sudden break in the crowd and she caught sight of horses and a few blood-stained soldiers. *Blood!* Her heart actually seemed to stop for a moment. If they were injured, then it meant there had been some kind of fighting already!

Where was he? Her eyes searched the riders with a new sense of urgency, but there was still no sign of him.

'It might be best if you go back to the villa.' Trenus, the quartermaster, tapped her shoulder.

'No.' She shook her head determinedly. How could he even suggest such a thing, that she ought to run and hide when Marius might be injured or worse?

'You might not want to see—'

'No!'

She leapt down the villa steps and broke into a run. Whatever protest Trenus was about to make, she didn't want to hear it. Instead she pulled her *stola* up around her knees and hurtled across the fort, heedless of her appearance. It was unseemly to run, particularly into a group of soldiers, but she didn't care. She had to find her husband, had to make sure he was all right and throw her arms around him…

She pushed her way through the crowd to the front and then stopped, still searching. The riders were all looking distinctly the worse for wear, but at least they all seemed to have come back. Up close, their injuries didn't look so bad either.

The last of the horses rode in through the gate and she pressed a hand to her mouth, stifling a cry of relief as she finally caught sight of Marius. He was still on horseback, looking as severe as ever, but unharmed.

She almost sank to the ground with relief. If she'd been in any doubt of her feelings for him before, she knew what they were now. She loved him, though until that moment she hadn't realised how much.

She was about to start forward again when she realised he wasn't alone. There was a man sitting behind him, although judging by his half-naked and tattooed appearance, he wasn't Roman. His hair was a long and vibrantly red colour like hers while his hands, when she looked closer, were tied up, bound together with rope... Horror clawed at her insides. He was a prisoner, that was obvious. What was even more obvious was that he'd been fighting. There was a livid cut across one of his cheekbones as well as a bloodied patch on his arm, while Marius's armour was scuffed and red-stained.

The contrast made her feel sick. Marius, the man she'd just realised she loved, had been fighting with him. One of her mother's people—*her* people—a mere youth, too, by the look of him, barely more than Porcia's age.

'Livia?' Marius caught sight of her at the same moment as she took an appalled step backwards. 'Are you all right?'

He looked concerned and she fought the urge to laugh. *Was she all right?* He was the one who'd been fighting! She ought to be asking *him* that question, except that she seemed to have forgotten how to speak.

She nodded instead, fixing her gaze on a point beyond his shoulder as she tried not to look at either him *or* his prisoner. The gesture seemed inadequate somehow, but what else could she do when all she wanted was to turn and run as far away from them both as possible? As relieved as she was to see Marius, if she didn't get away soon then she really was going to be sick.

'Some of the men are injured. I have to make sure they're taken care of.' He gestured around him and she seized on the words at once.

'Yes. I'll go.' She forced the words past her lips as she spun away, inadvertently catching the eye of the prisoner as she did so. He was regarding her curiously, she noticed, so that for a second she was tempted to say something, but what? What *could* she say to him? He might be her kinsman of sorts, but he was also her husband's prisoner. If it came to choosing sides, then she'd already chosen…

Hadn't she?

Chapter Eighteen

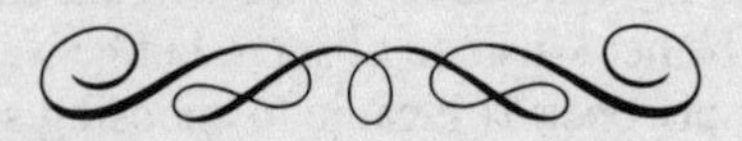

The prison door closed with a resounding thud. Marius nodded to the guard outside, hoping he'd done the right thing in bringing the patrol back so soon, though both he and Ario had agreed it would have been foolish to go on. The audacity of the attack suggested that there were more warriors ahead, possibly *too* many, and he wasn't going to risk losing good men simply to prove a point. He'd seen enough to convince himself.

As he'd expected, the young Caledonian warrior hadn't told them anything, though he hoped a few days on his own would be sufficient to change his mind. He had a few cuts and bruises, including a nasty gash on his arm—nothing dangerous, but one that could become infected if left untended for too long. He'd have to send the camp medic to him later after Ario's men had been seen to. Injuries in battle were one thing, but he didn't want the boy dying on him.

His conscience pricked him at the thought. He would have preferred a full-grown warrior to a boy, even if a youth was more likely to talk, but there was too much at stake for him to be squeamish about it. If the boy was old enough to wield a weapon, then he was old enough to suffer the consequences, no matter how unpleasant the thought.

He turned his weary feet in the direction of the villa. Would Livia be there? The sight of her standing, breathless and anxious-looking, beside the gate when he'd ridden back through had made his heart leap, even more than he would have expected, though her reaction when she'd actually seen him had bothered him for the rest of the afternoon. For a few hopeful moments, he'd thought she'd actually run across the courtyard to find him, but her expression when she'd finally met his eyes had been anything but pleased. She'd looked positively horrified. Had she been hoping to be widowed again so soon?

No, he dismissed the thought as too harsh. He didn't know exactly how she felt about him, but he was reasonably certain she didn't want him dead. Strangely enough, he'd had the distinct impression that her reaction had had little to do with him and far more to do with his prisoner. Something about the evasive way she'd been staring suggested that she'd been trying very hard *not* to look at either of them.

Was it the man's nakedness that had shocked her? No, she didn't strike him as the kind of woman who'd be so easily offended. Or was it simply that he'd taken a prisoner at all? If it was, her reaction appeared somewhat excessive, but then he supposed she wasn't used to life in the army, especially on a frontier. The reality of it could be brutal, but he had a job to do and orders to follow—above all, he had Roman lives to protect. He'd have to explain that to her.

He marched through the villa, resisting the urge to call out her name, not entirely convinced she wouldn't hide from him if he did. As it turned out, he didn't need to. She was in the courtyard again, perched on the low wall where they'd sat side by side the night before, hunched over with her face in her hands.

'Livia?' He came to stand in front of her, half-alarmed, half-irritated. How could she be so affected by the sight of one prisoner? 'What is it?'

She didn't answer, her shoulders going rigid, as if she were still reluctant to lift her head and look at him.

'It's nothing.' With her hands over her face, her voice sounded muffled.

'It doesn't look like nothing.' He frowned at her denial. If she were one of his soldiers, then he'd simply demand to know what was going on. If only women were so easy…

She dropped her hands at last, dragging them across her cheeks as if she were trying to rub some colour back into them. To his relief, her eyes, though wide and slightly wild-looking, were dry. At least she hadn't been crying.

'It's just the thought of it. The thought of you in battle.'

A wave of relief washed through him. 'You mean you were worried about me?'

'Of course!' She sounded angry and offended at the same time. 'You could have been injured!'

'I'm a soldier. That's always a risk.'

Her gaze raked him up and down. 'You have blood on your armour.'

'It's not mine. At worst I might have a few bruises.'

'Good!'

He lifted an eyebrow, even more confused than before. As much as he wanted to believe that such an extreme reaction had been caused entirely by worry for him, he wasn't completely convinced.

'So you've been right all along?' Her voice had a quaver in it this time. 'There really is a rebellion coming?'

'It looks likely. We were attacked by a war party who were trying to stop us from seeing something, preparations for an assault on the wall most likely, but one skirmish doesn't prove anything. Not yet anyway.'

'Yet?'

'We have a prisoner.' He watched her reaction as he spoke. 'With any luck, he'll talk.'

'I saw.' She dropped her eyes tellingly. 'He was injured.'

'Not badly.'

'He might still need attention.'

'So do Ario's men.'

'Oh...yes.' A guilty expression crossed her face. 'Were any of them badly hurt?'

'A few injuries, but no losses, fortunately.'

'What about the war party?'

'You seem very worried about them.' He narrowed his eyes and folded his arms at the same time. 'They're our enemies, Livia.'

This time she didn't flinch. 'They're still people, too, aren't they?'

'So they are.' He felt a shadow of suspicion at the back of his mind, something he couldn't quite put his finger on. 'We inflicted some damage, but it was just a skirmish. There were no bodies left on the ground if that's what you're asking.'

'Oh.'

'Livia?' Briefly he thought about sitting down beside her and then decided against it. The intimacy they'd shared the previous night seemed a distant memory, as if there were another wall between them suddenly, one that he couldn't cross to reach her. 'What else is it?'

She hesitated for a moment, drawing in a deep breath before she spoke again.

'What if your prisoner doesn't talk?'

'We're giving him a few days on his own to think about it.'

'Is that *all*?'

There was an accusatory gleam in her eye and he frowned, not sure what she was getting at.

'What do you mean?'

'I mean, is that all you're doing to him, leaving him on his own? Or will you do more? Will you hurt him?'

He stiffened at the accusation. 'Hopefully that won't be necessary.'

'But if it is...will you?'

'No.' He spoke in a clipped voice. Torturing prisoners wasn't a practice he approved of, though he knew of several Roman officers who had no such scruples. '*I* won't, but it might not be up to me.'

'You mean if you take him to Coria?'

'Yes.'

'What about afterwards? What will you—*they*—do to him after he's told them what they want to know? Will they let him go?'

'No.' He wasn't going to lie.

Her head jerked as if an invisible hand had just slapped her across the cheek. 'You mean they'll sell him as a slave?'

'Possibly. I doubt the decision will be up to me.'

'It's your responsibility! *You* took him prisoner!'

'Because he attacked us. He's a barbarian!'

'He's a boy!'

She leapt to her feet, her tone anguished, and the shadow of suspicion grew longer. He'd never kept slaves himself, but the practice was widespread throughout the Empire. Most Romans accepted it. But then her mixed feelings about Rome had been obvious almost from the start. Perhaps there was more behind it than he'd thought…

'You don't approve of slavery?' He arched an eyebrow. 'Didn't your family have slaves?'

Blue-green eyes sparked with some fierce emotion before she twisted her face to one side.

'Yes. That is, my brother and Julius both did, but my father freed all of his slaves before I was born. He thought it was wrong to enslave another person, Roman or not.'

'Then I applaud him.'

'You do?' She whipped her head back round again.

'Yes. Denying any man his freedom without just cause is wrong.'

'How can you say so when you've just taken a prisoner?'

'I said *without* just cause, but he was part of a war party that attacked us. Now he has to face the consequences. Under the circumstances, he's lucky to be alive.'

'You were in his territory.'

'What?' The words were so faint he wasn't sure he'd heard them correctly.

She lifted her chin, a look of defiance crossing her features. 'You were north of the wall, *outside* Roman territory. He might have thought you were the one asking for consequences.'

'Is that so?' He advanced a step towards her, speaking slowly and meticulously. 'And is that what *you* think?'

'No.' He noticed it took her a few moments to answer. 'I just don't think he deserves to be condemned to a life of slavery for defending his own territory.'

'He hasn't been condemned to anything yet.'

'But he will be!'

'Probably, yes.' He took a deep breath, trying to quell his own temper. 'Why the hell do you care so much about the fate of one warrior? Because your mother was Carvetti? It might have escaped your notice in Lindum, but the Caledonians are no friend to the tribes south of the wall.'

'This has nothing to do with the Carvetti! It's about what's right and slavery is wrong!'

'*Not* according to Rome.'

He turned and walked a few paces away, feeling bone-weary all of a sudden. It had been a difficult morning and the last thing he wanted to do was argue, especially when she seemed so determined to cast him as the villain. It was a long way from the reunion he'd been hoping for...

'Did *your* family keep slaves?'

He glanced back over his shoulder. She was still staring at the spot where he'd been standing, her face flushed with emotion now.

'I didn't have a family, remember?'

'The people you lived with, then.'

'I lived with one of my father's old soldiers and his wife and children. They hardly had the money to keep me, let alone anyone else.'

'So you've *never* had slaves?'

He frowned. Something about the way she asked the question told him there was more to it than just curiosity, as if his answer really mattered to her…

'No.'

She closed her eyes briefly and he almost turned back before thinking better of it.

'I ought to go and check on the men. As for the rest, I'm only following orders, Livia. My conscience is clear.'

He stalked out of the villa, struck by the uncomfortable realisation that he was lying.

Chapter Nineteen

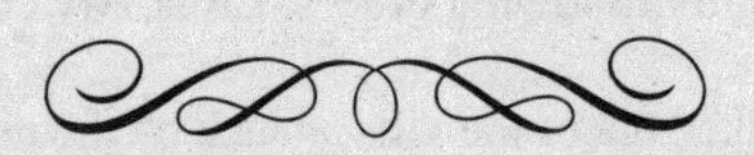

The morning was cold and bright. Livia could sense it through the window shutters, though she waited until she was certain Marius had left the room before opening her eyes. She'd been in bed, as close to the wall as possible, when he'd come back the previous evening and she'd been determined not to get up again until he'd left. She didn't want to speak with him. Until she'd calmed down, it was far better for them to keep out of each other's way as much as possible.

She was still furious. When he'd only been talking about leading a patrol north, it somehow hadn't seemed so dreadful. He'd said that he'd only been going to look around, but the fact that he'd been fighting—*fighting!*—her mother's people made her as angry as if he'd attacked her himself. It didn't help that she knew he was only doing his duty. In his mind, he was protecting Rome, holding the frontier, working towards his ambition of becoming Senior Centurion. It wasn't his fault that he'd married a woman with mixed allegiances. He didn't even know. Because she hadn't told him, not before their marriage or yesterday when she'd had the chance.

The thought brought with it an unwanted stab of guilt, although surely he'd guess the truth soon enough if she kept on behaving the way that she was. She couldn't help it. How could he talk about the boy's future so casually, as if slavery was acceptable just because Rome said so? He'd even called him a barbarian, as if he were just as prejudiced as every other Roman! Which perhaps he was and she'd simply been too blinded by attraction to see clearly before. In any case, she certainly couldn't tell him the truth now. Their whole situation was unbearable. She'd wanted to visit the wall for almost as long as she could remember, thinking it was where she belonged, but now she was trapped, caught between two sides in a war. Was *that* where she belonged? If it was, then she'd prefer to belong nowhere.

At least Marius had never kept slaves himself. She'd been unable to shake Julius's opinions on that subject—had actually shocked him by giving Porcia her document of manumission on the very day he'd purchased her as a gift—but then she'd given up hoping that he might change. She'd been unable to do anything for his other slaves either, ending up as powerless as she'd ever been in Tarquinius's household.

Well, this time, she decided, she *would* do something. She didn't know what exactly, but she wasn't going to stand by while anyone was treated as less than a human being. Marius wouldn't appreciate her interference, but there was no harm in making sure the boy was all right, surely?

She got to her feet and dressed with a new sense of purpose, trying to ignore the musky male scent of the blankets as she climbed across them, collecting a few items before marching determinedly out of the villa and across the fort. A few auxiliaries nodded to her as she passed and she nodded back, glad to see them all back safely, though struck with a twinge of disloyalty, too. She pushed it aside. Tending to the enemy didn't mean that she cared any less about them, but someone had to do the right thing and make sure the prisoner was properly looked after.

'I've brought some food.' She spoke to the guard outside the prison, prepared for an argument that never came as he immediately stepped aside to let her in.

The prison wasn't a single large room, as she'd expected, but a series of cells lined with wooden bars, all of them empty except for the last where the warrior was leaning against the wall in one corner, his eyes closed. Judging by the bandage around his left arm, his injuries had already been tended to. So had his comforts. There was a pile of blankets around him, as well as a cup of water, a jug and an empty plate to one side, and she felt a fresh pang of guilt for having misjudged Marius. Again. Whatever else he intended to do with the prisoner, he clearly wasn't mistreating him.

She crouched down, bringing her eyes level with the warrior's, though up close he looked even younger. His skin bore traces of woad, giving him an odd, bluish pallor, while his chest was decorated with a series of intricate, interlacing tattoos. She lifted her eyes to his face, looking for some semblance of her own features. There were no obvious physical similarities between them, but there was still something, a feeling of kinship that meant she couldn't ignore or abandon him. For all she knew, they might be related.

'Are you awake?' She dragged the words from her

memory, the Caledonian language her mother had taught her, and his eyes snapped open at once.

'I've brought you some food.' She rummaged in her bag and held out a chunk of bread. 'I thought…'

She didn't finish the sentence as he sprang forward suddenly, reaching between the bars and grabbing her forearm.

'You speak my language?'

'Yes.' She winced at the tightness of his grip. 'Let me go.'

He released her almost as quickly and sat back on his haunches, his eyes burning fiercely in the half-darkness. 'Who are you?'

'It doesn't matter, but you can trust me.'

'Trust a Roman?' He spat into the dirt.

'I'm not…' She bit her lip before she could say it. She *couldn't* say it. She couldn't deny that side of her heritage any more than she could deny her mother's and she didn't want to choose. 'I'm only half-Roman, but I want to help you.'

'How?'

'You need to answer their questions. They already know about the rebellion, so you won't be betraying anyone. If you tell them what they want to know, then they won't hurt you.'

His gaze narrowed, but she kept going.

'The rebellion won't succeed. It can't. No matter how hard you fight, the new Emperor will keep on sending legions to defeat you.'

'So you think we should just surrender and become slaves of Rome?'

The word made her look away. 'No, just hold your

own territory. Don't attack the wall. What's the point of dying in a fight you can't win?'

He stared at her for a long moment and then spat into the dirt again. 'Not all of us are prepared to make treaties with Rome!'

'Livia?'

A voice from the doorway made her spin round with a jolt.

'Ario!' She stood up to face him, feigning composure even though she felt as if her insides had just turned to water. 'I was just giving the prisoner some food.'

'I see that.' His gaze swept over the prison cell. 'Have you finished?'

'Yes.' She picked up her bag, resisting the urge to throw one last imploring look at the prisoner before making her way to the door, keenly aware of two pairs of eyes watching her. 'I'm all done.'

'Did Marius send you?' Ario's face was grave as they stepped back outside.

'No.' There was no point in lying when he could check her story so easily. 'But I don't see what harm taking the boy some food can do.'

'None the less, in the future…'

'I'll ask.' She flung the bag over her shoulder, adopting what she hoped was a convincing smile, but which she had a strong suspicion didn't fool him at all. 'I promise.'

'What is it?' Marius knew the Decurion well enough to know when something was wrong.

'Not here.' Ario jerked his head, leading him inside the camp headquarters, through the main hall and into the commander's office.

'Why the secrecy?' Marius drew his brows together as Ario closed the door behind them.

'It's something you might not want others to know. It's about your wife.'

'Livia?' Every muscle in his body seemed to go rigid at once. 'What about her?'

'I found her in the prison a few minutes ago.'

He felt a cold, prickling sensation at the back of his skull. 'And?'

'She claimed she was taking the prisoner some food.'

'Claimed?' The coldness seemed to be spreading, trickling down his spine as if there were a block of ice slowly melting against his neck. 'Don't you believe her?'

'I do. I just don't think it was all she was doing.' Ario muttered an oath. 'Look, Marius, what do you know of her loyalties? Where is she from?'

'Lindum and I trust her.' Even as he said it, he felt a cross-current of doubt. *Did* he really trust her? 'Get to the point, Ario. What are you trying to tell me?'

'She was speaking to him.'

'Who?'

'The prisoner. She was speaking Caledonian.'

The cold reached his toes and fingertips at the same time, as if all his blood had just frozen. 'Are you certain?'

The Decurion nodded gravely. 'I only caught the last of it, but, yes, it was definitely Caledonian. She speaks it better than I do.'

Marius gripped hold of a chair back, clenching the wood in his fists as he tried to understand. How the hell could she speak Caledonian?

'Do you think she might be a spy?'

'No.' He shook his head, certain of that much at least. How could she be? Her brother was a respected citizen of Lindum. He'd sent her north against her will. She'd never seen the wall before—her emotional response to it had proved that much—so how could she be spying for the tribes?

The wooden chair splintered apart in his hands as a new idea dawned on him. New and improbable and yet, he was suddenly convinced, the truth. It made all the small things that had puzzled him about her finally make sense—her eagerness to see the wall, her barely concealed antagonism towards Rome, her reaction to the prisoner, the momentary pause when he'd asked which tribe her mother had belonged to…

This has nothing to do with the Carvetti! That was what she'd told him yesterday and it was true because the Carvetti *did* have nothing to do with it. Because her mother hadn't been Carvetti at all. She'd been Caledonian. Which meant that even if Livia wasn't a spy, she was a liar.

'She's not a spy.' He said the words with authority.

'Are you certain?'

'Yes.' He nodded tersely. 'I'll deal with this. In the meantime, tell the guards not to let anyone but you or me near the prison and don't tell anyone.'

'What do you take me for?' Ario gave him a sharp look. 'Just make sure you find out where her loyalties lie. There's too much at stake here to take risks.'

'I know.' Marius was halfway out of the door already. 'I know.'

There was no sign of her in the courtyard. It was mid-morning, but the villa was silent, filled with dim and mysterious shadows. He felt an obscure sense of discomfort followed by a momentary panic. Had she run away? If she'd suspected that Ario had overheard her, then no doubt she would have guessed that he'd tell him. But if she'd run away, where would she have gone? In which direction?

'Livia?' He called her name, relieved to hear a faint answering call from the bedroom.

'In here.'

He followed the sound of her voice to the doorway. She was sitting in the middle of the bed, her knees drawn up to her chest with her arms wrapped around them and her hair tumbling loose over her shoulders, so much of it that she looked half-hidden beneath the red tresses. All this time he'd taken her loyalty to the Empire for granted, assuming that she was more Roman than Briton. Now he didn't know if she were Roman or rebel, but he had the uncomfortable suspicion that he might not like the answer.

'Have you spoken to Ario?' She got straight to the point.

'Yes.' He leaned a shoulder against the doorjamb.

'What did he tell you?'

'What do you *think* he told me?'

A look of defiance mixed with guilt crossed her features. 'I was only trying to help. I took the prisoner some food.'

'Did you think I would starve a boy?'

'No...maybe.'

'Because I'm such a monster?'

'No.' She pressed her teeth into her lower lip. 'But you called him a barbarian. I wanted to be sure he was all right.'

'And was he?'

'Yes.'

'So then you turned around again and left?' He folded his arms. 'Or is there something else you want to tell me?'

Her gaze slid to one side guiltily. 'I told him to answer your questions about the rebellion. I thought that if he told you what you wanted to know then you wouldn't hurt him.'

'I've already told you I've no intention of hurting him.'

'Not you, but...' she waved a hand '...others. I thought that perhaps you might let him go.'

'He's a prisoner, Livia. I can't just let him go.' He sighed. 'So you admit that you spoke to him?'

'Yes.'

'How?'

She dipped her head. 'I told you, my mother was a Briton. She taught me some of her language.'

'Is that so?' He felt a surge of anger, pushing himself up off the doorjamb and advancing slowly towards her. 'Except you told me she was Carvetti. According to Ario, you were speaking Caledonian. Or do you imagine us Romans don't know the difference?'

Her whole body tensed visibly and he took another step forward, looking down at her from the edge of the bed and lowering his voice dangerously.

'Tell me the truth, Livia. No more lies.'

For a moment he thought she wasn't going to answer. Then her face seemed to crumple abruptly.

'I never wanted to lie! I *had* to, or at least with Scaevola I had to, and then I didn't know how to tell you. I've spent the last ten years not being allowed to talk about it.'

'Talk about what?'

'The truth! I thought you might prefer not to know.'

'I would imagine every husband wants his wife to tell him the truth… What's so funny?' He scowled as she gave a bitter-sounding laugh.

'My first husband probably thought so, too, before he found out.'

'I'm not your first husband,' he growled. 'I'm your second and I *do* want the truth.'

'All right.' She pressed her lips together tightly before looking up at him again, a look of resolve on her face. 'The truth is that my mother was Caledonian. She came from north of the wall. She was also a slave.'

Chapter Twenty

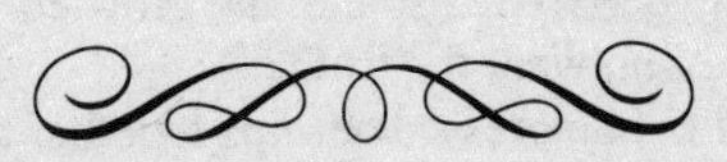

Livia held her breath, waiting for Marius to respond, to show some sign that he'd heard her at least, though his stern expression gave nothing away. She hardly recognised the man she'd gone to bed with two nights before. This one looked as impenetrable as marble. Seconds or minutes might have gone by before he slowly unfolded his arms.

'Go on.'

She let the breath go in a rush, her body shuddering with relief. If he gave her an opportunity to explain, then there was a chance, a faint one perhaps, but still a chance that he might understand, too.

'Her name was Etain. She worked on my father's country estate. He owned her for twelve years before they even met.'

'Twelve years?' He looked sceptical and she nodded.

'It's not so unusual. He lived mostly in town back then and he was still married to his first wife. It was only once he was widowed that he retired to the country. She was one of his kitchen slaves.' She smiled sadly. 'He used to say that he fell in love with her cooking before he even set eyes on her.'

'Wait.' Marius lifted a hand. 'Go further back. What was she doing there in the first place?'

'What do you think?' She gave him a hard look. 'What is any slave doing in a place that isn't their home? Her village in Caledonia was one of those that defied the Romans when they were building the second wall.'

'The Antonine?'

'Yes. Roman legionnaires attacked at night so they barely had a chance to defend themselves. Everyone she knew was either killed or enslaved. She was only nine years old when she was brought south in chains and sold at market like an animal. My grandfather's steward eventually bought her for his estate. She was a slave for thirty years.'

'Until she met your father?'

She nodded vigorously, fighting a swell of emotion. 'They fell in love. It sounds unlikely, I know, that she could love a Roman after everything they'd done to her, but she told me once that thirty years is a long time to hate. She said that my father wasn't responsible for what had happened to her village and that love was love, wherever and whoever it came from.' She rested her chin on her knees, looking inwards rather than out. 'Though even then she refused to marry him at first.'

'Why?'

'Because she wasn't his only slave. There were others, a dozen of them from all over the Empire. She told my father that she could never give herself to a man who denied happiness and freedom to other people.'

'That's why he set them free?'

'Every one of them.' She smiled proudly. 'When Tarquinius heard about it he thought he'd gone mad. He even tried to stop the marriage, but by the time he arrived it was too late. My mother said they had a huge argument about it. He made my father promise never to tell anyone about her and never to go back to Lindum.'

'His own father?'

'Yes. Tarquinius was afraid of what it would do to his reputation if people found out that his father had married one of his slaves, so it was all kept secret. He probably bribed or threatened anyone who knew the truth. Fortunately, my mother didn't care. She'd no desire to play the Roman lady and she loved my father. She thought that she was too old to have children, but then I came along and we were happy, her and Father and me. She taught me how to cook, as well as some Caledonian customs, including the language. She always told me that Caledonia was as much a part of my heritage as Rome. I grew up thinking of myself as belonging to both. It never occurred to me that other people wouldn't think that way, too.'

'Then what happened?' His expression was still inscrutable.

She lifted her chin from her knees, looking at him sombrely. 'She died. We thought it was just a cough at first, but it was more serious than we realised. One moment she was healthy and the next she was…gone. My father was heartbroken. It sent him into a decline, but he loved me and he knew that Tarquinius loathed me simply because of my mother. I think he clung on to life for as long as he could just to protect me, but eventually he got sick, too.' She took a deep breath, blinking back tears. 'Just before he died, he summoned Tarquinius and made him swear to take care of me, to treat me like a real sister.'

'Did he?'

'Maybe, although I don't suppose that was saying very much in the first place. After the funeral, he took me back to Lindum and handed me over to his wife, but she hated me even more. She made me attend to her every whim, treating me like a slave in my own brother's home. Then one evening, one of his business associates, Julius, a man twenty years older than me, noticed me standing in the background. I saw him staring, but I didn't think anything of it until Tarquinius summoned me to his office the next day.'

She shook her head at the memory. 'He walked around me, looking me up and down as if I were an animal to be inspected. Then he said that he'd arranged a marriage for me. He didn't ask or offer me a choice. He just told me I was going to be married.'

'To Julius?'

'Yes. I was horrified, but Tarquinius said that I ought to feel honoured, that I ought to be grateful to him even for arranging any marriage at all considering who I was.' Anger stiffened her spine. 'That was how he said it, *who I was*, as if I were somehow repellent to him. Then he said that I should never mention my mother, not to a single living soul, but *especially* not to Julius, and that if anyone asked, I was to say she'd been a Roman widow from a nearby village. He said that if I told...' She faltered over the words, the old fear reasserting itself.

'If you told...' Marius's voice had a sharp edge to it.

'If I told, then he wouldn't be held responsible for the consequences.' An icy shudder ran through her. 'I was only fourteen at the time. I didn't know what he meant, but he frightened me. He *still* frightens me… In any case, I went through with the marriage and I never told anyone. In ten years I've never spoken about her until now. It feels strange even saying her name.'

'So that's your excuse—' the muscles in his jaw were bunched, as if he were clenching them all together '—that it's simply become a habit not to speak about your mother?'

'In part—' she ignored the sarcasm '—although believe it or not, I wanted to tell you. I loved my mother. I was proud of her. She was so full of life and love and happiness despite how hard her life had been. I didn't understand why I couldn't talk about her. And Julius wasn't a bad man, not really. He was kind to me at first. After a while I thought that he wouldn't even mind if I *did* tell him the truth, but I was too afraid of Tarquinius to take the risk. Then he found out, just after Julia was born.'

'But if you didn't tell him…'

'Tarquinius. After everything he'd made me promise, *he* was the one who told.'

'Why?'

'Money. He'd arranged the marriage thinking an alliance would make Julius more obliging in business. It did for a while, but he kept on pushing for more until eventually my husband refused. So Tarquinius told him everything, about my mother, about where she came from, about her being a slave. He threatened to tell the whole of Lindum if Julius didn't give him the prices he wanted.'

'Blackmail?'

'Yes. He destroyed my life and my daughter's future over the price of a few wine barrels. But then the only thing my brother cares about is money. He probably never gave a thought to what would happen to me.'

'What *did* happen to you?'

She blinked, taken aback by the note of repressed anger in his voice.

'Julius was furious, but he didn't hurt me, if that's what you're thinking. He wasn't a violent man, although he wasn't a particularly clever one either. If he'd thought about it for even a moment then he'd have realised that Tarquinius would never have gone through with his threat. It was his own reputation he would have been damaging, too. But Julius was so afraid of what people might say, of his family name being *tarnished*, that he gave in at once. He gave Tarquinius the low prices he wanted and took his anger out on me instead. Everything changed after that.'

She picked up a strand of hair and wound it around her fingers. 'Julius had always said that he loved my red hair, but afterwards he hated it. He used to stare at me as if I were some kind of monster. He called me names. Barbarian. Savage. That's why I overreacted that night with Scaevola.'

'You didn't overreact.'

She glanced up, surprised by the conviction behind the words. She'd left her hair loose deliberately, so that he could see how much of a Caledonian she really was, although her appearance didn't seem to bother him.

'After a couple of years I got used to his coldness,

but then as Julia grew up he started to look at her in the same way, too. That was when the accusations started.'

Marius sat down on the edge of the bed, his back towards her, though he kept his face half-turned to one side.

'What kind of accusations?'

She swallowed, trying to find the words. It seemed strange to be talking about the intimate details of her life with Julius, but now that she'd started she felt as though a wall were crumbling inside of her, releasing all of the pain she'd held in for ten years.

'Livia?' he prompted her and she jerked her head up.

'He called me a lying whore and said that Julia wasn't his daughter. Maybe because she looked so much like me and nothing at all like him. He accused me of sleeping with other men behind his back. It wasn't true. I hardly left the house, let alone saw anyone else, but he was looking for reasons to divorce me and disown Julia, too. We were already leading separate lives, but he set his servants to watch me and report on everything I did. They saw his contempt, so they treated me the same way. I was despised and insulted every day behind my back and sometimes openly to my face. Only Porcia stood up for me.'

'Your maid?'

'Yes...' she smiled affectionately '...although she was my slave first, only a girl when Julius bought her as a gift. It was still early on in our marriage and he thought that I'd be pleased. I was appalled. I gave her a document of manumission the same day, but she stayed anyway. She doesn't know everything about me, but she suspects. She stayed even when I had nothing to pay her after Julius died.'

'He left you nothing at all?'

'Not a single denarius. After his funeral, I sent word to Tarquinius, though he didn't answer at first. I thought that perhaps he wasn't going to, that he was going to abandon us, but then he sent his henchmen to collect me. It was just like the first time. He didn't ask what I wanted. He just told me that he was sending me here to marry again. Scaevola must have seemed like the perfect solution to his problems. Two birds with one stone. A way to get rid of me and make another useful alliance at the same time.'

'So you think he was planning to blackmail Scaevola, too?'

'Probably, as soon as he thought of a use for him. I doubt he would have taken on his debt otherwise, although perhaps he thought it was a reasonable price to pay to get rid of us.'

She ran her hands through her hair, pushing it out of her face and over her shoulders. 'Part of me was excited when he told me where we were going. I'd always wanted to see Caledonia. I thought it would be a kind of homecoming even though I knew my marriage would be the same situation all over again. Then I met Scaevola and I realised it would be even worse. He didn't even need to know the truth to hate me. He was repelled just by the colour of my hair, though in a strange way that made me feel better. I knew that when Tarquinius finally did tell him the truth, he couldn't have hated me any more.' She drew in a deep breath and then let it out again slowly. 'I thought that there was no way out. I thought I was trapped.'

'And then I won you.' He twisted his face away again.

'Yes.'

Slowly she unfurled her legs and clambered to the edge of the bed, sitting down beside him. 'I'm not trying to excuse myself. I *should* have told you before we got married. I'm sorry that I didn't. After you stood up to Scaevola for me I owed you the truth, but it all happened so quickly. I was selfish and knew that you'd be a good father to Julia, and…the truth is, I liked you. I felt as though there was something, some kind of bond, between us from the start. I *wanted* to marry you, but I was afraid that I might have misjudged you the way I did Julius.'

'A bond?'

'Yes. I thought that we could be happy together, but I was scared that if I told you the truth then you might change your mind about me, too.'

'I wouldn't have.'

'You wouldn't?'

'No.' His voice sounded leaden. 'Your husband was a stupid man, Livia. Your brother and Scaevola are stupid, small-minded men. Your mother was captured and sold into slavery. Neither of those things was her fault. There's no shame in them either.'

'But she was still Caledonian. *I'm* half-Caledonian. They're enemies of Rome.'

'Rome has a lot of enemies.'

She stared at him. The words themselves sounded sympathetic, though his tone was anything but.

'So…you mean you *don't* care who my mother was?'

'I don't care if she was Boadicea herself. I don't care about the colour of your hair either. I *do* care about the fact that you didn't tell me.'

'I was going to, I promise. I tried when we arrived, but then the timing didn't seem right with the rebellion...'

'You didn't think it important considering *who's* rebelling?'

'I hoped that Nerva was right and you were mistaken. I hoped that I wouldn't have to choose sides. I've never wanted to do that.'

'If we're attacked, then you might have to.' His gaze turned accusing. 'This is why you were so upset about the prisoner yesterday, isn't it? You should have told me then what was wrong.'

'How could I when you spoke about him so cruelly? You called him a barbarian.'

'Because I'd been fighting! What did you expect?' He glared at her for a moment and then seemed to look inwards. 'But it was still wrong of me. I lost my temper and I shouldn't have.'

'So did I.' She looked across at him hopefully. 'You're right—I should have told you then, but maybe it's not too late...'

'It is. It's too late for any of this.' He got to his feet, his expression as stern as she'd ever seen it. 'I can't trust you now, Livia. You kept secrets from me and went to see a prisoner behind my back. How do I know you're not planning to help him escape?'

'I'm not.'

'But if you had the opportunity, would you?' He held her gaze steadily. 'Would you let him go?'

She hesitated for a moment and then nodded. No matter what his reaction, she wasn't going to lie again. 'If it came to a choice between that and abandoning him to a life of slavery, then, yes, I'd help him escape.'

'Then you need to stay here. Consider yourself a prisoner, too.'

'A *prisoner*?'

'Until things are settled. After that… I don't know.'

He made for the door and then stopped, his shoulders tensing suddenly as if a new thought had just occurred to him.

'Didn't you think your brother would try to blackmail me, too?' He turned around slowly, a look of suspicion on his face. 'Didn't *that* occur to you when you married me?'

'Ye-es, but I thought he'd leave us alone.'

'Because there's nothing he'd want from a man like me?'

'What? No!' She was shocked by the strength of bitterness in his voice.

'Or is that the real reason you married me?' Green eyes blazed with a burst of anger. 'Because you thought that with my family history I *couldn't* be blackmailed?'

'No, I told you I was going to…'

His lip curled. 'You know, I thought I was doing the honourable thing in marrying you, but it wasn't my honour that you wanted, was it? You wanted a man with no honour left to lose. That way your half-brother would leave you alone and you'd never have had to tell me the truth. I was just a means to an end.'

'No! It wasn't like that. I didn't think he'd try to blackmail you, but I thought that if he did then you'd be the kind of man who'd stand up to him, who wouldn't be threatened or intimidated. I never even thought about your family history. How could I when I don't even know what it is?'

'The details aren't important.' The anger in his eyes

seemed to dissipate suddenly, his whole face shutting down as if he'd just pulled a mask across it.

'Aren't they?' She shot to her feet, angry now, too. How *dare* he accuse her of using him so callously! 'I'm not the only one who's been keeping secrets!'

'It's no secret. I told you, there was a mutiny.'

'But you won't tell me what about!'

'Because I don't talk about my father. If you want to know more, then ask someone else. Half the legion could tell you.'

'I don't want someone else to tell me. I want *you* to do it! I've just told you everything about my mother. Why can't you do the same?'

'Because he dishonoured my family!'

'*Our* family now! Mine and yours and Julia's, too! And did he *really* dishonour it? Or was that just according to Rome?' She narrowed her eyes scornfully. 'You know the similarity between us, Marius? We've both been told that our pasts are shameful, something we ought to hide, but the difference is that you actually believe it! *I* don't. Yes, I should have told you about my mother before, but now that I have, I'm glad of it. I don't *want* to hide her away any more! I'm the daughter of a Caledonian slave, but she was a good woman, a better person than most Romans I've met. I've never been ashamed of her. I could never be ashamed of someone I loved, no matter how many insults are hurled at me, but you're so deeply enslaved to the Empire that it never occurs to you that Rome might be wrong!'

'I said I *don't* talk about him!'

'Do you really think that Rome is so perfect? Do you think that fools like Scaevola should be allowed to rule just because of who their fathers are? Was your father any worse than him?' She stormed up to face him. 'Even if he was, it doesn't reflect upon you!'

'If you can say that, then you really aren't Roman.'

'Then maybe I don't want to be Roman!' She shoved him hard in the chest, the words bursting out of her in a frenzy. 'Maybe I'd prefer to be Caledonian!'

'Exactly.' His tone was brutal. 'Which is why I can't trust you.'

Chapter Twenty-One

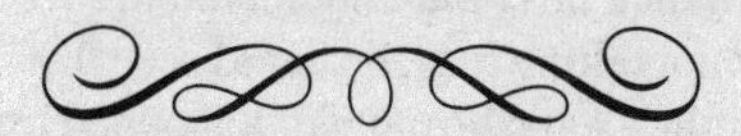

Marius stormed out of the villa and along the Via Praetoria, mind whirling as if there were some kind of tempest raging inside his head. He'd asked her for the truth and she'd given it, more than he'd ever imagined, so much that he'd had to get out, to get some space to think, to absorb everything she'd told him and then work out exactly how he felt about it.

More than anything, he was furious. How could she have kept such a secret from him, now of all times, just when he'd thought they'd been getting closer? Just when he'd thought… He stopped the thought in its tracks. He wasn't going to think it, wasn't going to acknowledge any feeling for her at all when he was so furious.

Ironically, however, it wasn't her story itself that enraged him, or at least not her part in it. When she'd told him about her marriage, he'd felt angry enough at her half-brother and first husband that he could cheerfully have wrung both their necks, though towards her he'd felt only sympathy. That and a strong desire to gather her up in his arms. The truth about her mother didn't horrify him in the way she'd seemed to expect either. The fact that she was half-Caledonian didn't bother him. Even the fact that her mother had been a slave didn't bother him, although he knew many Romans would regard it as something to be ashamed of. The fact that she'd been keeping secrets from him definitely *did* bother him.

Yet even then he *could* understand it. Much as he resented her not telling him, he could see why she hadn't. She was right—everything had happened quickly and she'd had Julia to think about. He couldn't blame her for wanting to protect her daughter and after everything she'd been through he could appreciate her lack of trust. And she'd certainly been acting strangely on the evening of their arrival in Cilurnum. Maybe she *had* been trying to tell him something then… Now that he thought about it, he'd actually discouraged her from doing so.

No, he conceded, he wasn't furious with her for either the details of her past or for not telling him. Both of those he could deal with. He wasn't even upset with her admission about freeing the prisoner if she could. Under the circumstances, he couldn't blame her. Imprisoning her in the villa, too, was only common sense, but lack of trust still wasn't the root of his anger. No, that was something else…something that his mind instinctively shied away from, but that, for once, he couldn't deny. It was the dent to his pride, the idea that she might have married him simply *because* of who his father was, that infuriated him, as if her secret would be safe with the son of a dishonoured soldier, a man who couldn't be blackmailed because he couldn't sink any lower.

Deep down, however, he knew even that was unfair. There had been an attraction between them from the start, a *bond* she'd called it—a word that seemed to describe perfectly what he'd felt, too. Despite everything, he believed that she'd wanted to marry him, a claim that might have warmed his heart the day before, but now left him cold. He believed that she was sorry. He even believed that his father had had nothing to do with her decision to marry him. But the very thought of his father had, as usual, made him see red.

Besides, it wasn't true that he couldn't be blackmailed. He *did* have something to lose, something he'd wanted and worked towards for the past thirteen years. Despite his recent, reckless behaviour, he *still* wanted to become Senior Centurion. It was the only way to redeem his honour after his father's disgrace, the thing he wanted most in the world, or so he'd thought. He'd jeopardised that ambition simply by gambling with Scaevola in the first place and now the truth about her past could destroy it completely. She had the potential to bring disgrace on him, too, in some eyes at least. How could she have let him risk so much?

On the other hand, she hadn't forced him to gamble—she hadn't even known about the game of tabula—and, as much as he resented the accusation, he hadn't exactly been open with her either. He'd hardly told her anything about his father at all. How *was* she supposed to know how badly his father's disgrace had tainted his life or how much he needed to redeem his own honour?

His father's disgrace... His own honour... He stopped abruptly, as if he'd just walked into a wall, standing stock-still and staring sightlessly ahead. Once upon a time it had been *both* of their honours that he'd set out to restore. Since when had it become just *his*? Since when had he stopped including his father in his ambitions and become ashamed of him instead?

It was raining again, he realised absently, heavily enough that pellets of water were dripping from his hair into his face. He hadn't even noticed when he'd stepped outside. In truth, he barely felt it now, though he was almost soaked to the skin. Anyone looking at him would think he was mad.

Perhaps he was. He *felt* mad suddenly, Livia's words pursuing him out into the open air, refusing to let him run away, demanding his attention. He'd gone to accuse her and she'd accused him right back—of hypocrisy, of putting Rome ahead of his father, of being enslaved to the Empire. And the worst of it was that she was right.

I could never be ashamed of someone I loved!

Those were the words that had really made him furious, the accusation that had sent him charging out of the villa and into the elements, fleeing the sudden onslaught of guilt. Now he couldn't escape it as a flurry of memories came back to him, the impressions of a thirteen-year-old boy listening to his father's dying words. He'd loved his father then, deeply and fiercely, only somehow over the years he'd forgotten it. He'd joined the army seeking redemption and yet at some point he'd let single-minded ambition and purpose take over from emotion, even from love. He'd let anger and bitterness get the better of him, allowing himself to be swayed by the opinions of others until finally he'd come to believe that his father really had betrayed and abandoned him. He'd become ashamed of someone he'd loved, someone he hadn't realised he *still* loved, and he hadn't even known it until Livia had told him. Was he going to turn on her now, too, like he had his father? Like her husband had on her?

He tipped his head back, letting the rain splash over his face as if it were some kind of cleansing force. Livia was right—they *were* similar. He knew how it felt to be torn between two conflicting loyalties as well. Deep inside, he'd always been just as divided as she was, torn between love for his father and loyalty to the Empire he'd sworn to serve.

Love and loyalty, two things that ought to go hand in hand, but which life seemed to have made very complicated all of a sudden. He couldn't think of a worse time to start questioning his loyalty to Rome, on the very eve of a Caledonian rebellion, but now that he'd finally come to his senses, it was too late to go back. He'd do his duty to the Empire, would stay loyal to his oath of allegiance, but if he had to choose then he chose her, the woman he suddenly realised he loved—he'd been a fool not to see it before—the woman he wanted more than any ambition. Which meant, if they were going to have any kind of future together, there was only one thing he could do.

He turned his feet in the direction of the prison, gripped with a new sense of urgency.

'Open the cell!' he bellowed ahead to the guard.

'Sir?'

'Release him.'

'Marius?' Ario came running across the fort as the prisoner staggered out, squinting in the daylight. 'What are you doing?'

'Letting him go.' He didn't flinch from the Decurion's interrogative stare, meeting it squarely. 'I can't explain, but it's something I have to do.'

Ario held his gaze for a tense moment and then ran a hand across his jaw. 'He hasn't told us anything yet. We don't know their numbers or when they're coming.'

'I know.' He glanced towards the prisoner. Despite an outward look of defiance there was a distinct glimmer of fear in the boy's eyes, as if he were afraid of what they were about to do to him. The thought made Marius ashamed and even more determined.

'I take full responsibility. I doubt the boy will tell us anything unless we force him to and I won't do that. We know enough. Those warriors would never have dared to attack us so soon in broad daylight if they weren't planning something bigger. I'll send word to Coria to prepare the legion.'

'Without the prisoner, you've no proof.'

'If I'm wrong, Nerva can demote me.'

Ario blew air from between his teeth. 'Perhaps the prisoner told us something before he died from his injuries?'

Marius arched an eyebrow. 'I don't ask you to lie for me.'

'But I will anyway.' Ario swore softly. 'I owe you a debt, remember?'

'You're a good friend.' Marius watched as the prisoner disappeared through the fortress gates, then turned his gaze back in the direction of the villa, his feet itching to go back to her, though he had a fort to prepare for battle first. If only the battle didn't arrive before he could set things right between them...

'Go.' Ario gave him a pointed look. 'I'll get everything ready.'

'Set double lookouts.' He clasped the Decurion's

arm gratefully. 'And tell the men to get ready for battle. The rebellion's coming.'

'You're back?' Livia looked up sharply as he reappeared in the doorway. She was still sitting on the edge of the bed, her face pale and drawn. 'I didn't think you would be.'

'Neither did I.' He took a step into the room. 'I've let the prisoner go.'

'What?' Her eyes widened, looking bigger and bluer than he'd ever seen them. 'Why?'

'Because I know what it's like to have divided loyalties, too. Sending that boy to a life of slavery might be the Roman way, but it would be wrong.' He coiled and uncoiled his fingers, concentrating on keeping his voice steady. 'It's not my way either. I'd just forgotten that until now. Most of all, I don't want to start our marriage with his fate coming between us.'

'*Start* our marriage?'

'Start again—if you want to, that is. Only listen first.' He put up a hand as she opened her mouth to speak. 'Then decide.'

He moved to the edge of the bed, planting his feet in the same spot where he'd confronted her an hour before, although it felt like days ago.

'I told you, my father was accused of mutiny. It was while he was stationed in Germania. He was a senior centurion at forty years old, a soldier who'd come from nothing and nowhere and risen in the ranks on his own merit. His men loved him and he loved them, enough not to waste their lives.

'There was an uprising amongst the Germanic tribes that year and my father was ordered to lead four cohorts east to stop it. It was already autumn, too late in the year for a campaign and in dangerous forested territory, but the Tribune who gave the order, a fool like Scaevola, wanted to win himself some acclaim. Everyone advised him against it, but the order stood. So my father led his men across the Rhenus. It didn't take them long to realise the extent of their mistake. The tribes attacked them over and over, day and night. My father lost a quarter of his men just on the retreat, but when they got back to headquarters the Tribune called him a coward and ordered them back again. My father refused. He said he wouldn't send good men to their deaths and was charged with inciting mutiny.'

'What happened then?' She asked the question softly.

'What usually happens to mutineers. He was sentenced to death. Fortunately, he had friends, senior officers who knew his real value and pleaded for him.'

'Nerva?'

'He was one of them. The case was taken before the Governor of Germania. He couldn't dismiss the charges or contradict a tribune in public, but he was able to spare my father's life, for all the good that it did. He was dishonourably discharged and sent home in disgrace.'

'I'm sorry.'

'When he came back to Rome he was a different man, as if something had broken inside him. Before he died he told me the truth about what had happened.' He gritted his teeth at the memory. 'I was so angry.'

'He didn't do anything wrong.'

'I know. I wasn't angry with him, at least not at first. I was angry at Rome, at the Tribune who'd punished him when he'd been doing the right thing. I hated Rome back then.'

'But…' Her brow creased. 'I don't understand. If you hated Rome, then why did you join the army?'

'Because I was young and alone. I wanted to belong somewhere, to redeem our family name, too. I thought that if I could reclaim my father's position then it would prove that he hadn't been the one in the wrong after all. I kept his sword, *this* sword, to remind me of that purpose.'

He reached a hand to his belt and sighed. 'But people treated me as if I were the traitor, as if I were responsible for his *crime*, and then I turned against him, too. I felt as though he'd abandoned me, as if he'd put his men ahead of me and left me to fend for myself, having to face all the insults and beatings on my own. I started to believe all the things they said about him, that he'd been foolhardy and stubborn. I started to believe that I ought to be ashamed.' He shook his head. 'I still wanted to become Senior Centurion, but I forgot why I wanted it in the first place. I forgot that I was doing it for him as well as for me. I had a choice between him and Rome and I chose Rome. I betrayed him, not the other way round.'

'You're being too hard on yourself. You were young.' She stood up in front of him. 'How do you feel about him now?'

'Now I feel the way I did when I was a boy. I loved him and he loved me. He would never have betrayed me. He only ever tried to do what was right. I see that now, thanks to you.' He lifted a hand tentatively to her cheek, gently caressing the skin with the backs of his knuckles, half-expecting her to flinch. 'I might have been a slave of Rome, but you set me free.'

'I'm glad.'

'Are you?' She didn't look it with her brow still furrowed. 'Livia, what is it?'

'You said that the Tribune who condemned him was a man like Scaevola. Is that why you married me? Revenge? Is *that* why you played that game of tabula?'

He cupped her cheek in his palm as he took a few seconds to consider the idea properly. Nerva had asked him the same thing. *Had* revenge been a part of it? Had he been mistaken in his motives there, too? No, this time he was certain. As much as he'd enjoyed defeating the Tribune, that hadn't been the reason he'd played.

She put a hand on his arm before he could answer. 'It's all right. I understand and I'm sorry about your father, truly. For what it's worth, I think he was an honourable man. He did the right thing, even if Rome didn't think so, and *you're* a good man, too. Whatever the reason you married me, you saved me from Scaevola and Tarquinius and I'm grateful. I'm only sorry that I've made life even harder for you.'

'You haven't...'

'I have.' Her fingers tightened. 'You made an enemy of a senior officer just to protect me. You put your career at risk and if anyone finds out about my mother then you'll have an even harder time becoming Senior Centurion. That's what you need to do, to fulfil your ambition for your father's sake. Julia and I can go away and live somewhere else—'

'No!' he interrupted her fiercely. 'I don't want you to go away. I thought I was angry because I risked my career for you, but you made me realise how worthless that ambition was, at least in the way I was pursuing it, without emotion, without *love*. I won't let ambition rule my life any more. If I become Senior Centurion, then I'll do it the way I want to do it, as the man I want to be, my father's son. Your husband, too, if you'll still have me? And I don't want you to deny who you are or lie about who your mother was either.'

'Do you mean it?' Her eyes were bright with emotion.

'Yes. I lost my way before, but I won't do it again. I think I always knew it deep down. *That's* why I risked my sword for you, because I knew some things were more important. I knew that *you* were more important. You still are. That game had nothing to do with revenge, Livia. I played because I couldn't stand the thought of Scaevola laying so much as a finger on you.'

'You didn't want him to touch me?' Her voice sounded faintly husky.

'I didn't want any other man to touch you. I wanted to be the one to do that.'

'But I thought...' She licked her lips, as if she felt the need to moisten them. 'On our wedding night, you didn't...and then the other night...'

'On our wedding night, you needed time with your daughter. The other night you seemed tense and I didn't want to force you into anything.' He raised both hands to her face this time, cradling it gently between his fingers. 'It wasn't that I didn't want you.'

'So you *do* want me?'

He leaned closer, sensing rather than seeing her sway towards him, too. 'I want you as much as I did the first time I saw you, more than any woman I've ever met. Whatever our reasons for marrying, whatever our loyalties, you were right—there *is* a bond between us. We belong with each other and I want you, Livia. Now.'

Chapter Twenty-Two

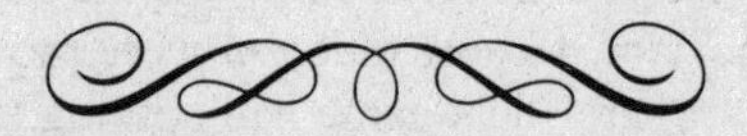

A swell of desire surged through her body, building in heat and strength as it went. Livia closed her eyes, swept up in the feeling. His words made her feel warm inside, too. There was a sense of rightness to them, as if this truly was the place she belonged, not outside on a wall between two enemies, but here in the arms of a man who understood how it felt *not* to belong.

She skimmed her fingers across his chest, amazed as always by its breadth, and for a moment her thoughts skittered back to Julius. He'd been reasonably tall and well built, but nothing like this… She pushed the thought aside. She didn't want to think about her first husband, not now. The only man she wanted to think about was the one standing in front of her. No, she corrected, she didn't want to think at all. She only wanted to feel.

'Livia?' Marius's voice was a low rumble, a vibration she seemed to feel in every part of her body. 'If you don't want me, tell me now.'

She didn't answer, flexing her fingers by way of response. He didn't ask again, taking a step back to pull off his mail shirt before wrapping his hands around her waist and hauling her against him again, so close that she could feel the strong pulse of his heartbeat pounding against her breast. Her own pulse fluttered faster to meet it, as if they were beating a rhythm together, one body already.

She lifted her face and then his lips fell upon hers, meeting them with an intensity equal to her own. His tongue slipped inside her mouth, tasting and sucking and stroking as his hands explored her body, trailing their way down the long column of her back and over the curve of her bottom, drawing her ever closer towards him.

She moved her hands, too, sliding them fervently over his shoulders and around the back of his head, holding his face against hers. Every part of her body seemed to be aching, straining towards him before they broke apart finally, both of them gasping for breath.

'Take off your clothes.'

He spoke like a centurion, issuing the words like a command, and she smiled, toying briefly with the idea of refusing him. But she didn't want to refuse. Instead she pulled herself loose from his grasp, dodging backwards as his fingers tightened convulsively, and then reached down, grasping the hem of her *stola* and pulling it over her head along with her *tunica*.

His expression didn't alter, though his breathing seemed to become even more ragged as he looked her up and down, taking in every inch of her body. She kept her arms at her sides, unmoving, making no attempt to cover herself, basking in the heat of his gaze. There was no criticism in it. For the first time in her life she felt as if she were being looked at as the person she truly was, as an equal, not a barbarian or someone who ought to be ashamed, but simply as herself.

'Now you.' She challenged him with the words and he did as she asked, unfastening his sword belt and greaves and setting them aside before removing his tunic in one sweeping motion.

She caught her breath at the sight of him. In broad daylight his chest looked just as impressive as it had the first time, though more damaged, too, pitted with scores and bruises.

'What happened?' She pressed a hand tenderly against one of the scars.

'I'm a soldier. It's part of the job.'

'But these bruises look recent.' She grazed her fingers over his abdomen, the muscles seeming to ripple as she touched them. 'From yesterday?'

'Probably.' His voice sounded almost hoarse. 'Livia…'

'Won't it hurt you if we…?'

He claimed her mouth again before she could finish the sentence, kissing her thoroughly before growling a protest against her lips. 'It'll hurt me more if we don't.'

'Then you'll need to remove these, too.' She smiled and tugged at the drawstring of his *braccae*, hearing his breath catch as the male part of his body strained beneath.

He gripped her wrist, holding it in one hand while he removed his *braccae* and boots with the other, his gaze never leaving hers until he stood naked before her.

'Oh!' She couldn't help but look downwards. In ten years of marriage, she'd never seen *that* part of Julius. Then she couldn't stop herself from staring.

'Do I pass inspection?' There was a hint of amusement in his voice and she lifted her gaze again, her cheeks burning.

'Yes.'

He moved suddenly, lifting her up in his arms and carrying her across to the bed. She tipped her head back as he laid her down in the centre, overwhelmed by a feeling of exquisite pleasure. Her whole body was tingling with a surfeit of new sensations, each one seemingly stronger than the last as his hands moved skilfully over her limbs, starting at her ankles and then moving upwards, pushing her legs apart as he bent his head to press kisses over her calves and between her thighs.

'What are you doing?' She didn't know whether to feel shocked or excited.

'Haven't you ever been kissed here?'

'No.' His voice was so deep it set all her nerve endings to quivering. She'd had no idea that anyone might *want* to kiss her there.

'What about here?'

His lips moved higher, hovering over her skin for a moment before his tongue darted outwards. She gasped aloud, seized with the powerful desire to start moving, to match the rhythm of her own heartbeat, pounding so heavily now that she could almost believe the whole room was shaking along with it. She'd never moved so much as a muscle in bed with Julius, had never even considered it, but now she felt as if she couldn't keep still. She didn't *want* to keep still.

'Or here?' The tongue darted outwards again and she groaned.

'No.'

'I told you your husband was a fool.' Marius lifted

himself up on his forearms, moving up the bed until he was covering her. 'I intend to kiss every part of you.'

'Every part?' She felt as though she were panting.

'Unless you have any objections?'

'None at all.'

He smiled slowly and she reached up, trailing her fingers down the sides of his face as he lowered his head and kissed her tenderly on the lips. She sighed into his mouth as she slid her arms around his waist, feeling as if every part of her were being caressed at once. At that moment, with their naked bodies moulded together, she didn't want to move. She simply wanted to lie there beneath him, to enjoy the feeling of contentment, the heady sense of warmth and mutual desire and togetherness.

Then he kissed her again, more deeply this time, and the feeling of contentment faded and raw need took over, bringing with it a throbbing sensation between her legs that seemed to intensify almost to fever pitch as she clasped her arms tighter around him, wanting more.

'Livia.' He murmured her name and she lifted her body, twining her legs around his and tilting her hips up towards his manhood. She was acting brazenly, but she didn't care. She felt abandoned and powerful, as if all the years of frustration and loneliness had led her towards this, this feeling of rightness accompanied by a fervency of emotion. She could feel the wetness between her legs, the hardness between his, and she couldn't wait any longer.

He must have felt the same way because he pushed inside her suddenly, entering her body in one powerful thrust. She sucked in a breath as her muscles tightened around him, stunned by a feeling of fullness, as if he fitted inside her perfectly. He groaned at the same time and then they were moving together, their lovemaking faster and deeper and more overwhelming with each thrust. She moved instinctively, writhing and bucking against him, pushing upwards and then retreating, her fingers digging into his shoulders as she felt herself building to some kind of completion.

Then a trembling sensation overtook her, a sudden spasm as if something inside her had burst. She heard herself cry out and then Marius, too, felt the warmth of his seed in her belly, but she was only vaguely aware of it, her whole body shaking with a dizzy sense of elation and happiness. Then he moved to one side, pulling her with him, and she tumbled downwards, dazed and satiated, on to his chest.

She didn't know how long they lay there, only that the air was cold and the shadows were lengthening across the room by the time she awoke. It felt fitting, seeing as her whole world seemed to have changed.

'Marius?' She ran her hands over one of his biceps, marvelling anew at the hard contours of his body.

'Mmm?' He didn't open his eyes though his arm tightened around her.

'Does this mean you've forgiven me?'

He gave a low chuckle. 'What do you think?'

'So what do we do now?'

'I can think of a few things.'

Green eyes opened lazily, regarding her with a wicked-looking gleam, and she batted a hand against him.

'You know what I mean. What now for *us*?'

He heaved a sigh and rested his spare arm behind his

head. 'Now we do the best that we can. I'm still a soldier of Rome and that means I have to defend the frontier. I made an oath and lives might depend upon it.'

'I know.' She rested her chin on his chest, looking soberly into his face. 'I wouldn't expect you to do otherwise.'

'Livia.' He tugged her closer again, frowning slightly. 'I understand that you have divided loyalties and I won't ask you to choose between Caledonia and Rome, but I need to know you won't do anything to help the rebels either.'

'I won't, I promise. Julia's in Coria. I want her to be safe and… What?'

There was a sound of running footsteps in the corridor and she shot upright in alarm, clasping the blanket to her chest.

'Centurion Varro?' A soldier burst through the doorway without knocking.

'The rebels?' Marius was out of bed in a moment.

'Yes, sir.' The soldier's expression turned from urgent to apologetic as he averted his gaze quickly. 'They're attacking the west tower.'

'I'll be there as soon as I can.'

'Yes, sir.'

'They're attacking now?' She scrambled to a crouching position as the soldier ran off again. 'But it's almost night!'

'It's dusk.' Marius was already strapping his armour back on. 'I should have expected something like this. Here.' He held out his *gladius*. 'Stay here, barricade the door and take this.'

'No.' She shook her head. 'I don't want it.'

'It's not a question of want. You need it.' He leaned

over the bed, touching his forehead against hers. 'I'll find another weapon, but take this one for me, please, Livia. I don't know what's going to happen, but I need to know you can defend yourself.'

'All right.' She pressed her nose against his. 'Just be careful.'

'I will.' He kissed her fiercely before picking up his helmet and charging out of the room. 'Just wait here!'

Chapter Twenty-Three

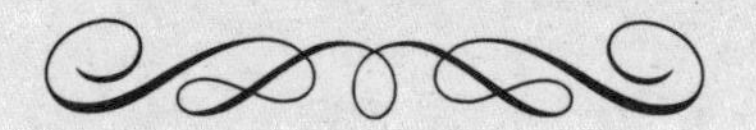

Livia sat on the edge of the bed, straining her ears to listen to the sound of muffled shouts and fighting outside, as if sound itself could tell her what was happening. The tension was agonising. Marius had told her to stay and wait, but for what? For him to return or for a horde of warriors to break down the door and burst in?

She turned his *gladius* over in her lap, hating the weight of cold steel in her hands. Would she be able to use it if she had to? The very idea was terrifying. Then she peered closer, noticing the pair of initials carved into the hilt. His and his father's. It was *their* weapon, the symbol of their family honour. It had meant a hundred times more to him than she'd realised and he'd risked it for her.

The thought brought her resolutely to her feet. How could she just sit there and do nothing when Marius had already risked so much for her? If he were injured, then she'd never forgive herself. He might need her and, even if he didn't, others might. The very least she could do was help the wounded.

She dressed quickly, tucking the *gladius* inside her

belt and then moving away the chest she'd barricaded against the door, peering nervously around the edge before making her way outside. The Via Principalis was deserted as she approached the west gate. Then she stopped, gripping the edge of a pillar for support as she stared, horrified, at the scene of chaos before her. Most of the fighting was along the top of the palisade, but a handful of rebels had already breached the defences and were battling auxiliaries inside the camp. Meanwhile, more warriors kept appearing over the top of the ramparts, so many that the Roman soldiers looked in danger of being overwhelmed. There was no sign of Marius.

A nearby groan drew her attention to a soldier lying on the ground a few metres away and she broke into a run as she recognised him. It was Trenus, the quartermaster who'd been so generous when she'd arrived, clutching his leg as blood spurted from his calf.

'I'm here.' She dropped to the ground beside him, trying to sound reassuring. 'It's going to be all right.'

'My leg.' His lips were already turning white.

'Hold on.' Quickly she unfastened her belt and tied it around the top of his thigh, pulling it tight with a heave.

'Good.' He gritted his teeth at the pain. 'As hard as you can.'

She heaved again, tying the ends in a knot before tearing a strip of cloth from the hem of her *stola* and folding it into a pad to press against the wound.

'Better.' His head fell back to the ground with a thud. 'Now get back inside. Marius will finish me off if he sees you out here.'

'It's not his decision. It's mine.' She tore a fresh strip

of cloth from her *stola*, tying it around the pad to hold it in place. 'Where's the surgeon?'

'No surgeon, just a medic, but he's fighting.'

'Then you *definitely* need me out here. There must be others who need help.'

'All right, but don't tell Marius I agreed with you.'

'Will you be all right?' She put a hand on his shoulder, looking around anxiously. He was vulnerable out in the open, but she couldn't lift him by herself and there was no one around to help.

'Don't worry about me. I'm not done for yet.' He held up a wicked-looking dagger. 'Do you have a weapon?'

'I have this.' She picked up Marius's *gladius*. It had fallen to the ground when she'd removed her belt, though lying next to a puddle of blood it looked even more terrifying.

'Do you know how to use it?'

'No.' She rose up on her haunches, spying another injured soldier close to the gate. 'But hopefully I won't have to. I'll be back as soon as I can.'

Trenus gave a twisted smile. 'I'm not going anywhere.'

She clasped the *gladius* in her hand, darting a quick look around before crossing the space at a run. There was fighting on both sides of her, but she kept her gaze fixed on the injured man for courage, finally sliding to the ground beside him.

There was an arrow embedded in his shoulder, she discovered, so deep that there was no evidence of the head, just a shaft of wood poking out of the flesh. She swallowed a wave of nausea, wishing that she had some kind of anaesthetic as the soldier cried out in pain. There was a bubble of blood around the wound and she tore another strip off her *stola* to staunch the flow, shaking her head as she did so. If she wasn't careful, she'd have no dress left.

'Hold this tight against the wound,' she instructed the soldier, yelping in shock as he suddenly reached up and shoved her to one side.

'What?' An arrow thudded heavily into the ground where she'd just been crouching and she scrambled around, heart pounding at the sight of a Caledonian warrior charging at breakneck speed towards them.

'My shield!' the injured soldier screamed at her. 'Pick it up!'

She reached for the shield and *gladius*, trying to hold them steady in trembling hands as she clambered back to her feet and braced herself. The warrior wasn't wearing any armour, she noticed, but she wished *she* was. He was almost twice her size and the look in his eyes was battle-crazed and terrifying.

Then he stopped, his wild gaze taking in first her hair and then her torn, bloodstained *stola.* She swallowed, uncomfortably aware that her legs were bare from the knees down, though she felt a faint glimmer of hope, too. Had he recognised who she was? Did he feel some sort of kinship with her as she had with the prisoner? Would he leave her alone if he did?

Then he spat out a word, one she didn't recognise, though she didn't need a translator to guess its meaning. It was obviously one her mother hadn't thought suitable for a child, one that revealed exactly what he thought of her and her relationship to the Roman garrison. It made her suddenly furious. As if being judged by one side wasn't bad enough, now she was being judged by the other, too!

'Livia!' She spun towards the sound of Marius's voice. He was standing in the midst of the fighting on top of the palisade, at least fifty feet away, drawing one arm back and then hurling it forward again as he loosed a *pilum* into the air towards them.

It was a warning call, she realised, turning her gaze quickly back to the warrior, a warning for her not to move. This was it, the moment she'd been dreading, when she had to make a choice between her Roman and Caledonian sides. She didn't want to choose, but in truth there *was* no choice. She was on Marius's side. And she wasn't going to let this warrior kill her because of it.

He was creeping forward now, closing the distance between them to within striking range, but she couldn't flinch or retreat, had to hold steady so that he wouldn't realise the danger until it was too late.

There was a hiss of air and at the last moment her attacker twisted his head sharply, diving away as the javelin came down with a thump, missing his leg by a hair's breadth. He gave her a furious look and then charged forward, but she darted to one side, lifting her shield and thrusting the boss towards him before swinging the *gladius* up with all her strength, aiming for his chest. It was no use. He blocked the blow with his axe, leering as though her efforts were nothing more than horseplay. She tried again, aiming lower, but this time he grabbed her arm, pulling her towards him and raising his sword to her throat.

'Oof!'

She dropped to the ground, landing heavily on her shoulder as Marius barrelled into the warrior from the side, knocking all three of them down in a heap.

Quickly, she wriggled away, readying her *gladius* to help, but it was impossible. The two men were rolling over and over in the dirt, fists pounding so ferociously that she couldn't get a clear aim.

'Marius!' she screamed out in horror as the warrior pulled a dagger from his boot, lifting it high in the air before stabbing downwards. Instinctively she threw herself on top of him, grabbing his arm and clinging to it, trying to loosen his hold on the weapon. He twisted around, face contorting with rage as he shoved his elbow into the side of her head, so hard that the world seemed to go black for a few seconds before she hit the ground again with a thud.

She reached a hand to her head, ears ringing, watching through a sticky red blur as the warrior lifted the dagger again and plunged. A cry rose to her throat, but no sound came out. Her vision seemed to be dimming, too, her eyelids closing against her will as she saw Marius's hand come up, blocking the warrior's wrist. There was another fierce tussle, a roar of anger followed by a bellow of pain.

The last thing she saw was the warrior's body slump to the ground.

'Livia?' Marius leaned over the bed, calling her name as he rubbed a hand softly over her forehead, willing her to wake up, to give some sign that she could hear him.

'It might take a while.' Ario stood opposite, his face and voice equally grim. 'Head injuries can take a long time to heal.'

'I know.' He grimaced at the thought. 'What the hell was she doing out there? I told her to stay inside.'

'Trenus says she was helping the injured. She tied a tourniquet around his leg before that savage attacked her.'

Marius swallowed. He'd been fighting on the ramparts when he'd seen them. The sight of Livia wielding a paltry *gladius* in front of an axe-wielding warrior had made the bottom fall out of his stomach and his world. For a moment, he'd thought his very heart had stopped beating. He'd been on the verge of losing everything—and everything, he'd realised in a moment of blinding clarity, was *her*. He loved her with every fibre of his being. He'd never thrown a spear so hard in his life.

'It still shouldn't have happened. I should have protected her.'

'You *were* protecting her.'

'He still managed to do this.'

'This—' Ario gave him a pointed look '—was because she was trying to protect you. At least this answers the question of where her loyalties lie. I think we can trust her.'

'We can.'

He sank into a chair and put his head in his hands. It was true. He *could* trust her, only he'd found that out the hard way, in the midst of battle, when she'd put herself in danger to help Roman soldiers. He'd told her that she didn't have to choose sides, but she had, risking her life alongside theirs and almost getting herself killed to save him. He should have trusted her all along instead of treating her like a prisoner, a traitor… She was no more a traitor to Rome than his father had been.

'You need to eat.' Ario rested a hand on his shoulder on the way to the door. 'I'll get some food.'

'Not until she wakes up.'

'Don't be a hero, Marius. She'll need you more than

ever when she does. That was just the start of the rebellion and you know it. They were testing our defences, seeing how many of us are here. We held them off for today, but they'll be back, probably in greater numbers, and then the real fighting will begin. You'll need to defend her all over again, but you'll be no use at all if you don't get some food and rest.'

'All right, but I'm not leaving this room.'

'I didn't expect you to.' Ario patted his shoulder again and then frowned. 'How long will it take Nerva to send reinforcements, do you think?'

'I don't know.' Marius ran a hand through his hair with a sigh. 'He should have received our message by now, but it'll depend on how many forts were attacked. I doubt that it was just us. If the rebels have broken through the wall, then the legion might be needed elsewhere.'

'So no reinforcements?'

'It's a possibility.'

'Damned Romans.' Ario swore. 'If they'd only listened when you told them…'

'They'll be listening now.' Marius turned his gaze back towards the bed. 'In any case, I need you to get four of your best men ready to ride to Coria.'

'Four?'

'Yes.' He nodded emphatically. 'I need them to take Livia back to her daughter. She's staying with Nerva's wife in the fort. If Hermenia has any sense, which she does, she'll take the girl to Eboracum for safety. Livia needs to go with them. I can't abandon my post, but she needs to leave the moment she wakes up.'

'Do you think she'll go?' Ario lifted his eyebrows. 'You told her not to go near the prisoner and she ignored you. You told her to stay in the villa and she ignored you. Something tells me she won't leave just because you tell her to either.'

'It's for her own good.'

'And if you think that telling her *that* will make any difference, then you don't know women very well, my friend. They're stubborn and she's already put herself in the way of a dagger for you.' He held his hands up as Marius glared savagely. 'I'm just saying that she might take some convincing, that's all, but I'll tell my men to be ready.'

Marius glowered after Ario's retreating back, assailed by a new set of worries. What if Ario was right and she wouldn't leave simply because he asked her to? He didn't doubt that she'd want to get back to Julia, but what if she decided it was her duty to stay and help? What if she wouldn't listen to reason? There was little enough chance of survival for any of them in the fort. They would be a few hundred against a few thousand. In which case, he *had* to convince her. He had to *make* her leave, any way that he could…

'Marius?' Her voice was little more than a whisper, but he was on his feet in an instant, leaning over the bed and cradling her face in his hands.

'Try not to move. You took a nasty blow to the head.'

'You're alive…and you're *smiling…*' She blinked a few times as if she thought she might be dreaming. 'You never smile.'

'I am now.' Despite what he had to tell her, he couldn't stop himself. The sound of her voice made his heart soar.

'It suits you.' Her own lips curved at last. 'You should do it more often.'

'Then I will.' He was struck with a pang of regret,

realising that he might not have time to do much of anything any more, ironically just when he'd found a reason to be happy. But at least he *could* still save her, which also meant that he had to hurry…

'What happened?' She tipped her head to one side as he smoothed his thumbs over her cheeks.

'You saved my life, though I'm afraid you're going to have a pretty big bruise to show for it.'

'Then the attack's over?' Her expression turned hopeful. 'Did we win?'

We? He felt a warm glow in his chest. Apparently she really had chosen sides…

'For now, but this is only a respite.'

'What do you mean?' She tried to sit up, but he moved his hands to her shoulders, holding her down on the bed.

'They'll be back. The rebellion's only just getting started.'

'Julia!' This time she succeeded in pushing past him, jolting to an upright position, her expression stricken with panic.

'Don't worry, she's safe in Coria. There's a thousand men based there, not to mention Hermenia. She's worth a few hundred herself, although under the circumstances I'd expect her to take Julia south for safety.'

'But she said that she'd never leave Nerva!'

'Trust me, she'll make an exception for your daughter. Hermenia's loyal, but she's sensible, too.' He took a deep breath. 'Ario's getting some of his men ready to take you to Coria to join them.'

For a moment, he thought she hadn't understood, her forehead creasing as she stared at him silently for a few moments.

'Livia?'

'You truly believe that Julia will be safe with Hermenia?'

'I do, but…'

'Then how can I leave?'

'Because you need to be with your daughter.'

'No.' She shook her head and then winced. 'If you think that this is only a respite, then it means the rebels will attack again soon. How can you spare men to take me to Coria when you need every soldier you can get?'

'They won't be gone long.'

'Long enough.' She lifted her chin, moving her head more carefully this time. 'I won't abandon you, Marius. As long as Julia's safe, I can face anything else. We'll fight the rebels together.'

'No!' He stood up, half-touched, half-appalled by her words. 'I won't let you fight.'

'Then I'll tend to the injured.'

'*You're* injured!'

'It was just a bump on the head.' She rubbed her fingers over the swollen area. 'I'll be back to normal in a few hours. I'm not even dizzy.'

'I don't want you getting hurt again.'

'Then I won't be.' She stretched out a hand towards him. 'I'll be more careful from now on. You can show me how to use a *gladius* and…'

'You're leaving!'

He said the words more forcefully than he'd intended, wincing inwardly as he saw her eyes widen with a look of surprise followed by hurt. He hardened his heart at the sight. Apparently Ario was right. She wasn't going to leave, not willingly, especially after last night. He'd told her that there really *was* a bond between them and now the only thing he could do was break it and persuade her otherwise. He had to tell her he didn't love her just at the very moment he wanted to tell her how much he did.

'I'm ordering you to go, Livia.' He forced the words out. 'You need to leave, you more than anyone.'

'What do you mean, *more than anyone*?'

Her eyes flickered with a look of suspicion and he clenched his jaw.

'Because I can't fight if I'm distracted.'

'I won't distract you! You don't have to defend me.'

'I didn't mean that. I mean that I can't watch you all the time. While you're here, I can't be sure you won't do something to endanger the fort.'

She looked as though he'd just struck her. 'But I told you I wouldn't. You said that you understood!'

'I thought that I did, but things are different now. I can't trust someone with divided loyalties.'

'But I saved your life! You just said so!'

'And I'm grateful.' He took a step back from the bed, adopting his stoniest, most resolute expression. 'But that's all. We had one night together, but it's over. I don't regret it, but this marriage will never work. I see that now. After this rebellion is dealt with…' He cleared his throat, forcing himself to pretend that there would be an *after*. 'You and Julia can live somewhere else as you suggested. We'll lead separate lives. That would probably be best for all of us.'

'Separate lives…' She sank back against the pillows, her gaze accusing. 'Last night you said that we belonged together.'

'I was wrong. In the real world, we all have to choose sides.'

'I thought that I had.'

Her voice sounded so hopeless that he had to resist the urge to go back to her, to hold her in his arms and say that none of what he was saying was true. Instead he braced himself for his last parting shot.

'I thought I didn't care where you came from, Livia, but I do. You're one of them. A Caledonian. A *barbarian*. You need to be ready to leave at dawn.'

Chapter Twenty-Four

Eboracum—two months later

'At last!' Hermenia looked up from her weaving as Livia traipsed wearily into the small *tablinium* of their borrowed villa. 'I was starting to worry about you. You've been gone for hours.'

'I'm sorry.' She kissed Julia first and then dropped down on to a couch, rubbing her eyes with exhaustion. 'I meant to send word, but we were almost overwhelmed in the hospital this morning. Some more carts arrived and the surgeon needed help.'

'You're working too hard. You need some sleep, too.'

'I'm all right.' She leaned back against the cushions. 'At least I'm healthy, which is more than can be said for some of those poor legionaries.'

'Any news?'

'No.' She shook her head despondently. They'd received word that Cilurnum had been overrun by the rebels the month before, but there had been nothing specific about Marius. None of the wounded who'd come back from the wall had been able to tell her anything about him either.

'Well, that's not necessarily a bad thing.' Hermenia's tone was reassuring.

'No, I suppose not.'

'At least the rest of the garrison should have arrived at the frontier by now. That will put an end to the rebellion once and for all, you'll see. The fighting will be over in no time.'

'I hope so.'

'Try not to worry.' Hermenia reached out a hand sympathetically. 'Nerva always said that Marius was one of the best soldiers he ever knew.'

Livia took the proffered hand with a heavy heart. Hermenia's confident tone sounded all too familiar, although it was reassuring to know that reinforcements had arrived at last. The last remaining units of the British garrison had marched through the city a month before, their shining armour a stark contrast to the battered and beaten-looking men coming back from the frontier.

But how could she *not* worry when Marius might still be fighting for his life? If he was even still alive at all! No matter how things had ended between them, with him lifting her on to a horse and practically pushing the animal out through the fortress gates, she still cared about him. Even if the bond between them was broken—his side of it anyway. Her side was damaged, but just as strong as ever. She had a feeling that it always would be. No matter what he'd said or how much she resented him for it, she couldn't help but worry about him. She resented that, too.

'It's the lot of a soldier's wife, I'm afraid, waiting for news.'

'I know.' She smiled at the older woman gratefully.

'And I know that you would never have left Coria if it hadn't been for Julia. I can never thank you enough for taking care of us.'

'There's no need. I had to make sure you found somewhere decent to stay here. There are *some* advantages to being the Legate's wife, after all. I'll stay until Marius comes to reclaim you.'

'When *will* Marius come, Mama?' Julia looked up from where she was sprawled on the floor beside Porcia, kicking her heels in the air.

'I don't know, love. Hopefully soon.'

Livia turned her face away, looking out into the courtyard beyond, trying to hide her expression. Julia asked about Marius every day, almost as if he were her real father, and every time she felt a stab of guilt, answering as if they really had a future together when in reality there was no hope for them. Even if he survived, there was none. Because she was a *barbarian* and he didn't trust her—and because he wasn't the man she'd thought he was either. Still, she couldn't bring herself to say it, to admit that her second marriage was over, not as acrimoniously as her first perhaps, but even more painfully. She hadn't even told Hermenia.

At least she had a purpose here in the town, helping tend to the wounded in the hospital. She had a plan, too, for after the rebellion was over. She wasn't going to go south again. She was going to stay in Eboracum and use the skills she'd learned from her mother to open her own kitchen and cook meals for soldiers in exchange for a few coins. It would be a way for her and Julia to be independent at last.

'There's a man here to see you, lady.'

'Oh!' She leapt to her feet at the servant's words, so quickly that she almost lost her footing and stumbled forward.

'Careful.' Hermenia reached out to steady her. 'There's no need to fall into his arms.'

'Marius…' Her heart was already racing. Could it be him? And if it was, how ought she to greet him? She could hardly kiss him, not now. A polite embrace maybe, though perhaps even that was too much… She clutched at Hermenia's sleeve, breathless with anticipation, her gaze turning towards the door at the sound of approaching footsteps…

'Sister.'

Her hopes hit the floor with a jolt. It had been three months since she'd last seen Tarquinius, but he hadn't changed at all. He still looked more like a bird of prey than a man, regarding her as if she were some stranger and not a blood relation, his pale eyes just as cruel and disapproving as ever. Only this time, she decided, she wasn't going to be intimidated by him.

'Hermenia.' For the first time in her life, she held his gaze, lifting her chin up rather than bowing her head. 'This is my half-brother, Tarquinius.'

'My respects.' His voice was an inexpressive monotone.

'Perhaps I ought to leave the two of you alone?' Hermenia looked at her enquiringly, but she shook her head.

'There's no need. I don't suppose Tarquinius is here on a family visit.' She lifted an eyebrow. 'Are you, *Brother*?'

'I see that your manners haven't improved in the north.' Pale eyes flashed, displaying not the faintest hint of pleasure at seeing her again. 'Although you're right. I've come to collect my debt.'

'Porcia?' She looked over her shoulder towards her trembling maid. The poor girl had always been terrified of Tarquinius. 'Perhaps you could take Julia to her room?'

'Yes, lady.'

'Thank you.' She smiled, waiting until they'd both left the room before adopting a look of exaggerated innocence. 'Now what debt would that be?'

'You know fine well what debt,' Tarquinius snapped. 'I received a message from Lucius Scaevola a few weeks ago.'

'A few weeks? Then it's taken you a while to get here.'

'I was hardly going to make the journey *before* military reinforcements arrived to impose order.'

'Of course. How very brave of you, Brother.'

His expression sharpened malevolently. 'Scaevola says that you refused to marry him.'

'He's lying.'

'Do you deny that you refused to carry out my wishes?'

'No, I simply deny whatever version of events he's told you. I came here with every intention of marrying him.'

'Then might I ask how it is that you came to marry someone else? A mere *centurion*, so Scaevola tells me.'

'Because he gambled me away in a game, although I don't suppose he mentioned that part. But it was all fair and legal. I simply followed the rules and married the man who won me.'

'Scaevola says he was tricked!'

'He would. He's a gambler. You ought to know that

their losses are never their fault. To be honest, Tarquinius, I'm surprised that you trusted him in the first place.'

'Enough! You will divorce this man, this lowly soldier, whoever he is, and marry Scaevola as planned.'

'No.' She bristled at his imperative tone. 'I will not. I have a husband. One worth ten hundred of you or Lucius Scaevola and I have no intention of divorcing him *ever*.'

He lifted a hand as if to strike her, his expression of restrained enmity slipping into one of pure poison before he seemed to control himself again.

'Perhaps we ought to speak alone after all.'

'I'm not going anywhere!' Hermenia's tone was now openly belligerent.

'It's all right.' Livia put a hand on her arm. 'He won't hurt me. He knows that I'm not under his protection any more. If he hurts me, then he'll have my husband to answer to and *who knows* what a *mere* soldier might do.'

'You were under my protection until you married Scaevola. Since you weren't married when he gambled he had no right to stake you in the first place! Therefore the game was invalid and your marriage to this Centurion is, too.'

'The thought did occur to me. I chose to ignore it.'

'Then we'll let a court decide, shall we? *Then* we'll see what your Centurion can do about it.'

'We could.' She tapped her chin thoughtfully. 'That is, *if* you really want to explain to the Emperor why you think one of his Tribunes ought to be relieved of duty in the midst of a rebellion.'

'Scaevola owes me a debt!'

'Exactly. *He* does. *I* don't. Now I think our business

here is concluded, don't you?' She squared up to him, unflinching. 'Since that's all I ever was to you, wasn't I, part of your *business*? Our father would have been ashamed. He asked you to take care of me, not to use me.'

'How dare you speak of our father!'

'Because he loved me, too, Tarquinius! Because love is love, no matter who we are or where we come from. Only you wouldn't understand that, would you?'

His lip curled contemptuously. 'Julius was right about you.'

She reacted instinctively, raising her fist and planting it square in his jaw.

'What…?' He staggered backwards, raising one arm in defence as she pursued him.

'I was faithful to Julius. He never doubted me until you turned him against me!'

'I only told him the truth about your mother.'

'You blackmailed him! You made him doubt me *and* our daughter! You made me hide something that should never have been a secret so that when he found out, he never trusted me again. You destroyed my marriage and you would have done it all over again with Scaevola!'

'What about your new husband?' His expression turned spiteful. 'Does *he* know where you come from?'

'Everyone knows about my mother.' She smiled triumphantly. 'Don't they, Hermenia?'

His face blanched. 'You've *told* people?'

'Yes. You can't make me hide it any more. But then you don't *really* mind, do you, Tarquinius? After all, you were the one who was always threatening to reveal it. Of course, Scaevola was a little surprised, since you didn't mention anything about it when you arranged our marriage, but I'm sure that's something you can discuss when you find him.'

Her brother's expression hardened. 'You're no sister of mine. I never want to see you again.'

'Then I suggest that you stay in Lindum from now on. In fact, I wouldn't come anywhere near the wall again if I were you. My *husband* wouldn't like it.'

He started towards the doorway and then stopped, looking back over his shoulder maliciously. 'And if your husband should die? It's a dangerous place on the wall. If he doesn't come back, what then? Don't expect to come crawling back to me.'

'I never would. Goodbye, Tarquinius.'

Livia waited until her brother's footsteps had receded before collapsing on to the couch again, her legs giving way beneath her. Now that their confrontation was over, all the tension seemed to catch up with her in a rush. She felt as if she were shaking all over, scarcely able to believe that she'd finally stood up to him.

'You were magnificent…' Hermenia sat down beside her '…if perhaps a trifle duplicitous. I thought you'd only told Marius and me about your mother?'

Livia smiled sheepishly. 'I might have exaggerated a little, but I wanted to see his reaction. Besides, I'm not going to hide it any more. If anyone asks, I'll tell them. Scaevola will probably find out eventually.'

'Perhaps.' Hermenia patted her hand. 'Although I have to confess I'm a little disappointed at you letting him off the hook so easily. Honestly, between the pair of them I don't know which is worse, but I don't suppose your brother will pursue him for the money now.'

'Probably not, but I expect Scaevola has enough to

deal with at the moment. And he might have suffered enough, worrying about it. In any case, if there are any more repercussions then they can fight it out between them. It's nothing to do with me any more.'

She let out a tremulous sigh. Now that her heartbeat was slowing again, she felt as though she needed to get outside, to get some fresh air to clear her head.

'I'm just going for a walk around the courtyard.'

Hermenia looked at her dubiously. 'You really ought to get some rest.'

'I will soon, I promise. I just need to calm down first.'

'Of course.' The older woman laughed suddenly. 'Do you know, I liked you the first day we met. I thought you were strong then, but it seems I still underestimated you. You and Marius are perfect for each other.'

Livia felt tears well in her eyes, enveloping the other woman in a swift hug to hide her face before walking quickly out into the courtyard. The open air felt liberating, soft and summery against her cheeks, even if there were tears running down them. She'd finally done it, finally broken free from her brother, and yet the feeling was bittersweet, her victory tinged with sadness. If only she could find out that Marius was alive and safe, then perhaps she could find a way to be happy again…

She leaned against a pillar, staring into what passed for a garden, though in reality it was just a single tree surrounded by paving stones. That was the funny thing about courtyards, she thought, trying to distract her mind from her anxieties. They were neither indoors nor outdoors, neither a garden nor a room. Not one thing or another, just like her life. She was neither Roman nor Caledonian, not a wife or a widow. It was strange how many significant events of her relationship with Marius had taken place in courtyards, too, but then their relationship had never been one thing or the other either…

Footsteps on the other side of the courtyard made her heart sink again.

'What is it now, Tarquinius?'

'Livia?'

She jerked her chin up and then froze, wondering if it were a trick of the light or whether she were imagining things. It *looked* like Marius, standing between the pillars on the opposite side of the courtyard, dressed in military attire, though his head was bare. His face was leaner and gaunter than she remembered, but the features were unmistakably his, as stern as ever, though his eyes were bright with emotion, shining with what looked like hope and something like yearning, though surely she was mistaken about that.

'Marius?' She hardly dared say his name out loud in case he denied it. 'Is it you?'

'It's me.' He hesitated, the look of hope in his eyes fading when she didn't say anything else. 'It's good to see you again, Livia.'

'It's good to see you again, too.' She hated how paltry those words sounded. *Good.* As if her heart weren't trying to beat its way out of her chest! As if she weren't tensing every muscle in her body in an effort to stop herself from running to him! *He was alive!*

'You thought I was your brother?' He was back to frowning again.

'Yes, he came to visit me, but it's all right. He's gone and I doubt he'll be back.'

'Good.' The frown deepened, the air of tension between them palpable now. 'You look well.'

'Thank you.' She clasped her hands in front of her, hoping she looked more composed than her palpitating heartbeat was making her feel. 'We heard about Cilurnum. What happened?'

'We had to abandon it in the end. There was no point in losing men to a lost cause.'

'That sounds familiar.'

'It does.' He gave an ironic smile. 'I think I understand my father even better now.'

'I'm glad.' She tried not to think about how handsome he looked. Despite everything, his smile still had the power to take her breath away. 'I still have his—*your—gladius*. It was in the bag you sent back with me.'

'I know. I put it there.'

'You did?' She'd thought that she must have picked it up in her semi-delirious state.

'Yes. I wanted you to have it in case I didn't make it.'

'Oh… I can go and fetch it if you want it back?'

'No. I can't fight for a while anyway.' He pushed his cloak back and she had to dig her toes into the ground to stop herself from rushing forward. His whole left arm was wrapped in a tattered white bandage.

'You're injured!'

'It's only a break. The surgeon tells me it'll be as good as new in a few months, but Nerva said it was about time I took some leave.' He shrugged. 'It's been twelve years, after all.'

'I see.' She didn't know how else to respond. What was he saying, that he'd come to spend it with her? The idea was exciting, insulting and unlikely all at the same time.

'How is everyone else? Trenus? Ario?'

'Both alive, only a little the worse for wear. They both send their respects.' He paused momentarily. 'I travelled here with another old friend.'

'Oh?'

'Scaevola, only not quite the man you might remember. It seems that war changes some people after all. He got more than he bargained for coming here, but it might be the making of him. He's actually proved a competent soldier. His father's found a reason to summon him back to Rome, but he wished us both well.'

'*Scaevola* wished us well?'

'Yes.' His brow furrowed again. 'Although it might be risky for him if your brother's here.'

'I doubt it. Tarquinius is probably on the road south already.'

'Ah.'

She turned her head, averting her eyes from the intensity in his. 'What's happening with the rebellion?'

'It hasn't been easy, but we're winning, slowly. Now that the rest of the garrison has arrived, we should push the rebels back over the wall before winter. We'll recapture Cilurnum. We'll get our villa back, too.'

'Oh.' She didn't know what to say about that either. 'So you were right about the rebels all along.'

He made a face. 'That doesn't make it any better.'

'No, I suppose not.'

'There was one consolation, though. Nerva offered me a promotion.'

'You don't mean…?'

'Not quite. Second Centurion of the Second Cohort. It's still a great honour, more than I could have expected.'

'Then I'm happy for you.' She forced a smile. 'You're getting closer.'

'I turned it down.'

'What?' She blinked. 'Is that allowed?'

'Not really, but under the circumstances… In any case, Nerva's more understanding than most Legates. I asked him for something else, a transfer to the auxiliaries. It doesn't usually happen—in fact, I'm not sure I've heard of it ever happening before—but I asked him to make an exception.'

'And?'

'He said I had some nerve. Then he asked me *why* I wanted it. I said it was because my wife was happy at Cilurnum and I thought it might make her happy again to go back once the rebellion was over.' Dark eyes flickered with a look of uncertainty. 'Was I wrong?'

'No, but…' Her voice trailed away as he took a step towards her.

'He said that the fort still needs a commanding officer and that the position was mine if I wanted it… I said I had to speak with you first. Being married to Hermenia, he understood that some marriages are based on equality.'

She stared at him breathlessly. Equality? He sounded as if he meant it. He was talking as if he wanted to take her back to the wall and give their marriage a second chance, too, but how *could* they go back? After everything he'd said, how could he think that she'd even *consider* such a thing? And how dare he change his mind again, as if she ought to just forget all his insults!

'You called me a barbarian.' She lifted her chin angrily. 'You said you couldn't trust me.'

'I didn't mean it. I didn't mean any of those things I said. I trusted you, even before you saved my life, but I knew you wouldn't leave unless I made you and I was afraid of you getting hurt again.'

'You mean you were trying to protect me?'

'Yes.'

A welling of hope turned into a fresh burst of anger. 'So you *lied* to me? And you expect me to forgive you for saying that *I* was untrustworthy? You tricked me!'

'Only because I had to get you away from Cilurnum. I was afraid that none of us would survive. I thought that *I* wouldn't. That's why I lied.'

She stared at him incredulously, replaying the scene when he'd ordered her to leave in her head, only now from a new perspective. She'd replayed it so often over the past two months that she knew every word and look by heart. Was it really possible that he'd just been pretending?

'How can I believe you?' She shook her head in bewilderment. 'How do I know you're not just being honourable again? Because you don't need to be. I have plans of my own. I'm going to start a kitchen here in Eboracum.'

'Then I'll ask Nerva to give me a job in headquarters here, too.'

'What? No!'

'The food would be worth it.'

'No, Marius, you don't have to feel responsible for me. I won't let you take a demotion to the auxiliaries.

If you do that, then you'll never become Senior Centurion.'

'I don't care.' He strode towards her, close enough that they were almost, but not quite, touching. 'Trust me, Livia, I know what I want. There's nothing like a horde of screaming rebels to focus the mind. I don't care about rank or promotion or being anyone other than your husband any more. I've spent years trying to prove a point, to overcome my father's dishonour, but there was never any dishonour to overcome. Rome might think so, but I don't. I'm proud of him and I'm not going to spend the rest of my life making up for a mistake he never made. I'm going to be my own man, just like he was.'

She felt her heartbeat accelerate even faster, his near proximity having its usual disorientating effect on her body. 'You mean sort of Roman, but not?'

'Yes.' There was a glimmer of hope in his eyes again. 'I love you, Livia. I couldn't tell you before, but I can now. I love you more than any promotion, any *gladius*, more than fifty thousand denarii!'

'Fifty thousand?' Her eyes widened. 'How much *did* you gamble on me?'

'Everything I had.' He lowered his face so that his mouth hovered just above hers. 'And I'd do it again if I had to. I'd risk everything for you. If you'll just…'

'Marius!' He didn't get any further as a small figure hurtled through the courtyard towards them.

'Empress.' He took a step back, bracing himself to scoop Julia up in his one good arm.

'Where have you been?' The little girl looked at him seriously. 'Mama's been worried.'

'Has she?' His eyes seemed to smoulder as they turned back towards Livia.

'Yes.' Livia looked between him and her daughter and then couldn't stop herself from beaming. 'Just because I'm a barbarian doesn't mean I don't love you, too.'

His answering smile was wider than she'd ever seen it. If she'd thought he'd been handsome before, he looked positively devastating now. 'Then you'll come back to the wall with me? When the fighting's over and the fort is rebuilt?'

'What do you think, Julia?' She leaned forward and wrapped her arms around both of them. 'Would you like to see the wall, too?'

'You mean where Grandmama came from?'

'Yes.' She met Marius's questioning look with a smile. 'I've been telling her some family stories.'

'I'm glad to hear it. Then how about it, Empress? Can you persuade your mama to say yes?'

'She doesn't need to.' Livia squeezed her arms tight. 'I've already decided.'

'And?'

'And it's a yes. You were right the first time—we do belong together, and as for Cilurnum…well, the edge of the Empire seems fitting somehow.'

'Sort of Roman, but not?' He kissed the top of her head, nuzzling his face against her red curls. 'I can't think of a more perfect place for us.'

* * * * *

If you enjoyed this story
you won't want to miss these other great reads
by Jenni Fletcher

Married to Her Enemy
The Convenient Felstone Marriage
Besieged and Betrothed
Captain Amberton's Inherited Bride